*Cleo wriggled back a little
and he opened his arms to release her,
half thankful, half regretful.*

Then he realized she was simply putting enough space between them so he could kiss her. *Who is seducing whom?* he wondered. He bent his head and took the proffered lips. *Just one kiss.*

Her mouth, hot and soft under his, opened without him needing to coax. She was willing, and yet, despite it all, shy. Quin took a firm grip on his willpower and kissed her with more gentleness than passion, his tongue sliding against hers, his palms flat on her back in the loosest of holds. She was trembling slightly, he realized, like a woman fighting emotion.

Quin raised his head. "Cleo?" Her eyes were wide and dark and flooded with unshed tears. "Cleo—"

* * *

Beguiled by Her Betrayer
Harlequin® Historical #1197—August 2014

Author Note

Several years ago I stood in the temple of Kom Ombo in Upper Egypt, fascinated by the graffiti left by French soldiers around 1800, very high up on the walls. I soon realized that the very tops of the monuments were all that Napoleon's troops would have been able to see because the sand had covered many remains to within feet of the roof.

Today, knowing so much about ancient Egypt, we still marvel at these monuments, but I began to wonder how they must have seemed to these men, right at the beginning of modern archaeology. The more I read about Napoleon's savants, the group of scholars he left with his troops in Egypt to explore this mysterious civilization, the more I admired them for their courage and endurance.

The Nile valley is so beautiful, and so romantic, that I knew I had to set a story there, and gradually the characters of Cleo and Quin began to take shape.

I hope you enjoy reading *Beguiled by Her Betrayer* as much as I enjoyed writing it.

Louise Allen

—

Beguiled by Her Betrayer

HARLEQUIN® HISTORICAL

Recycling programs
for this product may
not exist in your area.

ISBN-13: 978-0-373-29797-9

BEGUILED BY HER BETRAYER

Copyright © 2014 by Melanie Hilton

This edition published by arrangement with Harlequin Books S.A.

For questions and comments about the quality of this book, please contact us at CustomerService@Harlequin.com.

® and TM are trademarks of Harlequin Enterprises Limited or its corporate affiliates. Trademarks indicated with ® are registered in the United States Patent and Trademark Office, the Canadian Intellectual Property Office and in other countries.

Printed in U.S.A.

HARLEQUIN®
www.Harlequin.com

LOUISE ALLEN

has been immersing herself in history, real and fictional, for as long as she can remember. She finds landscapes and places evoke powerful images of the past—Venice, Burgundy and the Greek Islands are favorite atmospheric destinations. Louise lives on the North Norfolk coast, where she shares with her husband the cottage they have renovated. She spends her spare time gardening, researching family history or traveling in the U.K. and abroad in search of inspiration. Please visit Louise's website, www.louiseallenregency.com, for the latest news, or find her on Twitter, @LouiseRegency, and on Facebook.

Chapter One

Early April 1801—Upper Egypt

There was shade down there and water jars sweating themselves cool and the start of the green growth that ran from the desert edge into the banks of the Nile. *Too soon.* Quin lay flat on the hot sand of the dune's crest and distracted himself from thirst, heat and the throbbing pain in his left arm by concentrating on the tent below.

Tent was perhaps too modest a word. It seemed to consist of several interior rooms surrounded by shaded areas formed by poles and flaps of fabric which, he supposed, would collapse to make outer walls at night.

It was an immaculately neat and well-organised encampment, although there were no servants to be seen. To one side was an animal shelter with hitching rail and trough, on the other a reed roof covered a cooking area. A thin wisp of smoke rose from the banked fire, there was no donkey tied to the rail and the only occupant appeared to be the man in shirtsleeves who sat at a table in the deep shade of an awning, his pen moving steadily across the paper in front of him.

Quin narrowed his eyes against the dusty sunlight. Mid-fifties, burly, salt-and-pepper brown hair: that was certainly his quarry, or one of them at least. Sir Philip Woodward, baronet, antiquarian and scholar, neglectful husband, selfish widower and father and, very possibly, traitor.

A flicker of movement out of the corner of his eye betrayed robes caught in the light breeze. Someone was approaching. Quin shifted his gaze to where the monumental columns of the temple of Koum Ombo rose from the enshrouding sand, dwarfing the mud-walled huts of the little village of fishermen and farmers beyond it. The person leading a donkey must be familiar with the area, for they spared no glance for the great ruins as they passed them by. It was a woman, he saw as she came closer, clad in the enveloping folds of a dark blue *tob sebleh,* but like most of the country women of Upper Egypt, unveiled. A servant—or the other person he had been sent to find?

Madame Valsac, widow of *Capitaine* Thierry Valsac of Napoleon's Army of the East, daughter of Sir Philip Woodward and, maybe, another traitor. But unlike her father, whose safety was of little concern to the hard-faced men who had briefed Quin, Madame Valsac was to be extracted from Egypt and restored to the custody of her grandfather whether she liked it or not, and regardless of where her loyalties might lie.

That this might prove troublesome, hundreds of miles from the coast and the invading British army, in the path of France's fearsome Mameluke allies who were believed to be heading north at that moment, and in the midst of one of Egypt's periodic outbreaks of plague, had not concerned the gentlemen in Gibraltar. Quin was a diplomat who spoke French and Arabic and knew enough of antiquities to pass as one of the French *savants*, the scholars left by Napoleon to explore Egypt under the protection of his underpaid, diseased, poorly resourced army. That, so far as they were concerned, was sufficient qualification.

'*Classical* antiquities, my lord,' Quin had pointed out. 'My knowledge of Egypt is virtually non-existent.' *Nor am I qualified in kidnapping females,* he might have added, but did not.

'Plenty of time to read it up on board ship between here and Alexandria,' his unsympathetic superior had retorted. 'Just remember, the Duke of St Osyth wants his granddaughter back, never mind if she's taken an entire French regiment to her bed. Her father no one wants, but if he's a traitor, then we need to know the ins and outs of it. Then you can dispose of him.'

'I am not an assassin, my lord.' Quin had said it with an edge missing from the protest about his lack of knowledge of Egypt. He might be ambitious, but he drew the line at murder.

'Then introduce him to a hungry crocodile or lose him in the desert.'

Quin blinked to clear his vision and realised that the black dots swimming before his eyes were not flies.

The woman and the donkey were close now. She spoke as she passed the man sitting under the awning, but he made no reply. A servant, then.

She halted the donkey and began to heave the water jars from its back with the economical strength of someone accustomed to manual labour. She filled the donkey's bucket, poured more water into the large storage jars and finally carried a pitcher to one of the open-sided shaded spaces facing the dune where Quin lay.

Through the insistent throbbing in his head it took him a minute to realise what she was about. The woman pulled the cotton folds of the *tob sebleh* over her head, removed the twisted cloth that tied up her hair and was unfastening the sash around her waist before he assimilated not only the colour of her hair—honey-brown, waving and most decidedly not Egyptian—but the fact that she was about to strip off her under-tunic and bathe.

He did not ogle women in their bath like some Peeping Tom, any more than he fed inconvenient baronets to the crocodiles. Quin rose to his feet, surprised at how unstable the shifting sands were. Now was the time to put his plan, such as it was, into effect.

One step down the slope and he knew it was not the surface that was making him so unsteady. *Hell, I'm sick*, he thought, getting his legs under precarious control as he half-slid, half-ran. He hit the flat ground at the foot with a force that jarred his spine and took six weaving steps towards the woman. She made no move and no sound, simply stood there, her hands arrested on the knot of her sash, staring at him.

Quin halted a yard from her. *'Bonjour,'* he managed before his knees gave out and the ground came up to meet him. *'Mada—'*

Cleo regarded the sprawled, bareheaded figure clad in a dusty *galabeeyah* for a long moment, sighed, then raised her voice. 'Father!'

'I am working. Is it time to eat?'

'No. There is a man here, unconscious.'

'Leave him.' Her father sounded irritated at the interruption and not in the slightest bit curious. But then this slumped heap of humanity was a person, not a ruined temple, or an inscription, let alone a fresco, so his lack of interest was only to be expected.

'He will die and then he will stink,' Cleo retorted. Only a direct threat to her parent's comfort and convenience would shift him, she knew that very well.

There was a muttered curse, then her father appeared. He poked the recumbent figure with the toe of his boot. It shifted slightly. 'Not dead. And not Egyptian. Frenchman, no doubt. Where do you want him?'

'I do not *want* him at all, but on the other bed frame in my room, I suppose.' Cleo pushed aside the hangings and stripped the spare sheets and her few clothes from the bed, leaving only the thin cotton padding over the crossed ropes. By the time she got back her father had the man under the armpits and was dragging him in, still face-down.

An unpleasant possibility struck her. 'Are there swellings?'

'What?' Her father let the limp figure fall back with a thud.

Cleo winced. Now she'd have a bleeding, broken nose to deal with. 'In his armpits. If he has the plague, there will be swellings.'

'No. No fever either, he's as dry as a bone.' He went back to dragging the man inside. Cleo lifted the long legs when he reached the bed and they hefted the stranger up and on to his back. By some miracle the assertive nose was unbent.

'Heatstroke, then,' Cleo diagnosed. There was a dark dried mess on his left sleeve. 'And a wound.' Her father was already turning away. 'I need to get these clothes off him.'

'You were a married woman, you can manage.' His voice floated back from behind the hangings. He would be lost in his correspondence again until she pushed food under his nose.

'I might have been married,' Cleo muttered, laying the back of her hand on the wide, hot forehead, 'but I was not married to this one.' She took off the man's sandals, the easy part, then rolled and pushed the limp, heavy body and dragged at the cotton robe until it was over his head. The cord keeping up the thin cotton drawers snapped in the process, so she pulled those off too. There was a belt around his waist with a leather bag, heavy with coin. She set it aside, then stood back to survey the extent of the problem.

And it *was* extensive. Six foot, broad-shouldered, blond and lean with the look of a man who had recently lost whatever slight reserves of fat he might have had, leaving the muscles across his abdomen sculpted as though by the hands of a master carver. And he was very definitely male. The carver might have had the decency to provide a large fig leaf while he was at it…

Widow she might be, but she was certainly not sophisticated enough to gaze unmoved on a naked stranger. Not one who looked like this. Cleo fixed her gaze on his arm where a ragged wound was cut like a groove from shoulder to elbow, gave herself a little shake and concentrated on priorities.

Gunshot, not a blade, she concluded, eyeing the inflamed edges of the red, weeping mess. Removing the outer robe had torn it open, although it had obviously not been healing healthily. The first thing was to get some water into him, then reduce his temperature and then she would see what she could do with his arm. There was no doctor or surgeon with the small detachment of French troops camped on the far side of the next village, so she could expect no help there.

The man sucked greedily at the cup when she lifted his head to drink. The smell of water seemed to revive him a little.

'Slowly, you cannot have too much at once,' she began, then recalled that he had spoken in French before he collapsed. *'Lentement.'*

He moved his head restlessly when she took the water away, but he did not open his eyes. Now to get him cooler and covered up. She could start work on his arm once she had put some food under Father's nose.

'You, *monsieur*,' Cleo said in French as she shook out a sheet and dropped it into a bucket of water, 'are a thorough nuisance. Believe me, if my fairy godmother flew down and offered me whatever I wanted, another man to look after would be the lowest on my list of desirable objects.' She pulled the linen out and draped it dripping over the distractingly naked body. 'There. That's better.' *For me, at least.*

It was his favourite fantasy, the one that came when he was half-asleep, the comfortable, yet arousing, one about being married to his perfect woman. There was the rustle of skirts, the soft pad of feet, the occasional faint waft of some feminine perfume as she moved about the room close by. Soon he would wake up and she would come to his bed and smile at him, her blue eyes warm and loving, her face—he could picture it very clearly—sweet, with neat little features and a soft, pink mouth.

'Caroline.' He would hold out his arms and she would unpin her long blonde curls and begin to undress with an innocent coquettishness that made him hard and aching before they even touched.

When she came to him, her curvaceous body would fit against his big frame as though she had been made for him. 'Oh, Quin,' she would murmur and run her hands over his chest, lower, lower…

The smell of roasting meat distracted him. What were the staff doing to allow kitchen odours to penetrate to his bedchamber? He was the ambassador, damn it. His dream wife's fingers stroked down, exploring. Her blonde ringlets, unaccountably wet, fell on to his chest as she pulled him back from that distraction with impetuous little kisses that dotted his face. His body reacted predictably, hardening, his balls tightened, lifted. Soon he would enter her, love her, caress her into ecstasy. And afterwards they would talk, rationally and intelligently. They would be interested in each other's thoughts, respectful of the other's opinions. It would be peaceful, harmonious…

'Hell and damnation!' It was a woman all right, but that was all that meshed with his dream. A string of idiomatic expressions in Arabic confirmed that the speaker was no lady.

Quin realised he was conscious, in pain, devilishly thirsty and decidedly confused. 'Wha…?' he croaked. His blasted eyes would hardly open but, mercifully, a cup was pressed to his lips.

'Slowly,' a voice chided in French. The same woman's voice, clear, crisp, definitely unseductive. Definitely unsympathetic. The water was removed.

'Merci,' Quin managed to say and squinted up through sore lids. *And definitely not my fantasy woman,* he thought, some shred of humour emerging amidst the general misery. Tall, slender, brown haired, she regarded him down a long, straight, imperious nose with an air of tightly controlled impatience. Intelligent, certainly. Cuddly, sweet and pliant…no. 'More?' he added, hopefully. 'Er…*encore?'* He needed to keep his mouth shut except for drinking until his brain stopped boiling.

'No more water for a few minutes. It is dangerous when you have become so thirsty. You are not French.'

So, he must start thinking after all. 'Would you believe, American?' he offered.

'Really?' It seemed she would. Her brows lifted in surprise, but she did not reject the idea. The Americans were allies of France, of course.

'It is a long time since I saw Boston,' Quin conceded. A long time since he had visited his cousins in the Lincolnshire port of that name, that was. He was sent forth to die for his country from time to time, that went with the territory, but he preferred not to lie for it, if he could help it. Usually a little misdirection was sufficient. His lids drooped closed, then cracked open again as he became aware of his body as more than something painful and hot.

'Who took my clothes off?' He was naked under wet cloth that ran from collarbone to toes.

'I did,' his reluctant nurse stated crisply. 'Oh, really,' she added as his fingers tightened reflexively over the upper edge of the sheet. 'There is no need to blush, I am a widow. I can assure you that one man is much as another to me.'

Quin unclenched his teeth. Damn it, he was *not* blushing. 'But I can assure you, *madam,* that one *woman* is not much as another to *me.*'

'You would prefer that I left you to die? I was not making comparisons, so you need not be alarmed.' Now she was amused, although she did not smile. There was something about the way her eyes crinkled at the corner, the ghost of a dimple in her cheek. Then it was gone as her gaze swept over his shrouded form. He *was* going to blush in a moment. 'That sheet is drying out. I had best replace it before I deal with your arm.'

There was the sound of cloth being agitated in water, the swish of her skirts as she moved. Quin clung to the edge of his sheet with a prudery that astonished him. With a wet flap that showered his face with droplets the weight of another sodden sheet landed on top of him. 'Grip the edge of the top one,' she ordered and yanked the lower sheet away from the foot of the bed with a snap that left him covered even as it administered a sharp slap of wet linen to his wedding tackle in passing.

Quin suppressed the word that leapt to his lips and released his death grip on the sheet. As he squinted down the length of his body he reflected ruefully that with the way it moulded itself to his form he might as well simply be wearing a layer of white paint. And goodness knew what was the matter with him. His experience with women was not such as to leave him blushing like a virgin curate when one ran her eyes over his body.

On the other hand, the woman advancing on him with a beaker in one hand and a bundle of unpleasantly sharp-looking implements in the other, was hardly a cheerful member of the muslin company.

'You may have some more water and then I will clean up your arm.' She settled on a stool beside him and Quin, his temper ragged, reached out to take the beaker before she could hold it to his lips.

'It is merely a graze from a spent bullet.'

'It is a gouge I could lay my finger in and it is infected. I really do not wish to have to remove your arm.'

'Over my dead body!' Quin managed not to choke on a mouthful of water. Damn the female, he could believe she was capable of doing just that, with her screaming victim tied to the bed.

'Your choice.' She shrugged.

'Very well.' Quin handed her the beaker and pulled the sheet away from his left arm. He'd been about to sit up, but one look at the festering mess left him glad he was flat on his back. This was not going to be amusing and he had no intention of gratifying his tormentor by fainting.

Chapter Two

Madame Valsac seemed competent, Quin had to admit. Her array of unpleasant tools were sharp and clean, she had hot water and sponges and torn linen all set out. She turned and studied him, momentarily distracting him with speculation about the colour of her eyes. Grey or green or greenish grey? Greyish green… He took a surreptitious hold on the bed frame with his other hand and gazed upwards past her right ear. It was a nice ear, framed by the hair she had pushed back behind it. Neat and elegantly shaped and—*hell's teeth!*

'What is your name?'

Distracting the patient to keep his mind off things, Quin thought, enduring an exquisite pang in silence. 'Quintus Bredon,' he said when he could catch his breath. 'You can call me Quin.' Might as well use part of his real name, there was less chance of mistakes that way. 'And yours?' He knew perfectly well, there could not be two women of her age with Woodward, but it was necessary to play the game and besides, he had not been told her first name. Given that she had stripped him to the buff, that at least should put them on some sort of intimate footing.

'Madame Valsac. You may call me *madam*.'

Thank you, madam!

She did something that made his vision swirl and darken and then, suddenly, the worst of the pain eased. 'There, that is clean now. How did you do this?'

'I stood in the way of a bullet from a group of Bedouin raiders.' Quin matched the indifferent courtesy of her tone. 'Careless of me, but I woke to find them removing my camels and all my gear.'

'Careless indeed.' She began to bandage his arm. 'You were alone? What is an American doing in Egypt?'

'I was with a small group of engineers, but I wanted to get back further south to study the way the river flows and they intended to stay another few days. I am interested in building dams.' There was no way to avoid fabricating the story of how and why he was in Egypt. The books he had studied so carefully on board ship had left his head spinning with pharaohs, weird gods, indecipherable hieroglyphs and wild theories. Trying to fool a scholar about his level of knowledge was impossible, better to pretend something he was at least able to discuss in English.

'I had no idea the emperor had Americans amongst his *savants*.' She tied a competent knot and laid his throbbing arm back down. 'You will be glad to hear there is a small detachment of troops at Shek Amer, just to the south of us. They will be delighted to meet you, I have no doubt.'

'No doubt.' Hell and damnation, that was the last thing he needed. The plan was to warn Woodward and his daughter that the Mamelukes were advancing from the south. It was, in fact, the truth, although he had no intention of adding the rest of the facts, that this was in support of the French, besieged in Cairo by a combined British and Turkish force. No one, French ally or not, would want to be in the path of the lethal mounted Mameluke militias under Murad Bey. He'd intended to persuade the Woodward and Madame Valsac to take a boat north with him, not telling them they were heading straight into the arms of the British.

Now he had to deal with French soldiers who would know there were no engineers in the area and who might even have received the news that General Abercrombie was harrying the French out of Alexandria. And there was a strong probability they would also know there were no Americans amongst the motley group of scholars, scientists, engineers and artists who had found themselves stranded with the army when their beloved Napoleon abandoned them almost two years before. Bonaparte had returned to France and staged the coup that gave him complete power and the title *Emperor,* and had left his generals to manage as best they might.

Quin eyed the woman he was rapidly coming to think of as his adversary as she stood and began to clear her instruments away. Nobody's fool and apparently cool to the point of frigidity, she was not going to be easy to panic into flight. If the worst came to the worst, he was going to have to steal a boat, kidnap her and leave her father to his fate.

Madame Valsac turned at the doorway, the light behind her, and looked back over her shoulder, her figure outlined through the fine linen of her robe. His body, cheerfully ignoring the looming presence of nearby French troops, heat-stroke, fever and his feelings about the woman's personality, stirred under the weight of wet sheet.

'Is anything wrong?' she asked. 'I thought I heard you moan. I have opium if the pain is very bad.' From her tone it sounded as though she would as soon hit him over the head and render him unconscious that way, if it caused her less trouble.

'No, nothing at all,' Quin lied as he closed his eyes. 'Everything's just perfect.' *I really, really did not join the diplomatic service for this...*

He had actually joined it because sitting on his courtesy title as a marquess's fifth, and very much unwanted, son did not appeal, despite a modest estate and an equally modest competence to maintain his style. His four elder brothers—the wanted sons with the real names—they all had their roles. Henry was the heir, learning to be a marquess. James was the spare and learning to be a marquess's right-hand man in the time left in a packed schedule of wenching, gaming and sporting endeavours, Charles was a colonel in the Guards and looked so good in his uniform that one forgot that he was as dense as London fog and George was a clergyman, clawing his way up the hierarchy towards a bishop's throne with unchristian determination.

'It will have to be the navy for you, Quintus,' Lord Deverall, Marquess of Malvern, had announced on Quin's fourteenth birthday. It had been a convenient conceit, naming him for a number. It meant the marquess could always remember his name.

'No, my lord.' He was not used to contradicting the

marquess, simply because the man did not speak to the cuckoo in his nest if he could avoid it, so the opportunity rarely arose. 'I do not excel at mathematics and it is essential for a naval officer,' he explained.

The Marquess of Malvern, five foot ten of slender, sandy-haired refinement, the model that Henry, James, Charles and George matched exactly, had glowered at him. Quintus, already as tall, blond and, most inconveniently, the spitting image of his mother's lover, the late and unlamented Viscount Hempstead, had stared back. 'Then what the devil am I to do with you?' the marquess demanded.

'I am good at languages,' Quin stated. 'I will be a diplomat.' And that had been that. An appropriate tutor, a degree from Oxford, a few favours called in at the Foreign Office and Lord Quintus Bredon Deverall was neatly off the marquess's hands. And he was just where he wanted to be, on a career path that would, if he applied himself, see him with an ambassadorial post or a high government position, a title of his own and an existence entirely separate from his family.

And here I am in the middle of this God-forsaken desert, a war breaking out north and south and plague sweeping the land in a most appropriately Biblical manner. If I'd wanted to be a soldier, I'd have learned to shoot better, if I'd wanted to be a doctor, I'd have paid more attention to my science lectures and if I'd wanted to march across hundreds of square miles of sand, I'd have been a camel, he grumbled to himself, then grinned. It was, despite everything, an interesting change from endless negotiations, diplomatic dinners and decoding correspondence in six languages. Madame Valsac was going to be a thorn in his side, but he was confident that he could handle Woodward. How difficult could one scholar-turned-inept-spy be to manage?

'No,' Sir Philip said flatly without looking up from the letter he was reading. 'You are not gadding off to flirt with officers. Who will look after that damned man? You seemed to spend all day today dodging in and out attending to him. Who will cook my dinner? And I need you to take notes when I measure the court-yard of the temple.'

'I am going to the next village, Father, not Cairo. I have no desire to flirt with French officers, one was more than enough. I will be back in time to cook your dinner, for I will leave after breakfast, and if Mr Bredon is still not fully himself tomorrow I will leave food and water by his bed.'

Surely after twenty-four hours he would soon re-cover and she could get him out of her bed space? It had been tiring, rising every hour to sponge his face and get water between his lips and, however tired she was, it had been strangely difficult to get back to sleep each time. Mr Call-Me-Quin Bredon was a disturbing presence whilst semi-conscious and in a fever. Good-ness knows what he would be like in his full senses. She was not looking forward to another night with him.

Cleo finished sweeping the sand from the mat around her father's trestle table and gathered his day's paperwork into a tin box. He would want his supper soon, but there was the remains of the spit-cooked kid and some flatbread and dates, so that would take little time. Then, when he retired to his bed with a book, she'd clear up, water the donkey again, feed it, secure the tent flaps, check on her patient and, at last, go to bed herself.

'Mr Bredon can visit the officers himself,' a deep, slightly husky, voice remarked. Cleo dropped the lid of the box, narrowly missing her fingertips. The American, draped in a passable attempt at a toga, was leaning against the tent pole. He was white under the tan and he was supporting his left wrist with his right hand, but his blue eyes were clear and there was a faint, healthy, trace of perspiration on his skin.

'You must excuse me, sir, but I failed to ask Madame Valsac your name,' he continued with as much smooth courtesy as a man entering a drawing room.

Cleo got a grip on herself. This was becoming untidy and she disliked untidiness. Mr Bredon should be lying down so she knew where he was and what he was doing. If he made himself even more ill, she was stuck with nursing him that much longer. 'This is Mr Quintus Bredon, who should be in bed, Father.' Mr Bredon merely smiled faintly. 'He is an American and was set upon by Bedouin raiders,' she reminded him. 'Mr Bredon, this is my father, Sir Philip Woodward.'

'Sir Philip.' The blasted man even managed a passable bow while keeping control of his toga. 'I must thank you for your hospitality. May I ask, which day this is?'

'You arrived here yesterday at about this time,' Cleo said as she picked up her broom. 'And you have been feverish ever since. I suggest you go back to bed.'

Her father grunted and waved a hand at the other folding chair. 'Nonsense. He's on his feet now, isn't he? You're a scholar, sir? What do you know about this stone they're supposed to have dug up at Rosetta eighteen months ago, eh? Can't get any sense out of anyone, couldn't get to see it in Cairo.'

'I've heard of it, of course, Sir Philip, but I did not see it in Cairo either.' Bredon raised an eyebrow at Cleo and gestured towards the chair. She shook her head, flapped her hands and mouthed *sit*. He was too heavy to have to pick up again if he collapsed. With a frown, he sat. 'But I am an engineer, I fear I know nothing about it, nor about hieroglyphic symbols.'

'Yes, but *are* they symbols?'

Cleo rolled her eyes and left, abandoning her patient to his fate. He would not be able to beat a strategic retreat as Thierry had used to do by pleading military business and she had no time to wait around while her father lectured a new victim. On top of everything else she supposed she had better get his garments clean and mended if he was out of bed. The conceit that Mr Bredon might descend on the French camp, toga-clad like a latter-day Julius Caesar if she did not, almost stayed her hand. It was an amusing thought, but perhaps not practical.

She dropped the *galabeeyah* and his cotton drawers into the wash tub, grated in some of her precious store of soap and pummelled until they were clean. Once they were hanging up on a tent pole where they would dry within the hour she found a new cord for the drawers and a length of white cotton for a turban. Mr Bredon obviously did not know he needed to keep his head covered in the intense sunshine.

'Magical symbols…' Her father's voice reached her from the other end of the encampment. 'Don't agree. Obviously a secret priestly code…'

She could almost feel sympathy with Mr Bredon.

Almost. Cleo dragged his bed frame into the furthest section of the tent and found room for it next to the storage boxes. If he was well enough to talk to her father, he was certainly not in need of nursing all night in her own bed space, thank goodness. Her privacy was a precious and deeply treasured luxury. She removed the wet cotton quilt he had been lying on and made the bed up afresh, then went back to her own space to tidy it. She hated disorder. Hated it. And sand. Most of all, sand.

'Chinese?' That was Mr Bredon. Father must have got on to the theory that Egyptian writing was a form of Chinese. Or was it the other way around?

Cleo watered the donkey and tossed it the last of the wilting greenery she had gathered that morning by the waterside. She would fetch more tomorrow on her way back from the military camp. Her back ached and she leaned for a moment against the dusty grey rump of the little animal, scratching the spot on his back just where she knew he liked it. 'Your work is finished for the day,' she informed him. Now for supper.

Quin found Madame Valsac spooning honey from a jar into a dish with the concentration of someone who was bone weary, but was keeping going by a dogged attention to every detail. He had found his robe, clean and sun-dried, his mended underwear, a turban cloth and his sandals neatly piled on a bed that she must have dragged into the other room and made up by herself.

The donkey was mumbling the remains of its feed, the encampment was tidy in every detail and the trestle table was laid for a simple meal. And he had spent an hour or so doing nothing more taxing than listen

to Sir Philip lecture on Egyptian antiquities and try to
stay awake in the evening heat.

Quin changed into his clothes, made a sling out of
the length of cloth and went back out, steadying himself against the momentary flashes of dizziness and
cursing his weakness under his breath. There was a
basket of bone-handled cutlery on the end of the table
and he began, one-handed, to lay three settings.

'No need for you to do that. You should be resting.' There was no hint of weariness in the cool, un-
emotional voice, but she did not attempt to wrest the
basket from him.

'I have been resting while I conversed with Sir
Philip.'

'I doubt it was a conversation. A new audience always opens the floodgates. Here, sit down.' She poured
liquid into two beakers, pushed one across the table
to him and sat carefully, as though her bones ached.

They probably do. How old is she? Quin wondered
as he took the drink with a word of thanks and sat opposite her, trying to recall his briefing. *Only twenty-
three.* He sipped. 'This is good.'

'Pomegranate juice.' She sat for a while, her fingers
laced around her beaker as though she had forgotten
what it was there for. Then she took a long swallow
and called, *'Father! Supper.'* She lowered her voice.
'It will take several reminders before he comes, you
may have your peace until then.' That faint dimple
ghosted across the smooth, sun-browned cheek and
her tired eyes narrowed. He had not seen a real smile
from her yet.

'How do you bear it?' Quin asked abruptly and
watched all trace of amusement fade from her face.

The sooner he got her out of here and back to the sort of life she should be living, the better.

'The heat?' She was quick, for he could have sworn she knew exactly what he meant. *How do you stand this life, that man, the loneliness, the constant labour?* 'I am used to it, we have been in Egypt for five years now and one learns to live with it when there is no alternative.'

Was she answering his real question after all? 'What is your given name?'

The arched brows lifted in silent reproof at his ill manners, but this time she did not evade the question. 'Augusta Cleopatra Agrippina,' she said evenly and waited for his response.

Quin did not disappoint her. 'Good God! What were your parents thinking of?'

'We were in Greece at the time apparently, but Father was still in his Roman phase. I doubt Mama had any say in the matter. Look at it this way, I am fortunate that he had not become interested in Egypt then or I would probably be called Bastet or Nut.'

He had heard of Bastet, the goddess with the head of a cat, but, *'Nut?'*

'The goddess of the sky who swallows the sun every evening and gives birth to it each morning. *Father!*'

Quin decided he did not want to contemplate the mechanics of that. 'So which of your imposing names are you known by? What does your father call you?'

'Daughter! Where are my towels?'

'On the end of your bed,' she called back. 'He does not remember it most of the time, as you hear,' she said to Quin. 'He is in his head, in his own world. I doubt he recalls that Mama is dead, or my husband, most of the time. My husband called me Cleopatra, it appeared to amuse him.'

'Queen of the Nile,' Quin murmured.

'Exactly. So appropriate, don't you think?'

Chapter Three

Queen of the Nile? Yes, very appropriate, Quin wanted to say, throwing her bitter jest back at her. *You look like a queen with that patrician nose and those high cheekbones, that air of aloofness. A queen in exile, in disguise, in servitude.* He was saved from answering by Sir Philip emerging from the tent, fastening a clean shirt with one hand and running his hand through his wet hair with the other.

He sat without a word and reached for the platter of what appeared to be cubes of meat. Madame… *No, Cleo,* Quin decided, slid a plate in front of her father and passed one to Quin, then gestured to him to help himself. He realised his mouth was watering.

'You should try to eat. It has been a while since you did, I imagine.'

'Yes. I was hungry at first and then that vanished.' He had been on foot and without anything but a small flask of water for two days after his camels were taken. Before that he had been eating sparingly, moving too fast to settle down in one spot and cook himself a proper meal.

'It seems to with heat prostration. You must rest tomorrow.'

'I will rest tonight. Tomorrow I will acquaint myself with your military neighbours.'

'That is foolish. I can ask them what is the best thing to be done with you.'

They would shoot me as a spy, if they knew who I was. 'If I am to be disposed of, Madame Valsac, I prefer to organise it myself.'

'Very well. I will not go and you will not be able to find them by yourself.' She bit down sharply on a piece of flatbread as though to cut off all discussion.

Confound the woman. Is she trying to keep me away from the military because of her own compromised situation or is she merely being inconveniently protective of an injured man?

'No, I want you to go, Daughter,' Sir Philip pronounced, reversing his earlier opinion without a blink. 'I need you to take my correspondence for them to send north. I have finished my letter to Professor Heinnemann.'

Correspondence? 'The French are obliging enough to act as postmen for you, Sir Philip?' Quin asked casually as he spread goat's cheese on his bread.

'Indeed they are.' The older man put down his fork. 'A fine example of the co-operation amongst scholars. As soon as *Général* Menou realised I was having problems receiving my letters he arranged for them to be handled through Alexandria.'

And how did the general know? Quin shelved that question for the moment. He thought he had hold of the tail of the matter now and he had no intention of letting it wriggle out of his grasp. 'You have an international correspondence?' he asked, injecting as much admiration into his tone as he thought was plausible.

He need not have worried about arousing suspicions. Sir Philip was smugly confident of his own importance. 'Of course. England, France, Greece, Italy, Germany, India, Russia. Spain and Portugal…' He droned on, complaining about the paucity of news from the Scandinavian countries.

England, the Mediterranean, continental Europe— news from dozens of pens flowing into Alexandria, into the hands of the French. Traitors, agents and innocent scholars all writing to this man who was either so blinded by his obsessions that he had no idea how he was being used or was a willing participant in his French masters' games. Every scrap of intelligence was like gold to skilled spymasters who could fit it all together from dozens of sources.

'India,' Quin said out loud. India, the real reason the French wanted Egypt. If they controlled the Red Sea and the overland route to the Mediterranean, then Britain's vital link to its most important trading area was lost. And troops were on their way now from India to land on the Red Sea coast and march across the desert to the Nile, then downstream to join the British and Turks in the delta.

Had letters from French agents in India already reached Menou in Cairo on their way to this man? A cold finger trailed down his spine, chilling the perspiration. If the French marched out to cut off General Baird's long, desperate march through the desert, then the entire tide of the war in Egypt could turn.

'Yes, India. I think I may well move on there next,'

Woodward said. 'Fascinating country by the sound of it.'

Quin was aware of the tension in Cleo's still form. Yet another move where she was taken along like a piece of furniture with no choice and no opinion? She would be much better off back in England where she belonged than dragged around at her father's heels like so much luggage.

'I will go with you to the army camp tomorrow, *madam*,' Quin said and turned to look her in the face. 'I want to find out if they have news from any other engineers.' *And I want to get my hands on your damned correspondence, Sir Philip. I may yet be finding a hungry crocodile for you.*

'As you wish.' If Cleo Valsac had any worries about letting him observe the exchange of letters, she hid it perfectly. 'I will be taking the donkey so if you collapse we can load you on him,' she added with a sweet smile that did not deceive Quin for one moment. She thought him a nuisance and she rated his strength, endurance and, probably, his brains very low indeed.

We will see who is right, Cleo my lovely, he thought, meeting her cynical grey-green eyes. To his amazement she blushed.

And do not pretend you don't know what is the matter with you, my girl, Cleo chided herself and bit so hard on a date that she almost broke a tooth. *Lust. An intelligent man with a magnificent body ends up naked in your bed space, at your mercy. And then when he regains his wits he looks at you with those blue eyes and you don't know whether he is pitying you or mocking you or desiring you.*

Or all three, perhaps. Two of those were unwelcome and one was improbable, unless the American had a fancy for skinny, sun-browned widows with calluses on their fingers and not a social grace to their name.

But the widow… Ah, yes, the widow could have a fancy to discover whether those eyes became a darker blue with passion and how those long fingers he was so careful to keep still and inexpressive felt on her body. *Quin.* She indulged herself by trying out his name in her head. *Quintus.*

He was looking at her father now, listening politely to another lecture on hieroglyphs and the importance of measuring the monuments. His face in repose, or when he was guarding it, was all straight lines. Level brows, narrowed eyes, that nose with its arrogant jut in silhouette. His lips were straight until he spoke and the lines of cheekbone and jaw showed strong and regular under the growth of beard, a shade darker than his hair. He looked severe and impenetrable—and then he spoke or smiled and the lines shifted, the angles changed and his face was alive and charming. *And still just as unreadable,* she realised.

But then I am not a very good judge of men. Look at Thierry.

Cleo rose and began to gather up platters. Mr Bredon…*Quin*…immediately began to clear the table, ignoring her shake of the head. He followed her and dumped the scraped dishes into the pot of water that was sitting in the hot ashes and looked round, for a dishcloth, she supposed.

'Leave it,' Cleo said, more sharply than she intended.

'You are tired. Bone weary.' He stood there, arm still in the sling, an improbable kitchen lad.

'I know what I am doing, you will only be in the way.' Ungracious but true. He made her feel clumsy, off balance.

'Then promise me you will come to bed as soon as it is done,' he said softly.

It sounded like an invitation. *Oh, my foolish imagination.* She bent over the water and felt the brush of his fingertips as he lifted her heavy braid over her shoulder and clear of the surface. His hand lingered a moment at her nape, then was gone, leaving her shivering as though a warm cover had been removed in the chill of the night.

'You work too hard, Cleo.'

When she turned, he was gone and there was only her father, a book open on the table in front of him amidst the crumbs, taking advantage of the waning light.

Quin Bredon came out of the tent as soon as Cleo had finished bathing the next day. 'Good morning!' He looked well rested, the haggard hollows had gone from beneath his eyes and his arm was not in the sling.

Cleo returned his greeting with less enthusiasm. She had not had a good night, waking every few minutes, it had seemed, listening for Quin's breathing in the stillness, then cursing herself for a fool and trying to fall asleep again. It was unsettling the way in which he had just appeared, the moment she was dry and dressed and had combed out her hair. He could not have seen her, but it felt uncomfortably as though he had been listening, alert for what she was doing.

'There is water warming by the fire and a linen towel in there. And my father's spare razors.' She gestured towards the makeshift bathing area and went on with preparing a breakfast of coffee, dates, honey and the toasted remains of the flatbread. There would be bread to buy in the village today, and dates and oranges, and the officers might have coffee to spare. With luck she would be able to buy a scrawny chicken to stew into soup with beans and lentils. Another mouth to feed put a strain on supplies.

Her father, dressed in an *abeyah* tied with a sash, his nightcap still incongruously perched on his head, wandered out of the tent with a book in his hand. 'Where's my shaving water?'

'Mr Bredon is bathing and shaving, Father. I have put on more water to warm for you.'

'Humph.' He sat down and reached for a date without taking his eyes from the book. 'This man is an idiot.'

'Who, Father?' The question was automatic. He could reply *King George* or the *Great Chan of China* for all she cared, but Cleo had an instinct that, if she stopped responding to every remark, her father would simply cease to communicate altogether. It had been a relief, she realised, to have Quin there to talk to him last night.

'James Bruce. He let himself be ordered around by his guides, listened to fairy stories and was frightened away by rumours of bandits. This is all nonsense.' He jabbed a finger at a densely written page of text.

'But he was writing over forty years ago, Father,'

Cleo said reasonably. 'And there *are* bandits, as Mr Bredon discovered to his cost.'

'What have I discovered to my cost?' Quin strolled round the corner, his hair on end from a vigorous towelling, his face shaved clean of the dark week-old beard. His jaw line was as sharp and firm as she had thought it would be.

Cleo tried to read his face. There had been an edge to that question she did not understand. 'That there really are bandits out there,' she replied and saw an infinitesimal relaxation around his mouth. 'How is your arm?'

'I took the dressing off. It seems to be healing.'

She put down the honey jar and followed him into the tent. 'Let me look at it. It will need redressing, you cannot take any risks with wounds in this climate.'

He had made his bed. Army-neat, she thought, recalling Thierry's habits of order, as Quin rolled up the loose sleeve of his *galabeeyah* to the shoulder.

'It will not be a tidy scar,' Cleo observed, more to distract herself as she wrapped a fresh strip of cotton over the wound than to make conversation. It was healing well, she saw.

'That amuses you?' Bredon asked and she realised she must have smiled.

'That you will be scarred? No. But it was an unpleasant task, cleaning that, and I have no liking for causing pain, so I am glad it is healing.' She secured the knot and began to roll down his sleeve again. 'I could wish I had made a neater job of it. It is not as though you have a soldier's collection of scars already.' *And that is what happens when you let your tongue run away with you. He knows you are thinking about his naked body. You know he knows.* She took refuge in setting her medicine box in order.

'I compare badly to your warrior husband, no doubt.' He picked up the cotton strip and worked it deftly into a turban.

'Are you fishing for compliments, Mr Bredon?' Cleo said over her shoulder as she picked up the box and ducked under the flap. 'There is nothing amiss with your physique, as you are perfectly well aware, and it gives me no pleasure to see the damage one fool man can inflict on another.'

She bundled her father's letters together and tied them securely into a neat package almost as large as one of the local mud bricks. She dropped it into one of the panniers, added two large goatskins of water, her sharpest kitchen knife, a money pouch and a small sickle for cutting greens. When she bent to lift the two baskets on to the donkey's saddle Quin Bredon slipped in front of her, hefted them into place one-handed and tightened the straps.

'Are you certain you do not wish to ride?' she asked him. 'It is three miles at least in each direction and we can attach the various objects some other way.'

Quin looked down at the long skirts of his *gala-beeyah*. 'Side saddle?' he enquired. 'Or do I hitch up my petticoats and expose my hairy legs to the alarm of the populace?'

'I could find you a spare pair of my father's breeches,' Cleo offered and bit the inside of her cheek to stop herself laughing. There was something not quite right about Mr Bredon, something that made her uneasy, and she was not going to allow him to charm her into letting her guard down. It would be interesting to see what Capitaine Laurent made of him.

'I think not. The poor beast is so small that my feet would trail along the ground.'

Cleo shrugged one shoulder and started walking. It was up to him and he would look considerably less dignified if he had to return stuffed in a pannier. 'We are going now, Father,' she called as she passed the shaded writing area. He grunted and waved his hand without looking up. 'There is food under a cloth near the water jars. Please don't let the fire go out.' There, that was as much as she could hope he'd take notice of.

'You do not have to dawdle on my behalf,' Quin said

'Hmm? No, I wasn't.' She took a firmer hold on the leading rein and lengthened her stride. 'We will take the path along the water's edge, it is easier going than through the sand and there is some shade.'

'Your father has a wide circle of correspondents, he must be greatly respected,' Quin said after five minutes of silent walking.

'His interests are wide-ranging, Mr Bredon. It stimulates him to exchange views with scholars from many countries.'

'*Quin*,' he said. 'It seems ridiculous to observe drawing-room manners in the middle of the desert.' Cleo opened her mouth to demur, but he kept talking. 'And he writes to scholars from both sides in the present conflict and neutral countries, too. I'm amazed that the French authorities are so complacent about assisting him.'

It had puzzled Cleo, too, but she was not going to admit it. 'They are intent on assisting all of *les savants*.

They appear to consider my father as one of their own. After all, he had a French son-in-law.'

'Positively Romeo and Juliet,' Quin observed. She glanced at him sharply, but he was studying the temple now they were close. 'And this is currently the subject of your father's study?'

'He copies the inscriptions and measures it.' Father measured everything obsessively, as though the figures could unlock some key to the mysteries of the past.

'And that is helpful?' Quin stopped and studied the great golden columns rising from the piled sand.

'Apparently. I like to look at the wonderful pictures on the walls—you can just see the top of some of them if you climb right up. The soldiers have carved their names along the topmost frieze. I wish they would not.' She shivered. These things had stood here for millennia, so some scholars said.

'Sacrilege,' Quin murmured and touched her arm. 'I think you have a greater sympathy for these monuments than your father has, for all his scholarship.'

'For the people that created them, perhaps.' She made no move to shake off his hand. Men and women had stood and looked at these buildings since time immemorial, perhaps touching as she and Quin were, supporting each other, perhaps in fear, perhaps in awe. It seemed a small miracle that she had found someone who understood that.

The donkey moved, tugging the rein and with it, her arm. The moment was gone into the hot air, just like every moment evaporating in the heat and dust of this place.

'Come, we need to get to the camp before the sun gets too high.' She began to walk without looking back, listening to the familiar soft footfall of the little don-key and the faint slap of the leather sandals worn by the man who walked with her. It had been a long time since anyone had kept her company. It was strange that it should make her feel lonelier than ever.

Chapter Four

'Do you want to stop and rest?' Cleo glanced back at Quin. 'There is shade just ahead and another mile to go.'

To her surprise, he nodded. 'Yes, that would be welcome.' Then, when she continued to stare he added, 'What is it?'

'Nothing. Nothing beyond the fact that an adult male is prepared to admit to a woman that he would like to rest.'

'You think I am betraying weakness?'

'No, I think you are showing common sense,' she retorted and led the donkey down to the river's edge. 'There is a fallen column from some monument in the shade of those palms. A good place to rest.' She leaned on the donkey's rump while it drank and watched Quin covertly as he sat. His pace had not flagged, although he was pale under his eyes and around his mouth. Considering that he had been prostrate with heat-stroke, and was still carrying a wound that had been seriously infected, it would seem that Quin Bredon was both fit and hardy.

'Men do sometimes demonstrate common sense,' he said mildly when she rejoined him. 'Thank you,' he added as he took the proffered water skin and tipped it expertly so the water arced into his mouth without the neck touching his lips. 'How long does it take to get used to the taste of goat-flavoured water?'

'You never do.' She drank and pushed the stopper into the flask. There were boys herding cattle on the opposite bank and a flock of egrets flew upstream, their white plumage brilliant in the sunlight. A large pied kingfisher landed on a branch nearby and squawked loudly, claiming its stretch of riverbank before diving into the brown water and emerging with a fish. A few hundred yards beyond the ribbon of green on the opposite bank the sand dunes formed a glittering golden ridge.

'This is very beautiful. Timeless. One half-expects to see the pharaoh's daughter find Moses in the bulrushes or for a great barge to float downstream with banners flying and trumpets sounding,' Quin said. He leaned back on a palm trunk, eyes slitted against the sun dazzle on the water.

'It has always been beautiful. And hot, dry, poor and dangerous,' Cleo said. Egypt was somewhere to be endured, battled, overcome. It was a place where men fought to extract something, as miners struggled beneath the earth in heat and danger. Only here there was an ancient civilisation, not diamonds, political advantage, not coal. 'You relax and enjoy it and it will kill you.' She pointed to a small snake slithering into cover.

'I hope your army friends will have more information about the movements of the Mamelukes,' Quin said. 'I have no wish to encounter Murad Bey. He is rather more lethal than that snake, I think.'

Cleo shivered. Thierry had spoken about the Mamelukes, their bravery and savagery, and his hand had tightened on his sword hilt as if to still a tremor of fear. She had no wish to encounter them either. 'What will you do?'

'I am hoping the soldiers will have been recalled towards Cairo. I imagine they will go by river, will they not? It seems perverse to march in this heat.' Quin stood and stretched, six feet of lean muscle unselfconsciously displayed.

'I cannot imagine how I would persuade Father to go.' She got to her feet and made rather a business of straightening the panniers. 'He is very stubborn.'

'Nothing a sharp blow to the head would not cure,' Quin said. He took the leading rein and walked off down the path leaving her blinking at his retreating back.

Did he mean that? How wonderful if he did. She was certain he would accomplish it very neatly, with no more damage to Father than a sore head when he awoke. No, it had to be a joke. Respectable engineers did not go around hitting scholars over the head and loading them on to river boats. She took a grip on her imaginings and ran to catch Quin up.

The camp was small and orderly in the bleak, soulless way of soldiers without women. Capitaine Laurent was sitting on a folding chair outside his tent, his two lieutenants standing listening to him. When he saw them approaching he stood up, watching the stranger from under heavy black brows.

'*Madam.*' He sketched a bow and the other two men did likewise. '*Qui est-ce?*'

'Quintus Bredon, American engineer, Captain,' Quin responded in French before Cleo could speak. 'I have been rescued by Madame Valsac and her father. Bedouin raiders took my camels.' He pushed back his sleeve as he spoke, revealing the edge of the bandage.

'American?' Laurent still made no gesture of hospitality.

'The United States is the ally of France, is she not?' Quin said easily. But he could see that Laurent's stance was alert, subtly more aggressive. The two men were facing up to each other like dogs meeting on the edge of their territories, not convinced yet that a fight was required, but quite willing to scrap if necessary.

'*Oui.* But what are you doing here?'

'Indulging my curiosity. I was in the Balkans, I heard about your emperor's *savants* and I decided to see for myself. There is a brotherhood amongst scientists, I find. I had hoped to reach the Cataracts—an intriguing problem in navigation—but I hear that would be suicide now.'

'Ha!' Laurent gestured to one of the soldiers and the man ran forward with two more folding chairs. 'Sit, have coffee. Murad Bey is on his way north with a force of fifteen thousand, the latest intelligence confirms it.'

'And you have what…fifty men?' Quin glanced around the encampment. 'I imagine your orders do not involve suicide either.'

'Correct. We will strike camp and load up the barges.' He gestured towards the river bank and the moored vessels. 'I was about to send to your father, *madam*, to tell him to prepare to move by dawn tomorrow. We have room for the two…the three…of you and one small piece of baggage each.'

'But my father's books, his papers…'

'His life?' the captain enquired, one brow lifted. 'Yours?'

'It seems I may have to take you up on your offer to knock Father out after all, Mr Bredon.' *Escape, at last. A way to get across those hundreds of miles to the coast and there… And there, what?* she asked herself. She was a woman with no money of her own and no protection once she left her father's side in this dangerous country. But if she could get to France or England, surely she could find work of some kind?

Quin sat back in the chair, his relaxed stance steadying her circling, futile thoughts. 'We might not have to resort to anything so drastic,' he observed. 'Would he come if he could take everything with him? He is not so blinded by his work as to think he could sit making notes on Egyptian antiquities whilst the most dangerous fighting force in Egypt sweeps over your camp, surely?'

'No, I hope even Father would bow to the inevitable under those circumstances. The problem is to prevent the days of argument beforehand while we convince him the danger is real.'

'The village we passed on our way here had several feluccas moored. We could buy or hire two—surely that would be enough room for the three of us and all your possessions.'

'But I cannot sail and Father…'

'I can sail a small boat. The rig is different, but the principles are the same. Besides, we can hire some men.'

Laurent was watching them intently, his head moving from side to side, eyes narrowed in calculation. 'How will you pay for this, *monsieur*? I have no funds to buy boats for civilians.'

And that was all too true, Cleo knew. The emperor had left his troops short of everything from coin to boots, while promising to send them a shipload of clowns and entertainers from Paris to keep up morale. Thierry had once bitterly observed that he would be quite prepared to eat a comedian, provided he was roasted well enough.

'I have money,' Quin said and stood, his hand held out to help her to her feet. Quite how he managed to stand there, clad in a *galabeeyah* like any local peasant, and look as though he was in a drawing room, Cleo had no idea. Not that she had ever been in a drawing room in her life. '*Capitaine,* we will join you here tomorrow before noon.'

Laurent looked as though he was searching for reasons to argue and could find none. 'Your father's correspondence, *madam*?'

'No need to trouble you with that, I am sure you have a great deal to do, without having extra paperwork cluttering things up,' Quin said before Cleo could respond. 'He will be able to deal with it himself when we arrive in Cairo and probably he will want to add to it as we sail down river.'

Cleo opened her mouth to argue, then closed it again. What Quin said was perfectly true, her only objection was with his casual assumption of complete control.

'Shall we go, *madame*? The sooner we reach the village and open negotiations, the better.'

'One moment, Monsieur Bredon. I wish to have a word with the *capitaine.*' She held his gaze. 'In private.'

'But of course.' He bowed to the officers and strolled off to where the donkey was grazing.

'He is insolent, this American, but then I hear they all are,' one of the lieutenants observed as the junior officers walked away to leave her alone with the captain.

'What do you know of him?' Laurent demanded, as she knew he would. She had no answers for him, but she wanted to discover what he thought of Quin.

'Nothing.' Cleo shrugged. 'He had an infected wound and was burning up with heat-stroke. He carried money, but nothing else. I have no reason to suspect he is anything but what he says.'

'But it is strange to find an American here.'

'The frontiers are easy enough to penetrate for a single traveller, are they not? Many people beside the emperor are intrigued by Egypt.'

'The English certainly are,' Laurent remarked, his eyes on Quin's elegant back as he leaned one hip against the panniers and waited, apparently incurious about their conversation or the camp around him. His head was bowed and Cleo wondered fleetingly if he was very tired. 'And not for the antiquities either.'

'You think he might be a spy?' That had not occurred to her before, but then it would be madness to send an agent deep into the desert when there could be nothing of interest to the British here. 'He is not a soldier, I saw his body when I nursed him, he has no scars beyond old ones that must belong to his boyhood.' She shrugged and answered her own question. 'But what would a spy be doing here? In Cairo or Alexandria, I could understand it. No, he must be what he says.'

She was never quite easy with Laurent, who had been her husband's friend. Sometimes she wondered if she could ask him why Thierry had married her. Her father's enthusiasm for allying his daughter with an officer in the army of his country's enemy she understood quite clearly—it protected their position. But why had Thierry courted her with every appearance of passionate attachment and then proved such a distant and uncaring husband?

In the low times, in the hour before dawn when she lay restless and aching with unhappiness, she wondered if the mess her marriage had become was her fault or… *Or what? He knew who he was marrying. Anyone would think he was a fortune hunter, but I have no fortune.*

'Madam?'

'I am sorry.' He must have been talking to her and she had been far away in her head. 'I must go and see if we can secure those boats. If not, we will be here tomorrow with our bare necessities.'

'Of course. You are certain you do not wish to give me your father's correspondence?'

'Perfectly, thank you.' Surely he had more pressing matters to concern himself about just at the moment? *'Au'voir, Capitaine Laurent.'*

Quin pushed the twine back into place and dropped the package of letters into the pannier as he heard the tone of Cleo's voice change into an unmistakable *au'voir*. If he had no further opportunity to get his hands on them, at least he had memorised the names of the eight men addressed, including the Englishman, a Professor Smith of Portsmouth. Was it coincidence that the professor happened to live in the country's foremost naval town?

'And pigs might fly,' Quin muttered to himself.

'Are you well?' Cleo asked, right behind him.

'Well enough and better for the prospect of heading north.'

She nodded agreement as she took the leading rein and started down the path towards the village with the boats. 'It will be a relief to be back in civilisation.'

Then you are going to be sorely disappointed, Quin thought, fanning away the flies with a leafy twig. *We are heading into a plague-ridden battlefield and the best you can hope for is that your father is exposed as a gullible idiot. At worst, perhaps that crocodile might be the kindest option after all.*

Men were lounging around the ramshackle jetty where the boats were moored, but Quin made for the largest house. 'This will be the village sheikh, I imagine. Are you going to sit meekly outside with the donkey while I negotiate?'

He expected an argument, but Cleo simply slipped the tail of her headscarf across her lower face and went to sit under the shade of the wall. 'I know my place,' she said. It was said without inflection or complaint, but there was something in the way she spoke that made Quin look back. 'Yes?' She raised one brow. 'I assume your Arabic is up to it, or do you need help?'

'No, thank you.' *But you do,* Quin thought as he tapped on the door, clearing his mind of French and English. *'Salaam alaikum,'* he said to the elderly man who opened it and ducked through the opening as the sheikh gestured him inside.

Quin knew that bargaining required patience and persistence—he'd had plenty of practice when buying his camels—but the negotiations took more than two hours. No, they could not sell the boats. Yes, possibly they could be hired and the men to crew them. For *how* much? The *effendi* wished to beggar them, like the *Feranzawi* from the soldiers' camp who came to buy food?

Patiently Quin pointed out that if the boats and their crew were absent from the village when Murad Bey and his men came through they would be safe. If they hired them to him, they would be out of reach and earning at the same time.

By this time they had moved to the waterside and there was much murmuring and gesticulating at this suggestion. A price was named. Quin reeled back in exaggerated horror. He prodded a battered gunwale, curled his lip at the state of the ropes and named another figure.

When finally they had come to an agreement and he had drunk bitter coffee and handed over half the price, Cleo was still sitting in the same place, motionless. When he turned from the waterside in a flurry of jokes and waving hands from his new acquaintances she rose smoothly to her feet and followed him in silence until they were out of sight.

'Will it take long to break camp?' he asked when it seemed she was not going to say anything.

'No. Not with you to help.' Her voice was muffled behind the veiling cotton.

'What is wrong, Cleo?' Quin stopped and turned. 'Don't you want to leave?' This mission might be, quite literally, a pain, but at least he'd believed he was effecting a rescue. Now it seemed the victim might not want rescuing.

'Of course I want to leave.' She wrenched the veil from her face and glared at him. 'Only a fool would *want* to stay.'

'Then you worry that your father might be stubborn and refuse? I am certain I can—'

'If he refuses, then we leave him.' She kept walking, swept past with the donkey trotting obediently behind.

'Abandon your father?' he asked her retreating back, the set shoulders and reed-straight spine. This woman was going to be a shark in the ornamental fishpond that was London society.

'He abandoned Mama. He has abandoned me. She was simply an unpaid maidservant and so am I. I want him safe and looked after, but after that…'

It took Quin several loping strides to catch up with her. 'Abandoned? But you are with him now.'

'Abandoned emotionally, abandoned in his head. Family is just a nuisance, a tie, to him. Mama thought he loved her and eloped with him willingly.' Cleo snapped out the explanation as though she slapped down cards on a gaming table. 'He loved the dowry he counted on my grandfather handing over when the marriage was a *fait accompli*. But Mama's father simply cut her off. By the time she realised that she had tied herself to a profoundly selfish man I was on the way.'

At least her grandfather wanted her, although Quin refused to contemplate whether it was from love, duty or simply family pride. He found he could think of nothing to say so he reached out and laid his arm over her shoulders. A hug might help…

Cleo shrugged off his touch and stalked on. 'Mama was very good at explaining things as I grew up. Papa was a very busy man. Papa was very important and so was his work. Papa must not be disturbed. Papa loved me really. That worked all through Italy and Greece and Anatolia while I was a child. Then we came to Egypt and Mama died and I realised—'

'Realised what?'

'That it was time to stop being a little girl and become a woman. To stop expecting what he cannot give.'

'Love? Is that why you married Capitaine Valsac?'

'But of course.' She turned those mysterious greenish-grey eyes on him and smiled. 'Why else would I marry, save for love?'

Chapter Five

'Why marry other than for love?' Quin Bredon fell into step beside her. 'I can think of many reasons. For protection, for money, for status.' She sensed his gaze slide sideways for a second. 'For lust.'

Cleo winced, then hid the reaction with a slap at a fly. *To escape,* she added mentally. *And for lust, let's be honest. You desired Thierry, he was big and handsome and active. Alive. He looked at you and saw something beyond a drudge, so you thought.*

'I married my husband loving him,' she answered honestly. *And by the time I was left a widow three months later I hated him.* Pride kept her voice light and her lips firm. She had been a fool to marry a man she hardly knew. And she must still be a fool, because she could not work out why he had married her. But she was not going to admit any of that to this man who was also big and handsome and active. *And worryingly intelligent and curious.*

'I'm amazed you found a priest to marry you all the way down here,' Quin remarked. 'Or did you wed in a Coptic church?'

'We married in Cairo. Father and I were there when the French took the city in July ninety-eight.'

'Good God,' Quin muttered.

'It was not amusing,' Cleo agreed, with massive understatement. It took an effort not to let the memories flood back, filling her nostrils with the stench of smoke and blood and disease. She had only to close her eyes and the screams of the sick and dying would drown out the sound of the river and the cries of the hawks overhead. 'Fortunately there was no prolonged siege. Father made himself known to the new French authorities at once—he had heard about *les savants*, you see.'

'And they allowed him, an Englishman, his freedom, even after their defeat at the Battle of the Nile?'

'They saw he was harmless, I suppose. He talked to the governor and must have convinced them he was exactly what and who he said. They gave him protection and even facilitated his correspondence.'

'Why are you not still there?'

'We stayed for a year, then the next July they found the Rosetta Stone and brought it to Cairo, but they wouldn't let anyone but the French *savants* look at it. Father was livid. Napoleon left for France to stage his *coup* and things began to fall apart in Cairo—the generals were arguing, there was very little money or food and the plague got worse. Father said he wanted to go south and they said he could if we went with a party of troops that was going too.'

'And luckily Valsac was one of the officers? You must have been delighted.'

'I did not know him before. We were introduced when the plans were being made. Thierry began to court me. Then Father and the general said it was awk-

ward me being the only woman, and unmarried. So
he proposed.'

'How fortunate that a marriage of convenience
should turn out so romantically. And how sad it lasted
such a short time. How did he die? If you don't mind
talking about it.'

There was no hint of sarcasm in his words and Quin
sounded genuinely sympathetic. It must be her own
nagging unhappiness about the whole marriage that
was colouring her reaction to his words.

'He was killed in a skirmish when we came up
against Murad Bey's rearguard on his return south. It
has been peaceful since, which is why we live apart
from the troop now. They have found a better base
for themselves and Father wanted to be close to the
temple.'

'And you returned to your father's tent.'

'I was always there when Thierry was away from
camp.' *Who else was going to look after him?* she
thought and bit back the words. There was no point in
bitterness, she was the only one it hurt. 'Look, here
is our village. I must arrange some help tomorrow to
carry our things to the boats.'

There was no problem here, she was known and
trusted even though the villagers thought her father
was most strange and the women sympathised with her
lack of a husband. Cleo negotiated with the sheikh's
senior wife for men and donkeys to carry their baggage
to Shek Amer in return for her own little donkey and
everything that would not fit on the boats.

Quin did not enter the village with her, perhaps
sensing that his presence as a strange man might be
an embarrassment. He was quite sensitive, quite un-

like what she imagined an engineer to be like. He was more suited to being a diplomat, Cleo decided as she stopped on the river bank to cut some greenery for the donkey's evening feed. When she looked round for him Quin had climbed the piled sand around the temple and was standing in the shadow of one of the great pillars.

Cleo lifted the packet of letters, the knife and water flasks from the bottom of one of the panniers and heaped in the greenery, then laid the things back on the top, straightening the cord that tied the bundle of correspondence as she did so. When she had fastened it that morning she had wrapped it round once, then twisted it so the cord caught in the other sides of the little bundle like a parcel, before knotting the ends in the middle. Now one corner was creased and the cord not straight. Odd. Perhaps it had been knocked when the water bottles had been dropped in.

She lifted her gaze to the figure almost invisible in the deep shadows of the temple. *Or perhaps Quin pushed the cord aside to look at the addresses on the letters.* But why should he do that? She recalled her conversation with Laurent. Could Quin be spying? But all there was here was one English scholar and his daughter and a small troop of French soldiers, miles from base.

But we are going back to Cairo and he will come with us... No, that is too convoluted. To come hundreds of miles south, through all those dangers, only to find a small group to give him an entrée into Cairo? Preposterous.

She was being foolish, Cleo told herself as she took the leading rein and made her way across the scrubby grazing area and into the sand. He was just curious and she was lonely, isolated and had no one to talk to. It was a miracle she did not see suspicious characters around every corner or hold imaginary conversations with the donkey.

There was a whole world out there filled with people who had proper families, families who cared for each other and talked and shopped and went to the theatre and entertained friends. A whole world that seemed as remote as the world of the ancient Egyptians with their enigmatic monuments.

The donkey found a bush clinging to life at the foot of the temple and proceeded to eat it. Cleo dropped the rein and trudged up the slope of shifting sand until she reached the top. Here the great horizontal slabs were only a few feet above her head and she slithered down the slope inside to where Quin stood in the shadows, gazing upwards at the ceiling.

'Look,' he said, his voice filled with wonder. 'The roof is painted with stars.'

'There is Nut.' Cleo pointed up to where a woman's elongated figure spanned the sky. 'This is all so unimaginably old. I was there when Napoleon made his speech to the troops outside Cairo. *"Soldiers! From the top of these pyramids, forty centuries gaze down upon you."* But I know very little about it. Father just measures things. I want to dig all the sand out.'

'And find treasure? They say there are golden coffins and statues of lapis and gilt.'

'Is that why you are here?' she said before she could censor her thoughts. 'Are you a treasure hunter?'

'No, certainly not.' He looked bemused. 'It is obvious, even to someone as ignorant about this as I am, that one would need teams of workmen to clear these sites.' As her eyes became accustomed to the dimmer light she saw he was watching her. 'I told you what I am. Do you not believe me?'

'Yes. Yes, of course. But an engineer would know how to clear something like this—'

'I know how to clear it safely and efficiently, I just do not know what I would be looking for or what damage I might be doing,' he interrupted her. 'Is it very hard to trust me, Cleo?' Quin held out his hand. 'Let's go out again, those four thousand years are weighing down on me.'

She ignored his hand, but they scrambled up the internal sand slope together and stood just within the sharp edge of shadow that ran along the top. Quin seemed to want to touch, she thought, watching him out of the corner of her eye. That arm around her shoulders that she had shrugged off, his hand just now. But it did not feel sexual, he was not trying to grope her body as some men did before she showed her knife to them.

'Your colour is not good,' she observed. 'You are grey under your tan.'

'That makes me feel so much better,' Quin said with a grimace. 'I'm shattered, if truth be told.'

'I warned you.'

'There's no need to be smug about it.' He leaned back on a pillar and closed his eyes, his lashes thick and dark on the pale skin beneath his lids.

'I am not smug, merely right.' Cleo put her hands on his shoulders and pushed down. 'Sit. Rest.'

Quin caught her wrist and pulled her with him as he slid down the pillar to end up on the sand, knees raised. 'Your concern is touching. Sit down too and tend to me in the approved womanly manner.'

Cleo snorted, but settled next to him, her shoulder not quite against his. It was a novelty to simply sit during the day and do nothing. It was completely outside her experience to just sit and talk. He would think her pathetic indeed if he guessed how much this gave her pleasure. 'My concern is simply to keep you in good enough condition to be of some help packing.'

'I will be all right in a few minutes.' His eyes were still closed and he rested his head back against the golden sandstone.

It was interesting to hear a man admit weakness. Thierry would never have dreamt of such a thing, he would have considered it unmanly. Cleo thought that merely foolish. It was sensible to take a rest, that was all, it did not make Quin a weakling. She studied his big hands with their long fingers as they rested on his knees. There was nothing unmanly about those hands. As she thought it he lifted the right one and slung it around her shoulders, apparently gauging her position by instinct.

'What are you doing?' Cleo demanded, twisting against him.

'Hugging,' Quin said and settled her firmly against his side. 'Not groping, don't panic. I'm a great believer in hugging, we all ought to do it a lot more. Human contact is important, don't you think?'

I wouldn't know. Cleo shrugged. Her father never hugged her, Thierry had only taken her in his arms for sex. She supposed her mother must have hugged her, but she could not remember. Mama always seemed so busy, or so tired. But, now she let herself relax a little, it was pleasant to be close to another human being, a friendly, talkative human. His arm around her shoulders was heavy, but not unpleasantly so. He made no move to touch her in any other way. She could feel the beat of Quin's heart beneath his ribs where their sides touched and he smelt of her own familiar soap, and not unpleasantly of fresh male sweat. She probably smelled of dust and donkey.

'Who hugs you?' she asked. 'Your wife?'

'Not married.' He sounded half-asleep.

'Your mistress?'

The side of his mouth kicked up a fraction. 'Mistresses aren't for hugging.'

'Who, then?'

'My mother used to. My nieces and nephews do. My old nurse when she isn't telling me off for something. My brothers. Male friends.'

'You hug *men*?'

That almost-smile again. 'Well, you know—that embarrassed half-hug men do, then we slap each other on the shoulder and clear our throats and start talking about horses or women.'

No, she didn't know. This was obviously part of that unknown world that she understood as little of as any village woman. 'Your father?'

'Not my father.' There was no smile this time and no colour in his voice.

She understood about fathers who wiped the smile from your lips. 'You have four older brothers, of course. Is there a Sixtus?'

'No, I'm the only one with a number.' Again that careful avoidance of emotion. 'The others are Henry, James, Charles and George.'

It took no great degree of perception to guess that something was very wrong with his family, or, at least with his relationship with his father. What to talk about now? Or perhaps it was best just to let him rest. It was unexpectedly comfortable sitting quietly together, touching. Cleo closed her eyes. *What an idiot I was to be suspicious of him. He is a nice, uncomplicated man.*

'Tell me about your little troop of soldiers.'

Her eyes snapped open. 'What about them?'

'I just wondered what they would be like as travelling companions. Are they amiable or aggressive? Competent, do you think? Well-armed?'

'I have no idea about their efficiency or their arms,' Cleo said cautiously. 'I know little about such things. Why?'

'Because I am going to write it all down in a report and send it off to the British by carrier vulture.' He rolled his eyes at her. 'For goodness' sake, Cleo! Because our safety is going to depend to a great extent on that unit, of course. This is hardly going to be a pleasure cruise. I have no weapons. Has your father?'

'A musket and some pistols. A sword in the big trunk, I think. But they have been in there for years.'

'We will get them out and check them over this evening. Is your father a good shot?'

'I imagine he could hit the side of a pyramid if he was close enough, but I have never seen him with a weapon in his hand.' It was always Mama who had to deal with the chickens for the pot.

'We'll stick close to your soldiers then.' Quin pushed against the pillar and got to his feet with an easy grace that looked effortless and which must, given his state of health, have taken some will-power.

'They are not *my* soldiers.' She looked at the way he was favouring his left arm. 'Does that hurt?'

'I'll live.' *Yes, he hides a great deal under that pleasant face and reasonable manner.* 'You married one of them,' he added, not to be distracted from his point, it seemed.

Cleo marched off down the slope to the patient donkey.

'For love.' Quin's voice came so close behind her that when she stopped he bumped into the back of her.

'Of course. I told you so.' She set off briskly towards the camp so the donkey had to trot to catch up. 'You are a very curious man, Mr Bredon.'

'Strange or inquisitive?' He had lengthened his stride, too, which would probably tire him again, but she was too flustered to care.

'Both.'

'I only wondered because it seems a strange thing to do, for an Englishwoman. To marry an enemy. But if it was love, I can understand.'

'The French are no enemies of mine. I have never been to England and my grand English relatives do not want me, so why should I care for it? The only good thing I know of it is that it rains a lot there.' She glanced up at the relentlessly blue, hot sky. 'And there is no sand. But it rains in France almost as much as in England, Thierry said, and there are no deserts there either. I was looking forward to France,' she added under her breath.

But not softly enough, it seemed. 'It rains a lot in America, too,' Quin remarked. 'There are deserts, but those are easy to avoid if you want to.'

Cleo reached the tent and turned. 'Is that a proposal, Mr Bredon?'

She had hoped to disconcert him, embarrass him

even. Instead he laughed, a deep, mellow sound. 'No, and you are teasing me, *madam*. It was a geographical remark, as you know full well.'

'Daughter!' Her father appeared around the side of the tent. 'There you are at last.' He picked up the bundle of letters from on top of the wilting greenery in the pannier. 'Why have you not handed these over? And was there nothing for me?'

'The soldiers are leaving, Father.' Cleo led the donkey into its shelter and lifted off the panniers. Quin took them and began to dump the fodder out, tactfully, she supposed, leaving them to their exchange.

'Leaving? But who will deal with my correspondence?' Her father was going red in the face as he always did when thwarted.

'No one. We are going, too, because the Mamelukes are coming. Mr Bredon has secured two feluccas and the villagers are coming to help us move our things early tomorrow morning. We must start to pack now.'

'Nonsense. There is work to be done here. They will not trouble us, why should they? We are staying.' He turned back towards the tent.

'But, Father—'

Quin ducked out from the donkey shelter. 'I am leaving tomorrow morning and I am taking Madame Valsac and her belongings with me. Whether you come willingly or attempt to stay is entirely up to you, Sir Philip.'

Her father swung round. 'She will do no such thing, she will do as she is told and remain with me.'

'Madame Valsac is a widow and of age, Sir Philip. She does as she pleases. And it does not suit my conscience to leave you here, however pig-headed you are, sir. If you refuse to accompany us, then I am afraid I will have to knock you out and sling you over that unfortunate little donkey.'

'You would assault a man old enough to be your father! After I took you in, saved your life—'

Cleo slipped away into the tent behind them.

'It was Madame Valsac who took me in and saved my life, Sir Philip. I imagine you would have noticed me when my corpse began to stink, but not before, unless you fell over me,' Quin said calmly. 'And I would not leave a man old enough to be my father to the mercies of a war band of belligerent cavalry, armed to the teeth and set on killing. So, what is it to be? Co-operation or force?'

'Damn you, sir—'

'Here is the key to the arms chest, Mr Bredon. I have just locked it.' Cleo handed him the key and stood beside him, facing her father. 'It is for your own good, you know.'

Sir Philip turned and stormed back into the tent.

'I'll take that to be a yes, then,' Quin said. 'You are truly a soldier's wife, Cleo.' He tossed the key into the air and caught it again. 'Let us go and inspect our arsenal.'

Chapter Six

Cleo was extraordinarily efficient. Quin wondered if she had learned to be in her few months as a soldier's wife or whether she was naturally organised. Probably the latter, he decided as he helped a grumbling Sir Philip pack his papers into trunks. From what he could see the man's books and notes comprised most of the Woodwards' possessions.

There were a few portmanteaux he had glimpsed in their sleeping spaces, enough for a limited wardrobe, but Cleo seemed to possess no ornaments or trinkets, only tools, kitchen implements and her medical kit.

'We cannot do more this evening,' she said at last, coming out to find him feeding the donkey to escape her father's complaints. 'What is left are the cooking and eating things and tonight's bedding and of course the tent, but that comes down very easily.'

'It does?' Quin slopped water into the bucket and straightened up to look at the structure.

'It does when you have done it as often as I have,' Cleo said. 'Here, there are some spare clothes of my father's.' She thrust a bundle topped with a wide-brimmed

straw hat into his arms. 'You will find it easier to re-
late to the soldiers if you look more like a European.'
She shrugged when he looked a question. 'They do not
trouble to get to know the local people. As far as they
are concerned the villagers are either the lowest form
of peasants or brigands—or both.'

Quin shook out a pair of loose cotton trousers, a
shirt and a long, sleeveless jerkin. Not exactly the thing
to be seen wearing at Almack's, but ideally suited to
the heat. 'Thank you, I must admit to becoming tired
of my skirts.'

'They will be too big,' she said as she walked back
to the tent, 'but you can use a cord as a belt. I will find
something.'

'Cleo.' She stopped, but did not turn. 'Leave it, I
will manage I am sure. You look exhausted. Surely
there is nothing more to do tonight?'

'Just supper and heating the washing water and
some laundry.'

'*Cleo.*' That brought her round, a frown between
the dark slashes of her brows. 'Come here. Please.'

She trudged back towards him, her usual grace lost
in what must be a fog of tiredness. Quin opened his
arms and gathered her to him and after a moment she
slipped hers around his waist, leaned in, her face in
the angle of his neck and shoulder. She relaxed against
him and sighed.

Quin held her and breathed in the scent of hot, tired
woman, the herbal rinse she used on her hair, the faint
scent of mint tea on her breath, the dust that filmed her
skin. He was beginning to care too much for her welfare, he knew that. He had a mission to perform and it
was not certain yet that she was an entirely innocent

victim to be rescued. This was all too near spying to be comfortable and yet it was his duty. This was no place to strike fine attitudes about being a gentleman. He sneered at himself. *So anxious to be a true gentleman and not a bastard? This is the best thing for her, the authorities will bend over backwards to look after her welfare, if only for her grandfather's sake. Your sensitive conscience can rest easy, Quin.*

Cleo stirred in his arms and he forced himself to think clearly about her. She professed no loyalty to England, she had married a Frenchman for love and she carried her father's suspicious paperwork back and forth to the troops. Had she any idea what was going on? She was an intelligent woman, but curiously sheltered from the real world. An innocent, an obedient daughter or a willing servant of the French?

Having a woman plastered to him was having its natural effect on his body and the thin robe he wore was not exactly designed to hide the fact from someone as close as Cleo was. Quin realised the proximity was having an effect on her, too. He could feel her nipples hard against his chest and her breathing had changed.

He wanted to make love to her, but that was out of the question. Back to his blasted gentlemanly sensibilities, he recognised with resignation. To make love to Cleo while he was uncertain of her smacked of a ruse to gain her confidence and extract information through pillow talk. He would die for his country, he would kill for it if he must, but he was not going to seduce a woman for it and if that made him a hair-splitting hypocrite, then so be it.

Cleo wriggled back a little and he opened his arms to release her, half-thankful, half-regretful. Then he realised she was simply putting enough space between them so he could kiss her. *Who is seducing whom?* he wondered. *Or is this just for comfort? If it is, it must be hers, because it is most certainly not going to help me sleep tonight... To hell with it.* He bent his head and took the proffered lips. *Just one kiss.*

Her mouth, hot and soft under his, opened without him needing to coax. She was willing and yet, despite it all, shy. Quin took a firm grip on his will-power and kissed her with more gentleness than passion, his tongue sliding against hers, his palms flat on her back in the loosest of holds. She was trembling slightly, he realised, like a woman fighting emotion.

Quin raised his head. 'Cleo?' Her eyes were wide and dark and flooded with unshed tears. 'Cleo '

'Unhand my daughter!' Over her shoulder Quin saw Sir Philip emerge from the tent, his fists clenched. 'How dare you, you libertine!'

Quin felt something snap under the layers of carefully cultivated diplomatic restraint. Suddenly he did not care if the woman in his arms was writing a daily journal to Napoleon himself with intimate details of Lord Nelson's sailing plans, because, if she was, it was entirely the fault of the red-faced, selfish, blustering man in front of him.

He set Cleo carefully aside and took two long strides to confront Sir Philip. 'I have had more than enough of you, sir,' he said and when the older man swung at him he ducked under his guard, hit him on the point of the chin and watched with nothing but pure satisfaction when Sir Philip's eyes rolled back in his head and he fell full-length on the sand.

That was definitely what had been missing from

his diplomatic career to date: the opportunity for un-thinking violence, Quin thought as the anger cleared and he stared down at the unconscious man at his feet.

'Damn.' It might be satisfying, but neither particularly honourable, nor practical. 'Cleo—'

'Don't you dare apologise,' she stormed at him.

Quin rocked back on his heels. *You look magnificent when you are angry... No, don't say it. You should lose your temper more often, it is good for you? No, probably not tactful either.* The memory of those un-spilled tears nagged at him. 'But I should apologise.'

'No. Not for hitting him, not for the kiss.' She stood over her father. 'But we can't leave him here and he is much heavier than you.'

'We could, this side is in shade now.' Quin knelt and examined the unconscious man. He was breathing normally, there was no blood and nothing but a bruise on his chin and a small lump at the back of his head to be found. 'If you fetch me a mat, I'll roll him on his side so he doesn't choke and put something under his head. He'll wake up soon.' *And in no very good temper, either, but in the meantime...*

Cleo went to start preparing supper, clearly with no expectation that Quin would assist her. He ignored the chivalrous instinct to take over and make her rest and went into Sir Philip's workspace. The boxes were all packed, but the locks were still open. Quin knelt in front of the first and began to search, ears straining for the soft pad of feet on sand.

When he was through in there he went into the other man's sleeping quarters, feeling beneath the mattress pad and pillow, sliding his fingers between neatly stacked shirts and linen in the trunk, flipping through the pages of the books on the floor by the bed.

'Quin! Father is stirring, can you come and help him into a chair?' Cleo called. The table was laid when he walked round from the far side of the tent from Sir Philip's quarters, wiping his freshly washed hands on a towel.

'Yes, of course. There you are, sir.' He took hold under the man's armpits and hauled him to his feet, then dumped him unceremoniously into a chair. He expected an outburst, but all he received was a glower. Woodward truly was a bully who would back down when challenged.

Cleo put platters on the table, added a basket of flat bread and sat down. It seemed that everyone was capable of pretending that nothing untoward had happened, even if conversation eluded all three of them.

The silence gave Quin the opportunity to review what he had found. Or had not found. There was no sign of any cipher keys, but that meant little. Quin was not certain he would recognise anything very sophisticated in the way of codes and if one was being used that involved substituting letters in a particular book, then he could spend a week and not find it. On the other hand he did know how to check correspondence for signs of tampering and some of the seals on the letters to Sir Philip had, to his eye, been opened once with a thin hot blade and resealed before the recipient had cracked open the seal.

Possibly all of them had been opened, he could not be certain when the seal had been completely destroyed.

'More dates, Father?' Cleo pushed the platter across

the board and Quin watched the older man as he took a handful and began to strip them off the stalk. If the letters were being opened before he received them, then presumably he was unaware of what was happening, unless pains were being taken to protect him. But was he naïve or simply ignoring what was under his nose? Whichever it was, Cleo was surely innocent of any involvement, which would make the Duke of St Osyth a very happy man. It certainly made Quin feel better.

'What will you do when we get to Cairo, Quin?' Cleo asked.

'Depends what the situation is. But I'll be going home fairly soon, I suppose.'

'To your wife, sir?' Woodward said, so suddenly that Cleo dropped her knife.

'I am not married, Sir Philip.'

'Should be at your age. What are you? Twenty-seven?'

It was the first conversation Woodward had made that was not essentially about himself or his own interests. It sounded suspiciously like a father asking questions of his daughter's suitor. Quin controlled the wry smile that tugged at his lips and answered truthfully. 'I am twenty-eight, Sir Philip. And I intend setting up my household once I am settled back at home.'

A wife was a considerable asset to a career diplomat and his superiors had not been reticent in pointing that out to him. It might be an open secret that Lord Quintus Deverall was not his father's son, but, as the marquess acknowledged him, he was an eligible match for the daughters of the middling aristocracy. As his career developed he knew he would become even more of a catch and he had no hesitation about laying out his ambitions very clearly to a prospective father-in-law.

He was even prepared to be very frank about his desire to cut every link between his father and himself. His sense of self, his pride, his very honour, were tied up in being unambiguously his own man, not the tolerated cuckoo in the marquess's nest. The older he became, the harder it was to stomach the legal pretence that, as his mother's husband had not repudiated him at birth, he must be his son. The world was going to have to accept Quintus Deverall, gentleman, on his own terms, as his own man. Nothing else was acceptable.

Now what he needed in his calculated campaign was an intelligent, sophisticated woman with good conversational skills, several languages and complete competence in organising social events at a high level, someone who one day could be an ambassador's wife. All he needed to do was to get himself back to London without further bullet wounds, a dose of the plague or having his eyes scratched out by a Frenchman's furious widow and then he would be all set for the new Season.

Lady Caroline Brooke was top of his list. Blonde, as sophisticated as an unmarried lady was allowed to be, a superb organiser and the daughter of a leading light in the government. He had seen her deal with a tricky dinner-party encounter between a Russian grand duke and the Italian count who was sleeping with his wife with both aplomb and tact...

'Quin?'

He blinked and realised he was gazing absently at Cleo, fitting the piquant heart-shaped face of Lady Caroline, framed by her customary fashionable *coiffure*, on to the tanned oval of Cleo's face. If her hair had ever been in the hands of a lady's maid, let alone a hairdresser, he would be very much surprised. 'I apologise, I was miles away thinking about the…' *lady I intend courting* '…about tomorrow. What time must we be stirring?'

'Dawn,' Cleo said. 'Of course.'

He had a pretty good idea that she knew he'd been thinking about another woman, females had that uncanny instinct. *Very diplomatic, Quin. Ambassadorial-level tact, that.* 'I'll clear this away,' he said and got to his feet. When he returned to England he'd be fully qualified as a kitchen maid.

Cleo had no problem waking before dawn, not after a night where she had hardly snatched more than a few minutes' sleep at a time. Her carefully cultivated calm and resignation had completely deserted her. She was excited about returning to Cairo and worried that she could make no firm plans to escape from there and get to England or France. Under that was apprehension about the dangers of the river journey and the lack of privacy as the only woman in a small flotilla of men.

And deep down, beneath those practical concerns as though she had pushed it under a mental rug, was that kiss. That had been no friendly hug, even though she was certain that was how it started. Quin had wanted to comfort her because she was so tired, she had wanted someone to care, someone to hold her. And then that fire had flared between them. She had felt his body stir and harden against hers, as her blood had surged in her veins and her breath had caught in her throat.

Cleo shifted, restless on the hard bed, and rolled over so she could watch for the betraying greyness that signalled the approach of dawn. When she had all but asked for his kiss Quin had not hesitated. Yet he had not snatched at his own satisfaction... What would happen if she got up and went to him now? If she knelt beside his bed and touched his face, bent and pressed her lips to his temple, to the corner of his eyes, to his lips?

Nothing, she told herself as she sat up and wrapped her arms around her knees. Quin was not going to make love to her in a tent with her father only a few yards away, any more than she was going to act on these foolish fantasises.

There was movement, a stir in the air, and she saw the wall hangings move as someone brushed past them. Dim light filtered in under the bottom of her door cloth. Quin was up. Cleo tipped her head to one side and followed what he was doing by sound. The pad of leather sandals on the sand, the splash of water. A long silence, then scuffling noises from the area of the hearth, a murmur as he spoke to the donkey.

Cleo threw back the covers and found her robe and sandals, then went out to join him. It was cold still, the world was grey and white coils of mist hung over the river. She shivered and hunched into the robe.

'Here.' Quin stood up from the fireside where he had been hunkered down. 'I've warmed some water for you.'

'Don't you want to wash?' It was curiously difficult to meet his eyes, as if he'd read her heated thoughts in them.

'I have. I used cold water.' He handed her the jar and squatted down again, his focus apparently on the glowing wood. 'I couldn't sleep.'

There was no answer to that other than, *Oh? Why not?* And that risked receiving an answer she would not want to hear. Cleo went and washed, wishing she had cold water, too, then slipped back inside to dress and pack away her clothes and make a bundle of the bedding, shaking each piece vigorously. Whatever else a voyage down the Nile would involve, there should be a merciful absence of sand.

'What shall I do with the bed frame?' Quin called.

'Stack them all by the donkey's shelter. I will put everything we are leaving for the villagers there.'

From the far side of the tent she heard the sounds of her father waking, grumbling as he moved around. 'Hot water by the fire, Father,' she called and went to set out breakfast.

The villagers came straggling towards them, donkeys at their heels, by the time the big tent was cleared and their possessions piled into two heaps, one to stay, one to go. Quin left Cleo to discuss the loading and carried on pulling tent pegs out of the ground. She came running back as he finished that and began directing men to remove poles and collapse the structure in such a way that they could fold and roll it into series of bundles that were then tied with the guy ropes.

'Very efficient,' he remarked as he dropped the pegs into the drawstring bag she produced.

'I am.'

Quin grinned at her back as she marched off to supervise the loading of the donkeys. Cleo was being exceptionally crisp this morning and he suspected he knew why. That kiss. He could not regret it, although it had made for an uncomfortable night. But it was as far as things could go, even though his body was clamouring for more and the part of his brain that tried hard to ignore his conscience was protesting that Cleo needed comfort and human warmth.

You are not going to seduce a respectable widow, he told himself firmly. *She does not deserve it and she certainly is not going to end up as your mistress.* He watched her now as she saw to the loading of Sir Philip's trunks, showing no more concern for them than she did for her cooking implements. In contrast he noticed the way she kept an eye on the box containing the weapons and could only conclude that she had no idea that her father's correspondence might be in any way important or compromising.

I can acquit you of harm, Cleo Valsac. And I can hand you back to your grandfather the duke with a clear conscience when I tell him you are the victim of the piece. And you can become the lady you should be by birth and leave this drudgery behind. All I need to do is get you there despite, no doubt, your best efforts to do things on your terms.

Quin flexed the muscles in his injured arm, feeling the pull and sting of the healing wound, then went to keep an eye on the weapons chest. It was a long way to England.

Chapter Seven

What *hat excellent Arabic you speak, Mr American En-*
gineer. I wonder why you need that particular lan-
guage. Cleo sat on a pile of blankets and watched as
Quin organised the sailors into creating small enclosed
compartments midships on both boats, using parts of
the dismantled tent.

The crew, she knew, would sleep ashore each night,
but she was profoundly grateful to see the makeshift
cabins that would give her a little privacy in the midst
of all these men.

Feluccas could carry at least a dozen passengers, so
there was ample room for their possessions and those
of the four villagers who would come with them to
sail the boats. The great lateen-rigged mainsails were
large to catch every breath of breeze and manoeuvrable
enough to tack from side to side down the meander-
ing river to avoid the constantly shifting sandbanks.
They were halfway between the annual inundations so
there was still enough water in the main channels to
ensure a fairly smooth trip and, of course, once they
had beaten upstream to meet with the army barges,
they would turn and go with the current.

'Excellent. I will have this one.' Cleo glanced up to see her father was already organising all his luggage around him in the foremost felucca, filling the small cabin.

'You need to allow enough room for your daughter, Sir Philip.' Quin switched back to English.

'She can sleep on the other boat.' He was already opening boxes and putting his folding chair in place.

'I am on the other boat and you have left me no room on yours. In the absence of a female companion Madame Valsac should be with you at night.'

'Sleep ashore if the proprieties worry you. Who is to know in any case?'

Quin vaulted over the side to wade to the shore. 'I don't like to leave you alone on the boat, not when we are away from the area you are familiar with. Would you object if I slept on the deck?'

So close I will be able to reach out and touch you. So close you could come to my bed and no one would know. Only you will not, will you, my chivalrous American whom I do not quite trust?

'I would be grateful,' Cleo said, striving for a balance between gratitude and distance. The sight of Quin moving so effortlessly around the boat, his long legs encased in wet linen, the neck of his loose shirt open to reveal glimpses of the sun-bronzed skin of his throat, were all reviving pleasantly dangerous feelings that it would be most unwise to acknowledge. That kiss had been bad enough, but now she was recalling his naked body with accuracy.

'We are ready, *effendi*,' the oldest of the four boatmen called.

Quin raised one hand in acknowledgment. 'Ready?'

he asked her and, when she nodded, simply scooped her up, waded through the shallow water and deposited her in the boat. She might have been a sack of wheat, she thought resentfully, so impersonal was his grip.

The villagers had gathered on the bank to watch them, faces as impassive as Cleo hoped hers was. These *Inglizi* with their strange habits had descended on them as though from the heavens and now they were taking themselves away, Allah knew where. Their ancestors must have watched like this as the temple builders came and went and then for hundreds of generations after as the sand took over the sacred places and a new religion and new conquerors swept across their land.

She had no idea what they thought of them, but she waved and the children waved back, running alongside as the boats cast off and began to drift with the current. The great sails flapped and filled and the women turned and went back to their village, incurious and uncaring of where the *Inglizi* were going now.

'I hope the villagers will be safe when the Mamelukes come through.'

'They should be. They'll hide their livestock on the islands, I imagine.' Quin stood amidships and leaned against the main mast, one bare foot on the strakes, his wet trouser leg flapping in the breeze. The wind ruffled through his hair and his face was more relaxed than she had ever seen it. He had said he was twenty-eight and she wondered just what his life had held to give him that strange ability to switch between bland courtesy, warm concern and an almost dark intensity. There was something in his family background that contributed to the darkness, she had sensed that easily enough, but why did she have so much trouble picturing him as the engineer he professed to be?

He was intelligent enough and practical, too. And yet… 'How long will it be?' she asked as she settled down opposite him.

'To Cairo? Depends on the army barges, I suppose.' He shrugged. 'I assume they'll want to make all speed, but we cannot travel at night, not with these sandbanks. Within ten days, I'd hazard, unless there are problems on the river or with the barges.'

Ten days to plan what she would do when they arrived in Cairo. There, at least, she could leave her father with a clear conscience. He could hire an assistant, servants, a house. These past few days had shown her that if she let him he would simply suck the life out of her. But where could she go on her own? France or England? Both strange, both at war. And both requiring money to reach them.

Cleo watched Quin, who seemed intent on the great flocks of geese and ibis on the shore. Where was he travelling next? Home to America? He would have to go to France or England to get a ship across the Atlantic, her geography was good enough for that.

'Quin.' He turned his head, still tipped back lazily against the mast. 'Where will you take ship to America from?'

'Oh, anywhere in the Mediterranean. Greece, perhaps, or there might be one in Alexandria. They trade all over Europe.' He smiled at her. 'Why? Thinking of starting a new life on the other side of the world?'

'No.' She shook her head firmly. America was out of the question or he would think she was building dreams on that kiss. 'No, just making conversation.'

She needed the practice, that was certain. How on earth did one make small talk without sounding like a twittering female? 'Have you commissions to go back to or will you be seeking employment?' *Was that all right? Showing interest in a man always seems to be acceptable. Or will he think I am unduly curious?'*

'I have employment waiting.' Quin's eyes were closed now, he seemed capable of resting whenever the opportunity presented itself. 'But thank you for your concern.'

Silence fell. Cleo could not decide whether she had trespassed, or whether she should respond with another question or…

'I was employed before I came to the Middle East. I can take that up again when I get back home.'

'That must be reassuring.' She was getting the hang of this now. 'Is your family in the business?'

Quin, who had been, she could have sworn, motionless, became even more still. 'No,' he said at length. 'My family are not in the same…business. Or in any other, come to that.'

Aristocrats? No, that could not be right, there were no titles in America. But perhaps the upper classes were the same as she understood they were in Britain, living on inherited wealth and the income from land. So why did Quin have a profession? Had his father thrown him out, cut him off? She felt a surge of fellow feeling for him, then remembered that he had spoken of hugging brothers and male friends, young relatives, his old nurse. He was not alone.

'What is the sour face for?' Quin's eyes were open and he was watching her.

'An attack of self-pity,' she admitted. It was an unattractive trait and a weakening one, too. If she had given way to misery at her life of lonely drudgery she would have gone mad years ago. It was so much easier not to feel at all, to simply exist and manage from day to day and conserve her strength for when the opportunity for escape presented itself.

'Surely you did not want to stay at Koum Ombo?'

'No, not at all. Look, we have reached the barges.' On the next bend of the river the dozen barges were loaded with packs and folded tents, a few men on each, stacks of weapons amidships. Compared to the graceful feluccas they were unwieldy and heavy, but they were stable and, going with the current and guided with long poles, they would cope with the river easily enough.

Capitaine Laurent stood on the river bank, arms folded, watching the soldiers as they finished tying down the loads. 'You will precede us,' he announced the moment the feluccas bumped against the bank.

'Bonjour, Capitaine,' Quin said and countered the officer's peremptory greeting with a smile. 'We will follow you, I think,' he continued in the same language. 'I have no wish to have my vessels run down by one of those things if it gets away from your men.'

'Your vessels?'

'My money, my boats,' Quin said. 'Or we can leave now and get well ahead if you prefer.'

'No. *Madam* requires the protection of my troop.' Laurent turned his shoulder and began to shout orders at his men.

'And *monsieur* requires to keep an eye on us, I think is rather more to the point,' Quin observed as he sat down, put both feet up and watched the activity through slitted eyes. 'He really does not like me, does he? I wonder why. I am normally considered the most amiable of fellows.'

'He was Thierry's best friend.'

'And he thinks you need protecting from me? Or he wants you for himself and wishes he was here and I was there?'

'Wants me? I hardly think so,' Cleo said. 'He told Thierry he should never have married me, that I was a nuisance.'

'But Thierry had no choice, had he?' She looked sharply at Quin, but he added, 'A man in love is powerless.'

Control your reactions, Cleo told herself. Why she did not want Quin to know her suspicion that her husband had been ordered to marry her, other than her own pride, she did not know. It would have been easier if she understood why a French general should be so concerned about the protection of one insignificant Englishwoman that he would order an officer to marry her.

The pretence of love had not lasted long once they were deep into the desert. Confused, in love and horribly insecure, with only her parents' hopeless marriage as an example, she had floundered, trying to reach her taciturn husband in the little time he spent with her. She was frigid, she was too demanding. She talked too much, she was no fun, she sewed his buttons on wrong, she was aloof with his friends. She flirted with his friends so she was a slut. At that she had flared up, hurt and angry, and he had hit her, a back-handed slap across the face. Goodness knows what he had told Laurent about her.

Now she hunched a shoulder at Quin's comment. 'I have no intention of inviting Laurent to dinner, that is certain.'

'Hell.' Quin sat bolt upright. 'Food. I should have thought—I do not want to be dependent on Laurent.'

'I did think. We have enough to last several days, although once supplies run low I suggest we overtake the barges and get to the next village ahead of them or there will be nothing left to buy. Ah, here is the goat.'

'Goat? Where the blazes did that come from?' Quin demanded as the protesting animal was heaved over the side of their felucca. The steersman grinned and tied it to the second mast where it bleated irritably, rolling its strange slit-pupilled eyes at her.

'I sent a message when we were loading,' Cleo said. 'We cannot count on getting fresh meat every day and it will go off quickly in this heat when we do. We may need the goat.'

'And who is going to be the butcher?' he demanded, then cursed under his breath when she simply smiled. 'Me, I suppose.'

'Then catch fish and we won't need to lay a finger on it, except to milk it,' Cleo said. The goat was actually in milk and she'd had no intention of killing it unless things got really desperate, but it was amusing to tease Quin. 'You are very squeamish. Don't you hunt things?'

'Not things I am living with,' he said as another villager heaved a sack full of greenery on board. The goat stopped protesting and started munching. 'And it smells.'

'Poor Delilah.' Cleo leaned forward and put her hands over the goat's ears. 'You will offend her.'

'That does it.' Quin looked disgusted. 'I refuse to eat something with a name. Delilah, indeed!' He saw she was laughing at him. 'What is so amusing?'

'You! You are a big tough man and yet you are sentimental about a goat you have only just met.'

'It is not sentimentality,' he protested, but he was grinning. 'I will catch fish and if you give them names as I haul them out I will hand them to you, all slimy, to gut.'

Cleo shrugged. 'I always do.'

The laughter faded from his face. 'You should not have to. You are a lady, not a kitchen drudge.'

'A lady?' She held out her hands with their calluses and the black stains where the pomegranate juice had got on to her fingers and the half-healed cut from cutting up meat for the skewers.

Quin caught them in his and turned them so they lay curved upwards on his broad palms. His fingers closed over as he stroked the swell at the base of her thumbs. 'A lady,' he repeated. *'Are you not?'*

My grandfather is a duke. Or was. Is he still alive? 'My father is a baronet. I thought Americans were not impressed by titles and rank.' Her hands trembled a little at the gentleness of his touch. So unfamiliar, this sensitivity.

'We know how to look after the women under our protection, like any gentlemen.' He seemed in no hurry to release her hands, even though it brought them knee to knee. When she looked into his eyes they were intent and darkened by something that only increased her perturbation. Desire? Longing? Or simply the concern of a friend?'

'I will never live like a baronet's daughter does in

England,' she said when she found her voice. 'If…
when I get away from my father I will have to work
for my living.'

'Don't be so certain.' Quin shifted his grip so their
hands were palm to palm, his fingers sliding up to
press against the pulse points in her wrists. 'Like a
bird tramped against a window pane,' he murmured.
'The beat of little wings.'

'I am not trapped and I am not a powerless little
bird.' Cleo tugged her hands free and slid back on the
bench seat. 'There was nothing I could do here, deep
in the desert, but once we reach civilisation I will—'
She broke off at the intent look on Quin's face. 'I will
be independent. I have lived at the whim of men for too
long,' she finished. It would be just like him to decide
to *protect* her from whatever she wanted to do. When
she knew what it was.

Quin twisted round to get his back against the
mast again and tilted his broad rush hat, the better to
study the toiling soldiers. 'Laurent is efficient,' he remarked as though nothing had just occurred between
them. 'He has had to be, I suppose, for them to survive. Bonaparte left this army in a parlous state when
he made his grab for power.'

'At least under him the killing of civilians in France
has stopped.'

'You think it safe to go there? To find your in-laws
perhaps? I would not advise it. France is a country
at war on every front. You would do better to go to
England.'

So much for any little fantasy that he might ask her
to go with him to America. Not that she wanted to be
with him, of course, but it would have been protection

on the journey and she would like to satisfy her curiosity about Quin Bredon.

Laurent came striding over. 'We are ready. I would have you remember that I am in command of this troop, *Monsieur* Bredon.'

'But of course,' Quin rejoined. 'You command your troop, I command my feluccas and we sail in convoy with you while it suits me. I will see you at dinner, *Capitaine*. Or in Cairo.'

'He does not make a good enemy,' Cleo murmured, her eyes on Laurent's rigid back as he stalked back to his men who had begun to pole the heavy barges out into the current.

'Neither do I,' Quin responded with that wry half-smile of his. He turned to the man at the stern. *'Taiyib?'*

'Taiyib,' the man responded and shouted to the others to cast off the ropes and push off from the shore.

It is well, Cleo translated. And somehow she felt it was, even though Laurent made her deeply uneasy and the journey was filled with perils, expected and unimagined. She believed Quin when he said he would make a bad enemy, although why, she could not say. He was lean and fit, but he did not have the scarred body of a warrior. He had handled the weapons in their chest competently the previous evening, but not with the casual familiarity she had become used to with Thierry who had seemed to be almost part of his sabre and firearms.

Quin had tipped the hat over his eyes and relaxed against the mast as apparently boneless and limp as a sleeping cat. Cleo made herself comfortable and studied what she could see of his face beneath the tilted brim. The strong, stubborn jaw, the straight line of his mouth, the shadow of stubble where his morning shave had been hasty and in poor light.

He was confident and supremely determined, she decided. When he had been ill he had refused to give in to it. Faced with Laurent's hostility he would not back down. But he was not stubborn. He had stayed in his bed until the worst of the fever had passed, he had been prepared to rest and admit weakness, he accepted Laurent's aggression by smoothly deflecting it, not rising to it. Intelligent, then, and flexible. A man capable of playing a deep game. Dangerous.

A man she was not going to allow herself to trust. Desire now…that was another matter and one, she suspected, that was beyond her control.

Chapter Eight

Her bed shifted and rocked. *Earthquake!* Cleo woke with a start, bolt upright, clutching the thin sheet to her chest. Under her clenched fists her heart thudded.

The bed rocked again, there was a splash of water and she remembered where she was, on a felucca, moored against the bank at Asna.

'*Shh.* I am here.' The quiet words from the other side of the woven wall were deep and reassuring and came immediately on her moment of panic.

'I'm sorry,' Cleo whispered. 'I forgot where I was.' She parted the hanging and found Quin lying full-length along the side of her shelter. He was propped up on one elbow and his face was quite clear in the moonlight.

'There's no need to whisper. The men are all asleep on the bank, the sentry passed a few minutes ago and your father is snoring on the other boat. Even Delilah is asleep.'

'Who—oh, the goat, of course.'

His chuckle told her he was well aware she had been teasing him by inventing a name on the spur of the moment.

'But you are not asleep,' Cleo observed. 'Are you uncomfortable?'

'No, only restless.'

Quin Bredon was the least restless man she had ever encountered. 'No you are not, you are keeping guard. But the men are sleeping by the mooring ropes and there are two sentries.'

'Patrolling a considerable length of bank. No one seems very alert to dangers from the river. If I had designs on robbing these vessels, I would swim and haul myself over the side.'

'That is reassuring,' Cleo muttered.

'That is why I am here.'

'Across my threshold like a slave in some ancient palace?'

'Of course. Are you not Queen of the Nile?'

Cleo snorted. 'And you were awake, you must have been, to know about the sentry and to react so fast when I woke. You should be asleep.'

'I can sleep during the day. I am cat-napping now. Close your eyes and let go, Cleo, don't be afraid.'

'I am not at all afraid.' She dropped the flap and slid back under her sheet. The loud slap of something large hitting the water had her sitting up again the next moment.

'Fish jumping.' A hand appeared under the hanging and touched her arm. *'Sleep.'*

As dawn began to break Quin had closed his eyes and let sleep take him. *Half an hour, perhaps*, he thought as he drifted down, ignoring the stiffness in his right arm. Cleo had gone to sleep holding his hand

and he did not have the heart to risk waking her by pulling it free.

He surfaced again to find the sun just up and his hand empty. Small scuffling and splashing noises told him that Cleo was awake and washing in the bucket of water she had taken into the cabin the night before. When he sat up the goat bleated at him. Quin eyed the evidence that the creature was not boat-trained, dealt with it and then lifted the protesting animal over the side into the shallow water.

'Stay there and have a drink and we'll go for a walk in a minute when I've got my gear.'

'Who are you talking to?' Cleo called.

'Delilah. We are going for a stroll, a wash and, if there's some hot water to be had, a shave.' The goat bleated. 'You be quiet or I'll shave your beard off.'

Cleo laughed, the first time he had ever heard her give way to amusement without some edge to it. It was a rather nice laugh, although he suspected she didn't let it escape very often.

'Come on, Delilah.' He climbed over the gunwale, took the goat's rope in one hand and the shaving kit Cleo had found for him in the other, and splashed ashore to look for hot water and some grazing for the goat.

He stripped off, washed in the river and dressed again, then found the angle of a branch to wedge the small mirror into while he shaved and Delilah grazed placidly around his feet.

'Someone is going to have to milk you,' he told her, eyeing the heavy udder as he rinsed the razor and poured away the water. The goat raised her head and peered at him down her formidable Roman nose and the recollection of the only other Delilah he knew, the Dowager Marchioness of Dawlish, came to him. Other than the fact that the old battleaxe was as flat-chested as a plank the resemblance was irresistible. Quin sat down and laughed until he cried.

'Bredon? What the devil's the matter with you, man?' Sir Philip, clad in a blue-and-yellow banyan, his own shaving tackle in this hand, stared at Quin as though he had just encountered a lunatic.

Perhaps he has. Perhaps all this had addled my brain. Oh, lord, what am I doing, goat-herding in the heart of Egypt when I could be drafting communiqués, planning dinner parties or deciphering code letters? Obeying orders, he answered himself.

'Just something that occurred to amuse me, sir,' he said as he got to his feet and found the goat's trailing rope. 'Come on, Delilah. Let us hope Madame Valsac knows how to milk you.'

'There you are,' Cleo greeted him. 'You haven't milked her?'

'I have no idea how to. Do you?'

'Of course.' Cleo tied a bow to secure her long braid and tossed it back over her shoulder.

That was a pity, Quin thought as he lifted the protesting animal back on board. He would have liked to see her hair loose around her shoulders.

It seemed Cleo had been preparing breakfast as well as getting dressed. 'Here.' She thrust a platter and a beaker into his hands as he stood up to his knees in water. 'Can you give those to my father, please?'

The older man still was not back, so Quin laid the food on the cross-bench and splashed back to haul himself on board, conscious of Cleo's intent gaze on him while her hands worked rhythmically, sending milk hissing into a bowl. The half-healed wound on his arm pulled painfully, but the muscles held.

'You are very fit,' she observed. 'Is that because of your work?'

Diplomacy was hardly a physically strenuous activity under normal circumstances and Quin almost said as much before he remembered who and what he was supposed to be. 'I fence, box, ride and swim,' he answered truthfully. 'That helps. But engineers must be capable of climbing tall structures and scrambling about half-built machinery, of course.'

'Of course,' Cleo agreed. Her face was expressionless as she turned her attention back to the goat. 'I've almost finished—we can have milk with our breakfast.'

They reached Kene on the great bend where the river turned sharply west just as the sun was going down that night. Cleo was hanging on to her temper by her fingernails and her father was complaining that they had swept past Thebes without stopping.

For once Laurent and Quin had been in perfect accord. The captain had announced that he did not care how many of the *savants* were at work on the ruins that were said to have stopped the army in their tracks with wonder, Quin had declared flatly that they had no time to go chasing up the Valley of the Kings in order to sneer at James Bruce's book about one of the tombs and, when the furious baronet offered the felucca's owner a ridiculous amount to stop, both men agreed they would sail on the moment Sir Philip got on the shore.

Her father had to be content with glimpses of the temples at Luxor and Karnak as they had swept past.

'You should have let him go ashore,' Cleo said to Quin while the men were mooring for the night. 'And left him. The villager who owns this boat would have benefited from the money and Father would have been perfectly all right with the *savants* and their escort.'

'Leave your own father?' Quin asked, his voice gently mocking.

'He was prepared to leave me.' Cleo did not feel in the mood to be mocked, however mildly. 'You heard him—Laurent said he would not permit me to go with Father and he replied that I would be in the way and I could go to Cairo with you.'

'I could not square it with my conscience to leave him here. It is better that he is in Cairo.' Quin stood on the gunwale to help pass ropes.

Cleo shifted so she could watch him. There had been something in his tone just then that she could not understand and she was still absolutely convinced that whatever Quin Bredon was, he was not an engineer. That morning when she had commented on his fitness he had answered with a general statement about engineers, nothing personal, no example from his own experience as she would have expected. Men liked to talk about their own lives and interests. But not this one.

Capitaine Laurent came down to inspect what they were doing and nodded amiably at Quin. Apparently their mutual tussle with her father had muted the antagonism between them somewhat. Should she say something to Laurent? But what? That she was certain Quin was not an engineer? But if he was not, then surely the only thing he could be was a spy and Laurent would have no option but to shoot him.

'Look out below!' Quin swung down to catch the tumbling sail before it covered her. 'Daydreaming?'

'No, just undecided about something.' Cleo began to gather the sail up so Quin could tie it from one end while the boatman began at the other. He worked his way along, knotting as he went, until he was opposite her. She looked into the deep blue eyes that were so friendly, looked at the relaxed curve of his mouth and the dextrous hands. 'I will sleep on it.'

Sleep proved impossible. Cleo lay staring up, sightless in the stuffy darkness. If Quin was a spy, then who was he damaging? The French, presumably, and she was a Frenchwoman by marriage now. But she did not feel French, any more than she felt English. And what had the French ever done for her? Married her off to a man who lied, who was unfaithful and who hit her.

If she went to Laurent, told him her vague suspicions, then he would want to know Quin's mission and that meant only one thing. He would use torture and somehow she could not imagine Quin simply giving in at the first glimpse of a hot iron or whatever hideous methods Laurent would employ. So it would be prolonged and appalling and then they'd shoot him and she would never get it off her conscience.

'And I like you, you infuriating man,' she murmured to herself. More than liked, if the truth be told. She desired him. Her experiences of physical love had not been very satisfying, but she knew enough to suspect that it had been her ignorance and Thierry's lack of care that contributed to that. Quin with his hugs and his humour, *and his beautiful body*, she admitted to herself, he would be different.

But it would be madness, even if he wanted her, even if they found somewhere to make love. No man was trustworthy, not deep down. He would be good to her while it lasted, then his own needs, his own interests, would emerge and he would leave her without a backwards glance. That was what men did.

She curled up on her side, her nose inches from the hanging panel that separated her from the open deck and Quin on his self-appointed guard duty outside her door. The boat rocked in the current, fish splashed, a jackal gave its harsh call. None of that was strange now, but something was keeping her awake beyond worry and lust. Someone was whispering.

'I do not give a damn.' That was Quin and the whispering voice had been him, too. His voice rose. 'Don't care. Why should I?'

Cleo parted the flap and looked out. Quin was flat on his back, eyes closed, the light rug that had covered him tossed aside. He was clad in only the thin cotton drawers that all the local men wore under their robes and in the moonlight she could see the faint trace of sweat glistening on his chest.

'Quin?' Cleo murmured as she touched his arm. He was deeply asleep and dreaming, but if his voice became any louder it would bring the guard and she imagined he would hate that.

He quietened at her voice, or perhaps it was her touch. 'Not like my father. Either of them.'

That made no sense. He moved his head, restless. Cleo reached over and pulled the cover back over his body, concerned he would take a chill. Quin began to mutter again. She could not make out the words, but he sounded bitter and unhappy. For a moment she hesitated, wondering if it was his conscience speaking, and then decided she did not care. A hug had made her feel better, she would see if she could work the same magic for him.

Cleo slid down to lie close to the long, hot body, put her head on his chest and her arm across to hold him. '*Shh*, I am here,' she said, echoing his reassurance of the night before. 'Sleep, Quin. Just sleep.'

With a sigh he put his arm round her and held her to him, then fell silent, his breathing deep and steady on the still air.

Quin woke and opened his eyes on to the darkness that heralded the dawn. Everything was still, the only sounds the single calls of birds anticipating the sun, the gurgle of the river against the boat, the creak of ropes and the breathing of the woman in his arms. Comfortable, he closed his eyes to drift down into sleep, the memories of the old nightmare dissolving like mist in the morning.

Woman? Hell's teeth! It was Cleo, he would know the scent and the shape of her anywhere, even after the fleeting physical contact they had shared. 'Cleo,' he whispered as he shifted to face her. The last thing they could afford was for her to wake up with a shriek to find a man in her bed. Although she was in *his* and how the blazes she got there…

'Hmm?' She curled up tighter against him, her head burrowing into the angle between his shoulder and neck.

'Wake up. Quietly.' Her hair tickled his nostrils and he had to control the urge to kiss the top of her head. Or let his hands stray. Or shift his aching groin any closer to her soft, warm mysteries.

'Quin!' It was a shriek, but a whispered one, muffled against his bare shoulder.

Quin grabbed for the sheet as he pushed her gently back into the cabin, offering up silent thanks for the darkness. He was three-quarters naked and as aroused as any man who wakes up wrapped around an attractive woman at that time in the morning could expect to be.

'I fell asleep,' she whispered through the crack in the hangings. 'I'm sorry, I meant to creep back in here once you'd settled.'

'Why? What was I doing?' Talking in his sleep, he supposed. How damned embarrassing.

'Talking in your sleep,' Cleo confirmed. 'You were saying that you did not give a damn and that you didn't care. And something about your father.'

'And I woke you, I'm sorry. It was just an old dream.'

'It doesn't matter. Only your voice was getting louder and I didn't think you would want the guard to come over to see what was happening.' He could hear her shifting round inside as though uncomfortable. 'So I thought a hug might quieten you. And it did.' They sat there in silence for a minute, on each side of the barrier as the darkness began to break into shimmering grey.

'You said something about not being like your *fathers*. But that doesn't make sense,' Cleo said eventually. It wasn't quite a question.

Oh, hell. Quin dropped his forehead on to his bent knees. He supposed he had better tell her, because if he was going to spend the next few nights prattling about his sordid history goodness knows what she would make of it. And he had discovered, on the very few occasions he had confided in anyone, that the nightmares stopped for months.

'Put on a robe and we'll talk on the river bank,' he said, pulling on trousers and a shirt. He lifted the protesting goat over the side and tethered her to a tree as a convenient excuse for being out at that hour, then went back to help Cleo, who was sitting on the side of the boat, legs dangling.

She put her hands on his shoulders and let herself be swung to dry land with a soft chuckle. 'You are strong.'

'You are easy to lift. You should have more flesh on your bones, but you work too hard.' Not that the flesh that did cover her lovely, lithe body was not soft and curved and enough to ruin a man's sleep for months.

'You smell better than Delilah,' he added in an attempt to lighten the conversation. The goat bleated at him when he untied her rope and set off along the path, upstream to where the current had carved a tiny crescent of beach. 'Go and have a drink,' he told her and let the rope drop.

Cleo came and sat beside him on a water-washed tree trunk. 'I will get fat and lazy, lying about on the boat all the way to Cairo.'

'Good.' Quin leaned forward, his forearms on his thighs, and contemplated the sand between his feet. 'The lazy part, at any rate. You deserve a holiday.' And she would need her strength when they reached

Cairo because whatever happened, it was not going to be easy on her. It was the right thing, but even so…

'Tell me,' she said and, to his surprise, turned sideways on the log, put her feet up and rested back against him. 'Tell me why you have two fathers.'

Quin had no idea whether it was instinct or if she realised that she was making it easier for him by creating some distance and yet giving him the comfort of her touch. When she discovered the truth about his birth she might well decide to move away. He took a deep breath and put it to the test.

Chapter Nine

'When I was eight years old and my eldest brother was seventeen and about to go off to university, my… father called all of us, all five boys, into his study and said there was something he had to tell us because Henry was probably going to hear rumours.

'I was, he informed us, the son of our mother and another man, now dead. He had chosen to acknowledge me in order to spare the family scandal, especially as he had four legitimate sons between me and the title. He told us that the reason I looked so unlike my brothers was that I resembled my true father closely and was coming to do so more with every passing year. For all the emotion he showed he might have been discussing the sale of land or an unsatisfactory servant.'

Cleo had gone completely silent, but she drew a deep shuddering breath as though she had been holding it in tightly.

'He would not neglect my education, he said, and he would settle land on me so that I would not bring further shame on the family by ignorance, bad manners or a display of poverty, but he did not expect my brothers to associate with me. He certainly hardly spoke to me again.'

She did speak then, still facing the river. 'Oh, poor little boy! What did your mother say to you?'

'Nothing. She was dead by then and even before, we hardly saw her. I realise now that they were living separate lives. It was…a shock.' That was a simple word for the mixture of shame, anger and the strange relief of knowing that the man he had thought was his father ignored him for what he was, not who he was. 'I knew my father did not like me, let alone love me, but I had no suspicion why. I had nightmares from then on.' He leant a little against Cleo's warmth. 'I grew out of them, of course, but they still come back when I am very tired, or anxious about something.'

'And you have been sick. No wonder you are dreaming.'

At least he had not been ranting about the rest of the dream, the obsession to make good on his own terms, to follow his own path, become a leading diplomat or a high-ranking government minister in the Foreign Office. *I will be the best.* He would repeat that over and over, when his head ached from studying, or his tutor whipped him or the marquess swept past without a flicker of acknowledgment. He would succeed. He would earn his own wealth, his own title, his own reputation as a man of honour, a man who did his duty, come what may.

He was here because of that duty and he was here because he would demonstrate his skills with languages, show initiative, pull chestnuts out of the fire and lay them before one of the most powerful men in government. What he had been doing would have to be secret, of course, but the fact that he had accomplished a tricky mission well would be known to Lady Caroline Brooke's father. When he got back to London he would ask for leave of absence and embark on some serious courtship.

'What are you thinking about?' Cleo asked. She sounded as though she was dozing and her head was tipped back against the point of his shoulder. A curiously silent and restful female when she chose to be…

'Marriage,' Quin said, half-asleep himself. He jerked awake and cursed silently. *Great tact. What diplomacy. Tell her you are thinking about another woman, why don't you?*

'What is her name?' Cleo asked.

Oh well, might as well be hanged for a sheep as a lamb and tell her, he thought. At least she would have no expectations of him, which had always been a faint nagging worry, given that they were going to be travelling together unchaperoned for weeks.

'Caroline. Her father is a…a very influential man. It would be an excellent marriage.'

'*Would be?*' she asked. Was it his imagination or had her voice cooled and become closer to that of the woman he had first met. 'You have not yet told her you wish to marry her? Is she in love with you?'

'I haven't done anything yet to fix my interest with her, if that's what you mean. And, no, she doesn't know me well enough to have those kind of feelings.'

Cleo swung her legs down and stood up. 'And you don't love her?' she enquired, her gaze steady, and sardonically amused. 'What a chilly arrangement. Practical, though.'

'That is how society functions, on the basis of marriages of convenience and advantage between suitably matched partners,' Quin said, wondering why he could explain something so self-evident and manage to sound like a stuffed shirt at the same time. It was the right thing to do and the right way to go about it for a man of his upbringing, class and ambitions.

'I thought it was different in America,' Cleo said. She ran down to the water side and took hold of Delilah's rope.

'Society works the same all over the world.'

Cleo managed to make a one-shouldered shrug into something almost graceful as she turned, towing Delilah behind her. 'So you're intending to marry her father, in effect. Very romantic.'

'Who said anything about romance?' Quin demanded, nettled, as his calming morning turned sour. 'And who did you marry? The French army for a bodyguard?'

Cleo stopped and regarded him down her nose, every inch royalty confronted by a peasant. 'Oh, you *man,'* she said and swept on past towards the boat.

'I damn well hope so,' Quin said to her retreating back and received no acknowledgment beyond a toss of her head. *Curse the entire female sex,* he thought as he strode back to the boat in time to heave the goat back on board. And whose foolish notion was it to bring a goat of all things? Smelly, stubborn, needs feeding and watering and cleaning up after.

And I'm in a foul mood, he realised with sense of shock. Years of training and self-discipline had knocked that sort of futile fuming out of him. Or so he'd thought. All it took to rattle the composure of a man quite capable of dealing with seductive foreign widows, scheming, spying diplomats and apoplectic ministers was one gauche young woman with neither experience, education nor sophistication.

Quin settled his expression into one of bland courtesy and turned to Cleo, who was apparently admiring a large spider on the rushes. 'May I help you into the boat?'

'You may pass me the sickle, if you please,' she replied. 'We need to cut fodder for Delilah.'

'I will help you into the felucca and you can give me the sickle.'

'I would welcome the exercise.'

'You should not be performing manual labour.' Quin vaulted over the side of the boat, found the sickle, climbed back and surveyed the patches of scrubby foliage.

'I had better not milk the goat or prepare the food in that case.' Cleo sat down, spread her skirts around her in a flurry of blue cotton and began to unplait her hair with the air of a woman prepared to spend all day primping in the shade.

Quin slashed at the undergrowth for a few moments of blissfully violent activity, gathered up an armful of greenery and turned back, a well-crafted retort about suitable occupations for women on his lips. And promptly forgot every syllable.

He had wondered what Cleo's hair looked like loose and now he knew. It looked like liquid molasses flowing in sunlight. It looked like silk, woven by a master weaver, it looked… He shut his mouth with a snap and walked past her to throw the fodder into the boat, making Delilah snort and stamp.

'The men are stirring,' he said, nodding towards the huddle of boatmen and, beyond them, the soldiers.

As he hoped, Cleo got to her feet, swept her hair over one shoulder and paddled out to the side of the boat. 'If you please, Mr Bredon.'

So, I'm back to Mr, *am I?* Quin thought as he put his hands around her waist and lifted her to sit on the edge. As she swivelled round her hair swung, brushed across his hands, sending a shudder of desire through him. He closed his eyes, his hands still lightly resting on the curve of her hips, and searched for some sort of control.

Cleo put her hands on his shoulders and bent down, making it a hundred times worse as her breath brushed his cheek and her hair spilled around them. 'Quin?'

'I felt suddenly dizzy. I'm sorry.' Better to sacrifice his pride by admitting weakness than tell her the truth: *I want you so much it hurts.* He pushed away from the side of the felucca. 'I'll go and see where Laurent is aiming for today.'

He walked away without looking back. Was she watching him as he went, as unsettled by that moment as he had been? More likely she was thinking what a poor specimen he was, with his nightmares and irregular birth and apparent weakness.

He wants me. There had been no mistaking that intense stillness. Dizzy, indeed! That had been lust, rigorously controlled because, of course, what use would Quin Bredon have with her, beside the comfort of her body? He had his sights set on Caroline, the woman of influence he hardly knew. She could only hope that Caroline would not be disturbed by his nightmares because she could not imagine some well-bred lady hugging her husband out of his bad dreams.

Cleo eyed the minor chaos of the boat, considered what to do about breakfast, shrugged, sat down and braided her hair. That, loose, had been what had set Quin off, she was sure of it. Men were strange creatures.

The felucca was tidy when Quin returned. Cleo had given her father his breakfast and had done her best with the mess he had created since the day before.

'Here.' She pushed a plate towards Quin when he climbed on board, his face relaxed into something close to a smile. 'The men brought me duck eggs, eat yours before it gets cold.'

Quin took it with a murmur of thanks and settled down in his usual place, back to the mast. 'Laurent is picking up rumours,' he said without preamble after a few mouthfuls. 'The British have landed a force from India under General Baird at Coseir on the Red Sea, due east of here. They will be marching on Kene.'

'But that must be well over a hundred miles of desert.' Cleo stared out at the edge of the dunes, lapping against the green, fertile strip of farmland, half-expecting to see the British redcoats breasting the summit.

'They are used to hot climates and there are established caravan routes across from here.' Quin wiped the crust of flatbread around the remains of the egg. 'It has made Laurent anxious to reach Cairo.'

He seemed to find that mildly amusing, but perhaps his antipathy for the other man accounted for that. 'But there will be fighting,' she said, answering his mood rather than his words.

'There will. I expect Baird will march down the river to Cairo. Général Belliard must look to his fortifications.'

'Perhaps they will meet with the Mamelukes and that will hold them up,' Cleo said hopefully.

'Perhaps. Look, Laurent's barges are casting off.' Quin pitched his voice to the boatmen who were talking in the stern. 'Are you ready, my friends? Let us give chase to the soldiers.'

Cleo watched the river banks slipping past, her pleasure in the journey turning to apprehension. Cairo, when she had known it before, had been hellish, but she had hoped that almost three years of French rule would have restored the streets to order so that daily life could resume. Now she was fleeing from not one but two armies and straight into a city that would be preparing for a siege.

'Don't worry.' Quin came and sat beside her in the prow. 'I'll look after you.' He must have read the scepticism in the look she gave him, for his mouth curved in a wry smile. 'Trust me.'

'To do what? Make the war go away?'

'To do the best for you.'

'You know what that is? I am glad someone does.' She had stoically endured the time in the desert, not daring to dream when there was no escape possible. Now she was moving towards the city, towards the sea, and she still did not have a plan of any kind. In the place of numbness was fear, a fear she dared not voice or allow to show, or she thought she might give way to it.

She braced her shoulders, afraid that Quin would give her one of his comforting hugs. If he did that, she thought she would probably burst into tears and the prospect appalled her. But he did not touch her and she breathed out the air she had dragged down into her lungs.

'I think you need security, comfort, the normal life of a baronet's daughter or an officer's widow. I know a city under imminent threat of siege may not be the best first step, but we'll sort it out as we go along. Trust me,' he repeated.

Cleo looked at his confident face, the jut of his nose, the set of his jaw. *He's a man,* she thought, *with all a man's failings—but I do trust him. Am I a fool?* 'Very well, I will trust you.'

And then Quin did catch her in a one-armed hug and dragged her against his side for a moment. Cleo blinked hard and the tears did not fall. Inside a small, fragile flicker of something began to burn. At first she did not recognise it and then she realised what it was. She was looking forward with hope, curious about the future. This man, with all his flaws, had given her that.

Seven days brought them to Benisouef, one day, the boatmen agreed, from Cairo. It also brought the news that Murad Bey had died of plague on the march north and his men under their new leader had sided with the British.

'I doubt that makes them any more or less dangerous to us,' Quin said, as they sat around the fire on shore that evening. Her father was grumbling that they hadn't needed to leave Koum Ombo after all and Quin was showing far more tolerance than Cleo was feeling with her parent.

Cleo swirled her coffee around in the cup, her attention not on the thick grounds in the bottom, but on Quin's profile in the firelight. As Cairo approached he seemed tenser, more focused on his own thoughts, which seemed strange when she would have thought that he would have been relieved to be free of the burden of looking after her and enduring her father's bad temper.

He had even taken to sleeping as far from her makeshift cabin as possible on the small boat. When she questioned it, making a joke that her snoring must be driving him away, he smiled faintly. 'Delilah is more nervous at night than you are. She needs me more.'

'It is strange we have had no news from the north,' she said now as she tipped the dregs of her coffee into the embers. 'Did you notice, the past few days we have seen nothing large coming south, only local fishing boats.'

Quin shrugged, but she noticed he glanced towards the soldiers' camp a hundred yards away. 'The Cairo authorities may be restricting movement if they've heard about Baird's landing, which they must have done by now. They won't want large shipping down here to fall into his hands.'

'I suppose that's it.' She stood and began to gather up the cups and coffee pot.

'Have you sewing things I can borrow?' Quin asked. 'Scissors and needle and thread?'

'Why, yes, but if you need anything mended, I will do it.'

'I can manage. Is the sewing kit on our felucca?'

'The light is too poor to sew now.' Cleo dumped things into the bucket and straightened up, hands in the small of her back to rub out the slight stiffness of another day spent sitting on the boat.

'I can manage,' he insisted. 'Can you get them now? And an old *tob sebleh* if you have one. I'll replace it for you in Cairo.'

'A *tob sebleh*? But why?'

'I just need something dark blue,' Quin said vaguely.

He was determined to be mysterious, she could tell. Cleo climbed on board using the box someone had set by the stern as a crude step and went to dig out her sewing roll and her oldest *tob sebleh*. She found a voluminous black *habera* and a long *burko* to veil her face and laid those aside. She hated the veil, but it was risky to draw attention to herself in a northern city, until she was within the walls of the French compound.

When she got back to the fire her father had gone and Quin was hunkered down amongst the boatmen, talking Arabic, low-voiced with a great deal of gesticulation. The men seemed to be listening intently, but they all fell silent as she drew near and dropped the bundle of blue cloth.

'Thank you,' Quin said with an obvious intonation of, *And good night,* to the words.

'Good night.' Cleo retreated, controlling the impulse to flounce. *Trust me*, Quin had said and she had agreed and had meant it. Now all the nagging doubts that had almost sent her to confide in Laurent came back. *Foolish,* she chided herself. By this time tomorrow they would be in a French-held city and all the powers that had protected her and her father before would be there. And this time she was the widow of a French officer, which would give her some status of her own.

Even if Quin was some kind of spy, on a mission she could not begin to imagine, it did not affect her. *Trust me.*

Chapter Ten

When everything was in order for the night, Cleo paused, her hand on the flap of the cabin hangings, and looked back to the shore. One of the younger men was unwinding his long turban cloth, the fabric glowing red in the firelight. He handed it to Quin, straightened the brown felt *libdeh* that formed its base and began to wind a new turban, white this time.

Cleo shrugged, went into the cabin, lay down and tried to sleep. There was too much to keep her awake, she thought, grumpy with tiredness, as her eyes refused to close or her mind to let go. She still had no concrete plan for what she might do when they reached Cairo, for so much depended on what they found there. She felt guilty about leaving her father and angry with herself for being so weak.

And then there was Quin and the undeniable fact that she desired him, which was embarrassing and uncomfortable. The man was as good as betrothed to some female he hardly knew... *Which means he can have no real loyalty to her yet,* an insidious little voice whispered. *He could lie with you in good conscience.*

He doesn't want me, she argued back. *He kissed me, but that was just for comfort.* She had missed not only Quin's slumbering presence on the other side of the hangings every night, she realised, but also the countless small contacts. He was a tactile man, given to a touch to the hand along with a word of thanks when she passed him food, a brush of his palm over the crown of her head when he swung past her on the boat to help with the ropes, a swift hug when he thought she looked tired. All that had stopped ever since the afternoon he had pressed her to trust him.

Cleo shifted again, restless and puzzled. And where was he now? She had been lying awake for at least an hour and yet the boat had not rocked with him boarding and neither had Delilah bleated a welcome.

Cleo opened the flap to look over the side. Quin was still by the fire, alone. He had built it up and, bathed in its light, he was bent over fabric spread across his lap. Cleo shook her head, defeated by its folds and the shifting light. Was he making himself some kind of disguise?

Thoroughly awake now, she went back to her bed and found her little knife and its sheath by touch. There was nothing to be done until they reached Cairo. If Quin was a spy, then Laurent could deal with him. If he was a danger to herself or her father then she knew how to protect herself. And if she was wrong to suspect him, then he would have her silent apologies.

They reached the first of the pyramids by midmorning and her father was happier than she could recall him in months as he crouched at the rail making notes and exclaiming. 'See? Dashur!'

Cleo found herself almost as excited. The pyramids had fascinated and awed her on their way south, now she stared again, entranced until Quin distracted her by ordering the two feluccas to come alongside each other and then jumping aboard her father's boat.

'What are you about, sir?' Her father turned from his sketching and made a grab at his papers as Quin bundled those off the makeshift table into the nearest chest and began snapping the padlocks closed. 'Stop that! I need my papers!'

'They are safer locked up,' Quin said as he hung the loop of cord with the keys around his neck and jumped back to Cleo's boat. *'Yalla! Yalla!'* he shouted to the steersmen, for all the world, she thought indignantly, as if they'd been camels.

But the men grinned and began to work the boats out into midstream. Whatever Quin was about, they were in on the secret.

'Sakhara,' her father said, still torn between indignation and his obsession with the monuments.

'Never mind the pyramids,' Cleo said. 'We are going to run into the barges!'

She held on to the side, her heart in her mouth, but the boatmen handled the feluccas as if they were swallows, darting over the surface of the river, hawking for insects. The boats flashed between the lumbering barges with insolent ease, their sails full of wind, the current bearing them along.

On the barges men shouted. Cleo saw Laurent run to the side and wave his arms, his mouth moving, but his words were caught on the breeze and tossed away. And then they were through, past Tora, and ahead was

Gizah and the great pyramids on their left and the city on the right.

Cleo ducked into the cabin and pulled on her *habera* and fastened the *burko* so the long strip of fabric fell from nose to knees. When she came out Quin was fastening a bundle of cloth to the mast. He dropped it when he saw her.

'Get that off and put on European clothes.'

'No, it is safer if—'

'Do as I say or I will dress you myself.' He turned and tugged on a rope and the cloth stirred and rose up the mast. The breeze caught it and it flapped open, a pattern of crosses, red and white on a blue ground. On the other felucca one of the men was hoisting an identical flag.

'What are you doing?' Cleo stopped, the *burko* in her hand, and stared at the crudely sewn design. 'That's the British Union Flag.'

'Do you want to be fired on by the British?'

She stared at the shore, at the unfamiliar red uniforms, the mass of men and camels and tents on the bank, the flags. 'That is the *British* army?'

Quin pushed her towards the cabin. 'Do as I say, get changed. I want them to see there is a European woman on board.'

'But...*the British?* How did you know? Laurent didn't.'

'I have known all along,' Quin said as he scanned the shore. 'I landed with them in March.'

'*You knew? You betrayed us!*'

'How?' he demanded, turning a bleak face to her. 'You are English, your father is English. Why should you regard being brought out of hostile territory to our own army as betrayal?'

She realised she had no answer for that, other than the fact he had kept it secret. 'But Laurent—'

'Laurent is a soldier and this is war. Now, are you going to get changed or do I have to undress you?'

'No!' Cleo dived into the cabin and sat huddled on the bed, trying to make sense of it all. Why hadn't Quin told her that the British were besieging Cairo? And then his words struck her. *Our own army.* He was not American. He was British and he had lied to her from the start.

She dragged off the *tob sebleh* and lifted the hangings to give herself enough light to find the creased muslin gown and lawn petticoats that she had not worn since her wedding day. She dressed, her fingers clumsy on the unfamiliar tapes and seams, then strapped her little knife in its sheath around her leg, just below the knee. It felt strange to wear such thin clothes and to have her hair uncovered, but she resisted the instinct to put on a robe or a scarf. She did not want to give Quin any excuse to touch her and perhaps discover the knife.

They were almost past the wharfs of Cairo when she came back on deck, but the soldiers were still lining the banks. Behind them there was a sudden burst of gunfire.

'Laurent!' She craned to see, but Quin pulled her back and swung up on the gunwale.

'Damn fool.' He shaded his eyes. 'He can't hope to turn those barges or run the gauntlet of so many troops. Ah, now he has seen sense, they're surrendering, someone's hoisted a shirt.'

'He was doing his duty,' Cleo said. 'What will they do to them?'

'They will be prisoners. And much safer out here than in a plague-ridden city under siege, believe me.'

'You lied to me.'

'No, I never did, except about my profession. I am not an engineer. I deceived you, yes. Played with words, yes. I asked you if you would believe me if I said I was an American, but I never told you I was.'

'I suspected you were a spy,' Cleo said bitterly and sat down where she could see his face, try to read the lies he would doubtless tell her now. 'I thought I should tell Laurent.'

'Why didn't you?' The look he gave her was oddly intent.

'He would have tortured you. I couldn't have that on my conscience.'

'Thank you for that. I am not a spy. An agent would be a better description, a courier sent to collect two individuals.' He turned to call instructions in Arabic to the boatmen. 'There's Elkatta. Moor there on the west bank.'

'Collect us? Father and me? But why?'

'You don't know?' Quin raised one eyebrow quizzically. 'No, I really believe you do not.'

'I saved your life.'

'Yes,' Quin agreed. 'Twice, if we count not throwing me to Laurent's tender mercies. And I am grateful for that, but it is not only soldiers who must do their duty.'

'What the blazes is going on! Turn back to Cairo this instant!'

'Keep calm, Sir Philip,' Quin called back in such soothing tones that Cleo itched to push him overboard. 'We are going downstream as far as the main British base at Elkatta. Much safer there.'

'British! What's happened to the French?' her father demanded. 'What's happened to my correspondence?'

'Give me strength,' Quin muttered, then raised his voice to shout to the other felucca. 'We are in the middle of a war, sir. I suggest there are more important considerations than a few letters. The safety of your daughter, for one.'

'Much you care for that,' Cleo said and found herself ignored as Quin began to help the men drop the sail. They were heading into shore, towards a landing stage and beyond it, rows of orderly tents and a bustle of activity around some mud-brick houses.

'Hold off,' Quin called to the steersmen as half-a-dozen soldiers, muskets at the ready, formed up on the landing stage. He cupped his hands and hailed them. 'Lord Quintus Deverall and party. Sir James Houghton is expecting us.'

Lord Quintus? He is a lord? Cleo stared at the tall figure, dressed like a sailor off some small coastal trader, who sounded so authoritative and so, *damn him,* in control. *I thought him the bastard son of an American landowner and here he is with a title. How much can I believe of anything he has told me?*

A non-commissioned officer strode on to the dock. 'My lord! Sir James sends his compliments and asks that you tie up alongside and come ashore.'

'You had better pack your things away,' Quin said. 'I imagine you don't want the soldiers doing it for you.'

'How considerate.' He did not so much as wince at the bitterness in her voice.

It was the work of a few minutes to stuff the items that were loose back into their bags. It took rather longer to fight the tears of anger and, she had to admit it to herself, fear. Quin had told her to trust him and she had. He had given her hope and now she was caught up in something she did not understand and had no control over.

Such a fool to trust. Surely she had learned by now that men could be relied on to do only one thing and that was seek their own advantage and their own desires? She had liked Quin, wanted him, come perilously close to... *Close to liking him too well.* Cleo scrubbed at her eyes. She had not wept when she had realised how little concern Thierry had for her, she had never wept however tired and trapped she had felt after her mother died, and she was not going to start now.

The boat bumped against the quayside as she emerged from the cabin, bags in hand, a loose scarf over her hair. Quin raised an eyebrow at the combination, but she ignored him and allowed the very young officer who arrived at a run to hand her ashore. After months of dressing like the village women she felt positively indecent with a bare head and short sleeves.

'Miss Woodward. Welcome to Elkatta. We have a—'

'Madame Valsac,' Cleo interrupted him.

'Oh. Yes, right... If you would like to come this way, there is a room.' He peered behind her. 'And your woman, ma'am?'

'I have no one with me,' Cleo said. 'Please take me to my accommodation.' She dumped her bags at his feet and showed her teeth in a smile that made him take a step back.

'Jenkins! Take *madam*'s bags. This way, ma'am.'

She followed him without a glance back. The back of his neck was scarlet with heat and embarrassment.

The rooms he showed her to were simple but clean. A chamber with a bed, a chair, a small table and a lamp and beyond it a room with a wash stand and a covered pail. The windows in both rooms were tiny, a protection against the heat, and the door opened on to a shaded area where a sentry stood at ease.

'I'm sure it's not what you're used to, ma'am,' the young man apologised as the soldier brought in her bags.

Cleo relented. It wasn't his fault, any of this. 'I will be very comfortable—?'

'Ensign Lloyd, ma'am. I'll find one of the camp women to look after you, ma'am. One of the respectable ones.' He had gone vermilion now.

'Thank you.' Cleo walked out on to the veranda. 'Now, I will join my father.'

'You'll be better off here, ma'am.' He might be embarrassed, but his jaw was set and he looked determined.

Cleo took an experimental pace towards the edge of the shade. The sentry came to attention. 'Am I a prisoner, Ensign Lloyd?' *What the devil is going on? I am English, they are English.*

'For your own protection, ma'am. Best if you stay here. This is an army camp, no place for a lady.'

'I am an officer's widow, Ensign. I am used to army camps.'

'I have my orders, ma'am.' He snapped off a salute and marched away, radiating relief at escaping her.

Cleo turned to the guard. 'And you are?'

'Private Minton, ma'am.'

'I have been cooped up on a boat for days, Private. I am going to take a walk.' *Where is Father? Where is that lying, scheming, traitorous Quin Bredon or whatever his name is?*

'No, ma'am.' He was tough, battered and about as unconcerned about being confronted by an irritated woman as the ensign had been embarrassed.

'Just what will you do to stop me, Private? Shoot me?'

'Pick you up, bring you back and lock you in, begging your pardon, ma'am.'

He is only obeying orders, she told herself. *You cannot lose your temper with him. Save that for his lordship.*

Cleo went inside and sat on the bed. How long was she going to be here? She supposed she might as well unpack her things and make herself as comfortable as possible. She had three bags. Two containing clothes and the third for her sewing kit, medical equipment, toiletries, two books and a notebook, her wedding certificate, her few pieces of jewellery. All the small possessions of a simple life.

Almost as soon as she began to lift items out she knew it had been searched. So had her clothes' bags. Cleo was nothing if not tidy and methodical after years of camp life. She always folded away her clean clothing just so, rolled her scarves a certain way, coiled ribbons and belts, placed shoes toe to heel. The disturbance was subtle and the repacking almost perfect, but she could tell someone had been through her things. Her books were stacked with the spines together, while she always put them with the spines opposing each together, because that way they lay flatter. Her notebook had a crease on the page where she had listed the ingredients for *bamiyeh* and a smudge under the weight of hibiscus pods needed—the page had been pristine when she had put the book away.

It had not been a thief. Mama's locket, the pearl earrings Thierry had given her as a wedding gift and the Greek gold bangle she had received for her fourteenth birthday were all there. No, it was another kind of robber, one who stole trust. But what had he been looking for?

She shook out the clothes and hung them on the pegs hammered into the walls, then organised the small things in one of the empty bags. The lining was loose: whatever Quin—*Lord Quintus*—had been searching for it was small enough to slip between the layers of leather and cotton. Papers? *But I have nothing.*

Cleo closed her eyes and conjured up the memory of him standing by the donkey that day in the French camp, his head bent as though resting. *Or reading.* The slight disarray of her father's letters as though someone had riffled through them… Yes, he was looking for papers, which meant he had not stumbled into their camp by accident. The encounter with Bedouin raiders was true enough, she was certain. No one was stupid enough to wound themselves and then get into that dangerous state of dehydration and heat-stroke, just as a ruse.

What was his original plan? To appear on his camel, perhaps with some surveying instruments, no doubt. He would have been welcomed, for no one turned away a stranger in the desert, and then he would have found an excuse to stay and eventually lure them down river into his trap.

'You cunning devil. You lucky, cunning devil,' Cleo muttered. But why, *why* did an English lord, for goodness' sake, put himself to the danger and discomfort and sheer inconvenience of travelling the length of the country to entrap a scholar and his unimportant daughter?

You are not going to like the answer when you find it, Cleo Woodward. You have no clue and you cannot arm yourself against an invisible threat. I wish I had left you there where you fell outside my tent, Lord Quintus. If I knew then what I know now I would have dug a grave and rolled you in when you died and then stamped the sand down over you. In a thousand years some scholar would have dug up your bones and brittle skin and tried to understand what had led you to this fate. Perhaps I should have buried a plaque with you. Liar, betrayer, oath-breaker. Heartbreaker.

Chapter Eleven

'Mrs Valsac, mam?'

The young woman standing in the doorway was English, Cleo only had to look at the pale skin freckled from the sun.

'Yes, I am Madame Valsac. Did Ensign Lloyd send you?' She made an effort and smiled and the other woman grinned back.

'Aye, he did that. Lord, but that boy does blush!' She looked round the room and then back at Cleo and her few possessions spread across the bed. 'He said you didn't have a maid with you, mam?'

'No.' She had never had a maid, had no idea, to be honest, what one did, although this cheerful young woman was a far cry from what she imagined a lady's maid might be like. 'I'm afraid I do not have any money to pay you.'

'That's all right, Sir James is paying, so Mr Lloyd said.'

'Come in. What is your name?'

'Maggie Tomkins, mam. Is it true you were married to a Frenchie?'

It occurred to Cleo that a British soldier's wife

might not take too kindly to being asked to serve the wife of an enemy officer. 'Yes. Do you mind? Perhaps your husband wouldn't like it.'

'No skin off my nose who you were wed to. Besides, my man died three months back on the transport ship, bless him.'

'Oh, I am so sorry, Mrs Tomkins. Had you been married long?'

'Call me Maggie, mam, everyone does. Couple of months we was wed. He was my third.'

She seemed alarmingly matter of fact about it. Obviously married life amongst the rank and file was not always a matter of passionate affection. 'Thank you, I would welcome your help. Can you tell me, who is Sir James?'

Maggie shrugged. 'He's not military, so he must be diplomatic. No uniform, but they all jump when he wants something. The men reckon he's here to do the talking when the Frenchies surrender. Wish the buggers would get on with it, too much sitting around in the dust for my liking.'

'Have you got any children?' Cleo asked, feeling a strong sense of sympathy for another woman who was being dragged around at the whims of men, having to make the best of things in a dusty campsite.

'Got a boy by my first husband.' Maggie's face grew soft. 'He's home in Chatham with his pa's parents, learning to be a shoemaker like his grandpa. That'll keep him out of the army, praise be.' She got up. 'I'll bring you some hot water and some dinner from the officers' mess in a while when it's dinner time.'

Cleo smiled her thanks and sank back on the bed when Maggie went out. There was nothing to do, nothing to look at beyond a patch of bare sand, stamped flat by drilling soldiers, the back edge of the tent line and a fringe of palm trees. Faintly, in the distance, she could hear gunshots. Closer to hand there were shouted orders, the clash of pans from the kitchens, the grit of coarse sand under her guard's boots.

That left her with composing exactly what she was going to say to Lord Quintus Whatever-his-name-was when he had the nerve to show himself. Cleo fingered the little knife in its hidden scabbard. Private Minton was only doing his duty, keeping her here, he certainly didn't deserve a knife in the back. But she could imagine sticking it between Quin's broad shoulders.

But Quin didn't come. Maggie had brought hot water, towels and soap after about half an hour, just in time to stop Cleo getting up and pacing back and forth outside the hut in sheer boredom.

Now, an hour later, she sat outside with a dinner tray on the table Private Drury, Minton's relief, carried out for her. She lifted the cover and the tantalising scents rising from the food made her realise she was starving hungry. Half a small chicken, golden and roasted, nestled on a bed of rice, vegetables swam in a thick, spice-fragrant sauce and another dish held a custard studded with sliced fruits.

Bliss. This was better food than she had seen in years and she hadn't had to prepare it, or cook it and she wouldn't have to clear up afterwards. Cleo ate until her hunger disappeared and then kept eating until her stomach ached and every grain of rice and scrape of custard was gone.

I will kill Quin Bredon in the morning, she thought

hazily as she plaited her hair for bed, already more than half asleep. *Just now I haven't the energy to be angry with a scorpion, let alone a worthless man.*

It was Maggie who woke her with the luxury of more hot water and then fresh rolls, crisp outside and fluffy white inside, and a pot of coffee and fresh eggs and a bowl of yoghurt studied with pomegranate seeds.

'I will grow fat on all this luxury and no work,' Cleo said as Maggie laid out the last of the dishes. 'There is too much—share it with me, please.'

Maggie needed little persuasion. 'Oh, this is good,' she said, grinning through a moustache of yoghurt, then using the back of her hand in lieu of a napkin. 'Sorry, mam, I'm not used to this fine dining.'

'Nor am I,' Cleo confessed. Although this would not count as even a picnic for the likes of Lord Quintus, she was sure.

Ensign Lloyd came marching across as they were finishing, very formal. 'Sir James requests the pleasure of your company in half an hour, ma'am.'

'And if I do not choose to join him?' Cleo sipped her coffee and tried to imagine what a well-bred society lady troubled by a tiresome invitation would do.

'Um, it isn't a request, ma'am.'

'So if I say *no* you will toss me over your shoulder and carry me, Ensign?' It was unkind to tease him, she knew, but he was the only man around to take out her anxiety on.

Ensign Lloyd actually lost colour, but he squared his shoulders and met her gaze. 'If I have to, ma'am. With the deepest respect.'

'You have courage, Mr Lloyd. I didn't mean it. Will you collect me?'

'Ma'am!' A sharp salute and he wheeled and marched off.

'Madame Valsac.' The tall man with the lined face and the cropped grey hair pushed back his chair and rose as she came into the room. Ensign Lloyd closed the door behind himself and she was alone with the stranger. Then there was another scrape of chair legs on mud brick and she turned to see Quin at a table in the corner, papers spread before him and an inkstand by his hand.

'I am Sir James Houghton of His Majesty's Foreign Service. This is—'

'I know who that is.' She did not look at Quin again. 'That is to say, I thought I knew who he was, but it seems he lied to me.'

'I am Quintus Bredon Deverall,' Quin said. 'I fear I misled you about being an engineer.'

She still did not turn. 'And much else, I am certain, *Lord* Quintus.' There was a seat facing Sir James and she took it without waiting to be asked. 'Where is my father?'

'He is perfectly comfortable elsewhere in this building. I trust you are adequately housed and looked after, *madame*?'

'Adequately, yes. For a prisoner. Why are we confined? And why did Lord Quintus lure us here under false pretences?'

'I can assure you that the Mameluke threat is in no way a falsehood.' Sir James did not appear in the slightest bit disturbed by her hostility. 'Despite the fact that they have changed their allegiance to the British on the death of Murad Bey, I can assure you they would be most unsafe to encounter.'

'So his lordship was acting out of purely uninterested concern for our welfare. How touching.'

'No, *madam*, he was not. He was acting on my orders as part of our attempts to counter espionage.'

'Espion—' Cleo closed her mouth with a snap. 'I do not know any spies. Other than his lordship, of course.' To her right there was the scratch of pen on paper and she swivelled on the chair to glare at Quin. 'Only he appears to be a clerk now. How confusing.'

'Are you sure, *madam*?'

'That I am confused, or that I know no spies beyond Lord Quintus? I am sure about both, Sir James. I married a Frenchman. Is that what this is about? I can assure you I am not spying for France—I owe it as much loyalty as I do to Britain, another country where I have never set foot. And what, exactly, would I be reporting on? The number of ibis flying past every day? The hieroglyphs on the temple at Koum Ombo? The amount of sand that I sweep out of the tent in a week?'

'We quite accept that there is nothing *you* could tell a French agent that would be of any interest to them.'

How dry he is. Does he ever show any emotion? Cleo tried to imagine Sir James in the throes of passion, which was a small help to her nerves. He would have skinny buttocks.

'You find something amusing, *madam*?'

'Not at all. So, if you do not think I am a spy, what am I…? Oh, I see, you think my *father* is one. What nonsense! My father is an English baronet and a scholar. He is probably the most boring man on this earth and he would not know anything of interest to your enemies if he fell over it. Unless it came decorated with hieroglyphs, that is.'

'Why do you think the French helped you when they arrived in Cairo?' Sir James asked, without the slightest indication he had heard what she said.

'Because of the *savants*. My father is a scholar and they, being more observant, or perhaps less insanely suspicious than you are, thought he would contribute to their efforts.'

'So they facilitated his move to an area they controlled, they arranged a marriage between his daughter and a French officer and they took over his postal arrangements?'

'Yes.' *Postal arrangements...* 'That is what this is about, isn't it? My father's correspondence.' She stood and confronted Quin, who sat back in his chair, but made no move to stand. 'You were prying into his letters. Did you search our tent? Is that why you locked up his boxes when we landed here?'

He nodded. 'And you did not suspect anything?'

Cleo put her knuckles on the table and leaned forward so she could stare deep into his eyes. 'Suspect that you were up to something? Yes, of course I did. And like a fool I did not tell Capitaine Laurent of my suspicions because I knew he would torture you and I was too soft-hearted to contemplate that. And this is how you repay me.'

There was colour over Quin's cheekbones, but he did not rise to her taunts. 'Did you suspect that the French were using your father's correspondence to channel information from spies and informers across the world?'

'Why should they bother with one man's antiquarian gossip?' She sat down again, twitching her limp skirts around her feet with a disdainful flick.

'Because that is how intelligence operates.' It was Quin who answered her. 'Endless tiny details building into one large picture. Agents wrote to your father from major English ports, from London, from militarily strategic parts of India, from all around the Mediterranean. Their outgoing letters would have raised no suspicions. Antiquarian gossip, as you say—but it was full of codes. The French in Cairo slit the seals, read the letters and passed them on to your father.

'Troop movements, ship movements, political intrigue, economic intelligence. Tiny grains of sand, just like the ones that irritate between your toes— and which mound up when the wind is right into vast dunes that can swamp a village.'

'Or an army, or a fleet,' Sir James added.

'And you think my father knew this?' There was an odd buzzing in her ears. Her fingers hurt and when she looked down she found they were twisted tight into the muslin of her skirts.

'That is what I need to find out,' Sir James said. 'If he is innocent of anything except gullibility, then he can help us establish just who is genuine and who is not. There is a mass of paper to sift through.'

'And if he is not innocent?'

Sir James just looked at her.

If they find Father guilty of this, they will... For the first time in her life Cleo knew she was about to faint. The air darkened, as though someone was slowly drawing a curtain. The buzzing sound filled her ear and she was falling.

'Very convenient,' said a dispassionate voice.

'I think it is genuine,' said another, close to her. One she knew.

'I never faint…' Cleo reached out her hands and found fingers, warm, strong fingers that held her as the world went black.

She had been dreaming, Cleo decided. She never fainted and she was in bed, so it must have been a dream. Only…it had all made sense. Her father's letters, the French assistance, the way Quin had acted.

If she kept her eyes closed, none of it would be real. That was what she had told herself when she was a little girl, frightened in yet another strange town where she did not speak the language, where she was hungry or uncomfortable, where Mama was crying quietly.

It hadn't worked then and it would not work now, she knew. Still, she would huddle under a sheet and pretend to be asleep while she thought. No one could expect her to speak when she was asleep. Speak and risk saying something that would condemn Father.

What was the worst possibility? That he was a deliberate spy, that he had bought French protection and the opportunity to study his beloved ruins unmolested at the cost of betraying the country of his birth. They would shoot him for that.

The best she could hope for was that the British believed he had been an unknowing dupe. He would be shamed and humiliated, his precious circle of correspondents shattered.

She did not think she loved her father. Any affection for him had been worn out over years of indifference, of emotional neglect, of learning painfully that he was a selfish man who had broken her mother's heart. But he was still her father and she would not have left him unless she had been certain he would be cared for.

Cleo had wanted to walk free from him with her conscience clear and now she would always know that by saving Quin, not once, but twice, she had condemned her own father.

But she could not go back and undo it and lying here was not going to help either. There were soft sounds in the room, someone was there with her.

'Maggie?' Cleo opened her eyes, blinking into the bars of strong sunlight that crossed the bed from the windows. It was still late morning then.

The bed frame behind her creaked as someone sat down on it and she rolled over on to her back. 'You.' Of course, he would not leave her in peace, he had to carry on harassing her.

'Yes, me.' Quin reached out and brushed her hair from her forehead. 'How do you feel?'

She could not bat his hand away, she was so tangled in the sheet. Cleo struggled free and sat up. 'How do I feel? Like a fool. Like a woman men lie to and who is stupid enough to believe them. Like a daughter who could not see what was going on under her nose. Like a sentimental female who wants to think the best about a man because he offers hugs and smiles and…'
And kisses.

'I am sorry. We had to find out who was involved, you must see that? We had to be certain you were innocent too.' He sat and watched her face, his own serious and open. There was regret in his voice as well as in his words.

She wanted to believe him, began to form the sentences to tell him that, to tell him she understood why he had lied to her and used her, that she believed it must have been hard.

'It was for your own good,' Quin added.

'My own good?' Every iota of empathy and understanding fled. 'You expect me to believe that? Of course it was not for my own good! Of course you had to know whether I was guilty or innocent and it doesn't much matter which, does it, provided you know? Innocent is probably less messy, I suppose. Do you shoot women? Or would I have had a nasty accident? That would have been neater.'

'Cleo—' Quin reached for her and she struck his hand away with the edge of hers, bone against bone.

'Ow!' Tears sprang to her eyes and she cradled her bruised and stinging hand against her chest.

'Let me see.' He held out his hand again, the mark of the blow red against the side of the palm. 'You abuse these poor hands enough without trying to break them on my hard bones. Come,' he urged when she glared at him. 'Show me.'

She laid her hand in his and closed her eyes as he straightened out the fingers, one after another. *So gentle. And so implacable. He knows it hurts me and he is going to do it anyway. For my own good.*

'Nothing broken. Keep still.' He began to wrap it in something soft and when she opened her eyes she realised that the bandage was his neckcloth, pulled free so his formal collar gaped open.

She had seen that vee of brown skin, the curl of hair, every day they had spent together up to now. She had seen him stark naked, for Heaven's sake! But this seemed both a shocking informality and a sign of tenderness that touched something deep inside. Something that hurt.

'Quin.' Cleo realised she was weeping. Great welling tears splashed down on the sheet, on his wrist, on her shift. 'I never cry,' she stammered. 'I never faint and I never cry and...'

'And you never let go, do you? Come here.' Quin shifted so he was sitting with his back to the wall and pulled her into his arms. 'There is a lot to cry about, I would say.'

Chapter Twelve

He thought she would resist. Cleo went rigid in Quin's arms and then, with a little gasp, burrowed deep against his chest and wept. His nice clean shirt, borrowed from Sir James, stuck wetly to his chest, his hand where she had struck him ached, there was a lump in the plaster behind his head—and his arms were full of soft, fragrant woman. Cleo, who might never forgive him, Cleo, who certainly needed him at this moment.

The discomforts faded. Quin bent his head and nuzzled the top of hers, his lips moving against the shifting texture of her hair. He felt no need to try to stop her weeping. She would be better for the release and, selfishly, he enjoyed having her in his arms.

When she sat up, red-eyed and endearingly snuffly, he found his handkerchief and offered it without a word.

'Sorry,' she muttered into the depths of the linen.

'Don't be.' Quin stayed where he was and waited until she emerged. 'Cleo, we believe you. And we believe your father now we've talked with him. The man isn't that good an actor.'

'What…what did he say?'

'He is furious that he was deceived and appears to regard it as an insult. The implications for national security do not appear to concern him anything like as much as the thought that we might cut him off from his correspondents.'

Cleo gave a moan of what sounded like pain. 'Typical! Has he no idea what would have happened to us if you hadn't believed him?'

Quin grinned. At the time he had wanted to hit the man, but in retrospect Sir Philip was so predictable it was almost funny. 'He is an English baronet and a noted scholar. Naturally, in his opinion, we would take his word. I doubt it occurred to him for a moment that we might not. I thought Sir James was going to lose his temper, which would have been a novelty.'

'Did Father ask about me?' Cleo had recovered her poise, as much as a young woman sitting up in bed in her shift and mopping red eyes could. Her question was put calmly, with an air of indifference that made Quin want to wince.

'He was rather preoccupied,' he prevaricated.

'In other words he did not.'

'Cleo—'

'I am used to it,' she said with a smile.

He had seen that smile before, knew it well enough now not to be convinced. 'The lack is in him, not in you,' Quin said as he traced the curve of her lips with his fingertip. As he suspected, her flesh felt tight and unyielding as she forced the smile.

He expected her to move her head, to reject the caress. Instead her lips parted and her eyes closed. Quin caught his breath as the shock of arousal swept through him. He bent and touched his lips to hers. *Sweet, soft, salty with tears.* The desire to taste more, to reach the essence of her, was overwhelming. Quin cradled the back of Cleo's head and opened his mouth over hers.

That kiss back in Koum Ombo might have been just a moment ago, so familiar was the feel of her lips, of the feminine essence that was simply Cleo. Her un-injured hand curled around his neck without hesitation, as direct and brave as she was herself, and he felt himself go achingly hard with the need to possess her. *Here, now. Mine.*

Cleo gave a little growl and Quin smiled against her mouth. No needy little whimpers from her, she was as fierce and demanding as Bastet the cat goddess. He stroked his hand up her side, shaped it to cup the globe of one small apple breast and heard his own answering growl as the nipple responded to the pressure of his thumb.

Her reaction was instant as she arched into his caress and lifted her free hand to pull his head closer, her teeth nipping at his lower lip. The trailing edges of the makeshift bandage brushed over his arm and cheek, confusing him, breaking his focus.

Hell. What am I doing? This is Cleo and she's disorientated, distressed and uprooted. I have done enough to hurt her. The last thing she needs is a man taking advantage of her need for comfort and someone to cling to. He broke the kiss and gently lifted her hands free of his neck.

'Cleo. I am sorry, this is not a good idea.'

Her chin went up and her lips thinned into that look of haughty disdain he had first seen when he had regained consciousness in her tent. Quin wondered why he had never recognised it for what it was, the legacy of generations of blue-blooded ancestors. This was a duke's granddaughter and it showed in every fine line of her face and the erect bearing of that lovely, over-worked body. And beside any other consideration, he had no business in her bed, desiring what he did, how-ever unconventional her upbringing had been.

A gentleman made love to a lady with only one outcome in mind—marriage—unless he was a com-plete blackguard. And for Quin marriage was a care-fully calculated step in his master plan. If he had to draw up a list of well-bred women in order of their total unsuitability for a diplomat's wife, Cleo Wood-ward would top it easily. Not that the Duke of St Osyth would countenance his suit for one second if he were so foolish.

'I am certain it is not a good idea,' she agreed with an icy control at odds with her reddened eyes and her tumbled hair. 'How very considerate of you to stop.' She dragged up the slipping shoulders of her shift. 'Who undressed me and put me to bed?'

'I did.' It had hardly been an intrusive act. She had not been wearing stockings or stays. All he had done was slip off her gown and tuck her under the sheet. 'There is no need to look as though I was some dirty old man stripping the clothes off a defenceless female for my perverted pleasure. I left you in your shift. *You* stripped *me* naked.'

'Tit for tat?' There were flags of furious colour fly-ing in her cheeks now. 'I had to in order to nurse you and you know that perfectly well.'

She was quite right, which did nothing for Quin's own temper. His balls were probably turning blue with frustration, his bruised hand gave a twinge every time he flexed his hand, he had pulled the almost-healed scar on his arm carrying her and his conscience was playing merry hell. 'And what the blazes were you doing with a knife strapped to your leg?' he demanded.

'I was hoping to find you with your back turned,' Cleo snapped back.

'Then I shall take care to keep my back to the bulk-head all the way to England,' Quin said as he stood up. 'The knife is on the table,' he added as he reached the door.

'England?'

'If you still want to go.' As though he would give her a choice, he thought with a stab of conscience. There was no way he could be open with her now, she would refuse to go with him if she suspected that her destiny had been neatly arranged, he was certain of it. *It is for her own good.* 'Oh, and Sir James would be pleased if you and Sir Philip would join him for din-ner this evening.'

The door closed gently behind Quin. The air stirred in the draught, dust moved in the light from the win-dows. It was hot and quiet and suddenly, quite empty.

He will take me to England. He begins to make love to me and then he loses interest. He is kind—and then he is...not. I want him, but he, it seems, does not want me, even after he had undressed me, even after I had thrown myself at him.

But what do I know of men? I thought Thierry loved me. I believed the French general wanted to help us. I trusted Laurent and all the time he was using us. I am not able to read men at all. All I know is that they will use me for what they want and tell me what they think I want to hear in order to do so.

Cleo got out of bed and went to the closet to dip her sore hand into the water jug. Why had she hit out at Quin? She couldn't remember now. Thierry would have struck back, but not Quin, the English gentleman. The diplomat. The liar she could not trust.

But surely he would not tell me he would take me to England and not mean it? He would have nothing to gain from that. Cleo found the arnica in her medicine box and soaked a handkerchief in it before she bandaged it on to her hand.

England. Independence. And no money to live on. Cleo took her notebook from the bag, sat down at the table and made herself think about something other than a man with blue eyes, a wicked mouth, broad shoulders and an unreadable mind. *There must be something I can do that someone in England might want to employ me for.*

Ensign Lloyd came to fetch her for dinner. 'The private stationed at your door will escort you anywhere you would like to walk tomorrow,' he said and waved a hand vaguely at the encampment. 'There isn't much to see, I'm afraid.'

'So I am no longer a prisoner?'

'It was protective custody, ma'am,' he said, colouring up.

He showed her into another part of the house where she had met Sir James that morning, a long room, whitewashed and carpeted with layers of colourful rugs. The table was covered in a pristine cloth and two men in white turbans, trousers and tunics with coloured sashes were laying it with six places.

Cleo took a deep breath, managed not to look around for Quin, and walked in.

'Madame Valsac.' Sir James came forward and shook hands. When she looked up she saw Quin behind him with two other men, one in uniform. They bowed. Her father, who had been holding forth to the civilian stranger about hieroglyphs, turned, frowned and nodded at her.

The men were all immaculately turned out. The officer was in what was obviously dress uniform. The other men wore swallow-tailed coats, knee breeches and stockings and someone had even found a suit to fit her father.

Cleo felt like a drab duck amidst a party of elegant drakes. Her skirts were limp, her gown was presumably years out of fashion, and her bare feet were pushed into backless slippers. Maggie had done her best with her hair, but without any idea between the two of them what a fashionable *coiffure* would look like, the best she could hope was that she looked clean and tidy.

When confronting footpads, stare them down, Mama had told her one day after an unpleasant encounter in an alleyway in Constantinople. *Never show fear.* She drew herself up to her full height, arched her brows, looked down her nose and produced a coolly confident smile. It was not her purse or her life that was at hazard here, only her dignity, she reminded herself. She was damned if she would let Lord Quintus Deverall see how much he affected her.

No one recoiled in distaste at the sight of her, or burst out laughing. But of course, they were diplomats.

'So glad you could join us,' Sir James said, for all the world as though she had somehow made space in a crowded social whirl to fit in his dinner party. 'Lord Quintus you know.' Quin's expression was politely bland. 'Major Grainger is our military liaison and Dr Kent has been sent out by the Royal Society to assist with the recovery of Egyptian artefacts from the French once we have obtained their surrender. Meanwhile I am sure he and your father will find much to discuss. Gentlemen, Madame Valsac.'

'I think I will revert to my maiden name,' Cleo said. She could think of no reason to keep Thierry's name now and it would surely ease things in England if she had no obvious French connections.

'Miss Woodward, then.' The gentlemen bowed all over again. Cleo dipped what she hoped was a passable curtsy and eyed the elaborate table setting with disquiet. This was a glimpse into the world that she had always known existed out there somewhere and it appeared to require levels of esoteric knowledge that made understanding hieroglyphs straightforward.

She had to do several things at once, beside attempting to keep her countenance and not lose her temper again with Quin. There was posture and what Mama had called *deportment.* Poor Mama had died before she could instil much into Cleo's head, but she did recall, *Keep your voice and tone moderate, your back straight and your head up. Do not wave your hands about to emphasise a point. Smile, do not be shy, nor forward, do not contradict the opinions of those you are conversing with.*

Conversing. That was the next thing. She must make small talk with these men. But what about? Mama had said that a lady did not discuss politics, religion, war, money… What did that leave, especially in the midst of a siege?

'Your wife does not accompany you, Sir James?'

'No.'

'I am so sorry, you must miss her. Perhaps your demanding work is a help under the circumstances,' she ventured.

'My wife would tell you that my work is always a distraction, Miss Woodward.' Could he possibly be smiling? Yes, it seemed he was.

Cleo managed a stiff little curve of her lips in response. 'Is this your first visit to Egypt? Although I suppose *visit* is hardly the word.'

'It is.' He placed one white-gloved hand under her elbow and steered her towards a footman who held a tray full of glasses. 'Champagne, Miss Woodward?' He took her silence for consent and handed her a glass. 'Difficult to get it adequately chilled, I fear. Yes, I am finding Egypt a most interesting country and the opportunity to use my Arabic is stimulating.'

'Do many British diplomats speak it?' Cleo asked. 'I assumed it would be uncommon.'

'What with the need to keep the trade routes to the east open and the constant dealings with the Barbary pirates, quite a few of us have had to acquire a facility. I cannot say I found it the easiest language to learn.'

'I suppose I came to it quite young,' Cleo said. 'Although I learned Turkish younger and I am less confident with that. Or perhaps I have had to use my Arabic more.'

'You speak several languages, Miss Woodward?' Major Grainger strolled to her side.

'French, German, Italian, Turkish, Greek and Arabic. Oh, and Classical Greek and Latin, of course.'

'My goodness, you are quite the scholar, Miss Woodward.' The major did not appear to consider it to be a quality she should be congratulated upon.

Cleo took a gulp of wine and almost choked. This was supposed to be enjoyable? She swallowed both the cough and a grimace. 'No, not a scholar, Major. I am the practical member of the family, the one who has to take the notes and do the shopping. If my understanding of the ancient languages is faulty, I am unable to assist my father. If I cannot buy provisions, then we starve.'

She was conscious of heads turning. She had raised her voice, she had spoken tartly to a gentleman. *Tut, tut, Cleo* chided herself. *They'll think you've been brought up in a tent.* She took another sip of the wine. It was not so bad this time, now she was prepared for the bubbles.

The glass was empty so she plucked another from the tray and took a defiant sip. Alcohol was not so different from a sherbet drink, to judge by the taste of it.

'The weather seems quite temperate,' Sir James remarked. 'Hot of course, but not as bad as I had feared.'

When all else fails, fall back on the weather, Mama had advised. 'This is normal for the time of year,' Cleo said. 'It will rapidly get hotter, of course, and then the plague will increase in severity.'

'Dinner is served, Sir James.'

Was it her imagination or did they all look relieved? The major and Sir James could stop making conversation and Quin and Dr Kent might hope to escape from her father's views on temple architecture for a few moments.

Sir James took the head of the table and showed her to the seat on his right. Quin took the foot with her father on his right, the major sat next to Cleo and the doctor took the remaining seat opposite her father.

Cleo eyed the array of silverware. Outside in, inside out? At random? And why did they need three glasses each?

Tureens were brought to the table and soup bowls laid out. At least she could work out which spoon to use for that.

Somehow she got through the soup and three removes without apparently committing any great social sin, although she had to admit that after two more glasses of wine, she might be missing the subtler clues. Alcohol, she was discovering, was potent stuff and it certainly helped with this business of making light conversation. She even felt vaguely friendly towards the major and lost all fear of saying the wrong thing. What did it matter what they thought?

The doctor and Quin stopped her father from completely monopolising the discourse, which impressed her with Quin's diplomatic skills, and Quin did not reveal by so much as a look or a word that anything in the slightest improper had happened between them that afternoon.

She knew she should be relieved, even though she did not expect ever to see the other men again once she had left the camp. A pleasant sensation of drifting, of unreality, was beginning to take possession of her. It was quite delightful.

'Why are you feeling your forehead with the back of your hand?' Quin spoke in her ear.

'Why are you creeping up on me?' she countered.

'I'm not. I advanced around the table with all the secrecy of a full cavalry charge.'

'I was checking to see if I have a fever, if you must know. I feel a trifle…light-headed.'

Quin took her wrist between his fingers and felt her pulse. 'You're not feverish, you are tipsy, Cleo.'

'Tipsy?' Somehow she managed to turn the shriek into a strangled whisper. The other men were talking amongst themselves and she remembered something vaguely about ladies retiring after dinner so the men could relax and drink something or another. *And tell* risqué *stories, no doubt. Pity, I'd like to hear a* risqué *story…*

'Tipsy, half-seas over, fuddled,' he whispered back. 'Have you never drunk wine before?' Those flexible, wicked lips held a smile, but it was reassuring, not mocking. Quin slid his hand under her arm as she shook her head. And then wished she had not.

'I think it is time I saw you home, Miss Woodward. You must be exhausted after the events of the past few days,' he said, guiding her towards the door. 'Sir James, gentlemen, I think Miss Woodward should be resting and as there are no other ladies for her to retire with I will see her across the camp.'

Chapter Thirteen

Cleo said her good-nights and thanks without tripping over her feet or slurring her words or saying anything untoward.

'Being drunk is very strange,' she remarked as she clutched Quin's arm and let him steer her towards her hut. 'I feel all floaty. It is rather nice, I think.'

'You'll have the mother and father of headaches in the morning,' he warned. 'Drink something before you go to sleep, that will help. And have a big breakfast whether you feel like it or not.'

Cleo stopped suddenly, jerking Quin to a halt beside her. 'You're being very kind to me, Lord Quintus. I don't know why.' She squinted at him in the moonlight that had turned his hair silver and black and threw dramatic shadows, making a severely beautiful mask out of his strong-boned face.

'Because I like you, Miss Woodward. You are as much trouble as a basketful of monkeys and as easy to understand as the Sphinx, but you've got courage and brains and a certain *je ne sais quoi*.'

'Then I am sorry I hit you this afternoon,' she said

on a wave of warmth and generosity. 'Does your hand still hurt? Perhaps I should kiss it better.' *I would like you to kiss me better.*

'That's very kind of you, but I think we might give the sentries a bit of a shock.' Quin started walking again. 'Here we are, back to your room.'

Private Minton slammed to attention with a thud of boots on the hard ground that made Cleo wince.

'Tomorrow we'll discuss arrangements for getting to the coast and taking ship to England,' Quin said as they stopped outside the door. 'Private, could you just check all around the building, make certain all the shutters are secure?' He waited while the soldier saluted and marched off, then turned back to Cleo. 'I really do better without an audience.' He tipped up her chin and bent his head so close that when he spoke his breath warmed her lips. 'Good night, Cleo. Sweet dreams.'

The kiss was gentle and respectful and shockingly thorough. And beautifully timed. As Private Minton marched round the corner again Quin was standing a good foot away from her. 'Good night, Miss Woodward. Good night, Private.'

'Sir!'

Cleo was beyond words and, for an awful moment, without the strength in her shaking legs to move. Minton leapt to open the door. 'Thank you,' she murmured and staggered inside to collapse on the bed.

The wine or Quin's kiss, or perhaps both, were making the room whirl above her head. It went on spinning when she closed her eyes so she sat up and groped for the covered glass beside the bed and gulped down warm well water. Cleo had a horrible suspicion that she was going regret a number of things in the morning and probably the least of them was going to be the wine she had drunk.

'I am not going to think about it now,' she said out loud and lay down again. *I am not going to think about him now, either.*

'You will be glad to know that your banker in Alexandria has come through all the recent disruption quite safely,' Sir James said, shuffling a pile of papers on his desk.

'Disruption?' Sir Philip looked blank.

Behind her Cleo heard Quin sigh, but he answered patiently. 'Being occupied by the French, being invaded by the British, having several battles fought in the vicinity, plague, Turkish troops...'

'Oh, yes.'

'He released the last lot of funds you requested several months ago to my safekeeping. Here is the receipt.' Sir James pushed it across the table. 'I imagine you'll need to employ a staff and a housekeeper. Dr Kent will see to finding you a house in Cairo as soon as we gain possession, meanwhile you are, of course, welcome to stay here. I assume you will be giving Miss Woodward a note of hand so that she can withdraw money as she passes through Alexandria.'

'What for?'

'Clothing, luggage, the necessities for a sea voyage, personal items. The hire of a maid. Miss Woodward will also require a bank draft on your London bank so she can establish herself when she arrives,' Quin snapped.

'All very extravagant,' her father protested. 'I'm not made of money. I'm a poor man.'

'Indeed? Your banker in Alexandria was indiscreet enough to let slip that he was concerned about the way your income from the trust fund was building up, Sir Philip.'

'Trust fund.' Cleo clenched her hands together to still their shaking. '*Trust fund?* You had money all the time that Mama was working herself into a shadow making ends meet, all the time I have been scratching around economising with every *piaster*?'

'It was a pittance a great aunt left me.' Her father stuck out his lower lip like a small boy confronted by a misdeed.

'The banker gave me a statement of account to pass to you,' Sir James added. His face was perfectly bland, but Cleo had the startling impression that he was enjoying this.

'Thank you.' She got to her feet and took the sealed letter from his hand before her father could reach for it. The wax shattered under her impatient thumb and she spread out the single sheet with its rows of figures. They danced in front of her eyes as she blinked at them. 'This is over a thousand pounds. A thousand pounds sterling.'

'It has accumulated slowly,' her father huffed.

'We could have had a doctor for Mama. A proper doctor. A house, servants, you selfish man.' Cleo looked at the figures again. 'I want half of this. I have earned it.'

'Ridiculous. You are a woman, you haven't the slightest idea—'

'I fear it may prove very difficult to find the keys to the locks on your chests, Sir Philip,' Quin interrupted. 'In fact, it may well be that the chests themselves may have been shipped off to Cairo in error. I doubt my memory of their whereabouts will come back to me until I stop worrying about Miss Woodward's very reasonable claim for funds.'

'That's blackmail!'

'No, the stress of his experiences, I fear,' Sir James said. 'Unfortunately Lord Quintus suffers from these blackouts from time to time. I am sure it will all come back to him. Eventually.'

'Might I suggest this?' Quin handed the enraged baronet a piece of paper. 'Just sign and date it. You'll see there is a request to release a sum of money to Miss Woodward immediately and to give her a draft transferring funds to the London branch. Ah, my memory is coming back,' he added as her father scrawled his name across the foot of the page. 'See, here are the keys.'

'Quin, you are wonderful!' Cleo bounced out of her chair and threw her arms around his neck. 'Thank you.' She stood on tiptoe and kissed him, full on the mouth.

It took only a second to realise what she had done. What was the matter with her? Lingering alcohol fumes and relief over the money, she supposed. This was Lord Quintus, the man who had betrayed her, for heaven's sake.

Quin went quite still, then stepped back out of her embrace. 'Your enthusiasm is enchanting, Miss Woodward,' he said politely and Cleo felt the chill in her veins. 'However, no thanks is expected or required. Now we have the finances settled, would you be ready to depart for Alexandria in the morning? I wonder if the woman who has been attending to your needs would be prepared to travel with you until you find a suitable maid and we locate a ship.'

Once, not very long ago, she had grown a carapace

of glass over her feelings, had learned to ignore emotion and show none. Then Quin had entered her life and it seemed her shield was crazed with cracks and weaknesses.

Cleo reached for the tattered remains of her dignity. 'Certainly I can be ready,' she said. 'And I will ask Maggie now. Thank you, gentlemen. Father.' She picked up the letter for the banker, considered attempting a curtsy and, instead, simply nodded and walked out.

Quin reached the door before her and opened it. 'I will find us a more comfortable river boat than our little feluccas,' he said.

I wonder if that is a peace offering. 'Excellent. Thank you, Lord Quintus.' And she smiled and he bowed and she swept out into the baking sunshine, wondering if she was ever going to recover from the embarrassment of throwing herself at a reluctant man in public.

Tomorrow she was going to have to face Quin again. She was going to have to travel with him for weeks. And he was going to be kind about it. And gentlemanly and pretend nothing had happened. That none of those kisses had been exchanged, that she hadn't made a fool of herself just then.

Once she had believed that all she needed to be happy was to be free of her father and independent. *What an innocent you were, Cleo Woodward,* she thought as she walked back, her soldier escort at her heels. *What you need to be happy is freedom, money and no men. Ever.*

Even after three days at sea the freshness, the cool breeze, the lack of dust were still pleasures to be sa-

voured. Quin drew a deep breath down to his dia-
phragm and folded his forearms along the ship's rail
as he watched a school of dolphins playing in the bow
wave of the *Dorabella.*

The merchant ship, bound for London from the Le-
vant, was making good progress towards Sicily and the
next friendly harbour at Syracuse. It hadn't been the
first possible ship, but it combined good lines, strong
armaments and a captain Quin felt knew his business.
Almost as important as the good navigator and the
guns, it had as a passenger Madame da Sota, the ex-
pansive—in every sense—wife of a Levantine merchant in London.

Madame might be flamboyant, but she was also obviously respectable and kindly. She would be delighted
to chaperon Miss Woodward, who must have the spare
cot in her cabin, she declared. Her maid could share a
cabin with Maggie, they would all get on delightfully.

Maggie Tomkins was another woman for whose
presence Quin was giving thanks daily. Given the
chance to accompany Cleo to Alexandria she had offered to go all the way to England, explaining that
life as an army wife had lost its charm for her and she
wanted to be home with her son.

Quin, with a vast inward sigh of relief, had surren-
dered Cleo to the care of the women and took himself
off, whenever possible, to the opposite end of the ship
to wherever they were.

Sir James had taken him to one side the morning
they departed for Alexandria on the large felucca he
had hired. He had not needed Sir James's words of cau-
tion, but he had listened patiently anyway.

'Her grandfather is expecting her back in perfect

condition,' the diplomat said. 'His support for our department and our work is invaluable, especially when it comes to securing the ear of the king and the purse strings of the Treasury. Never forget that, Deverall.'

'Certainly not, sir. Although there is a limit to how perfect Miss Woodward's condition can be, given that she's a widow. I suppose the duke does know that?'

'He does and he's not best pleased about it. Still, we want to make sure she doesn't arrive home even less of a virgin than she is now, don't we?'

Quin had no illusions about what his superior was saying and could understand his concern. If he was in Sir James's shoes, he'd be laying down the law, too. 'Miss Woodward is impulsive and unused to society, Sir James. I believe that her display of…affection yesterday was simply an innocent reaction to excitement and relief over the money. She doubtless regards me in the light of a brother.'

'And you appear to regard me as a blind old fool, Deverall,' Sir James said, the hint of a dry smile on his lips. 'However, I have every confidence that your zeal for this particular mission and your ambitions for a suitable marriage to advance your career will trump any unsophisticated charms Miss Woodward may possess.'

'Sir.' Quin swallowed his irritation at such an explicit warning. How could he resent what he thoroughly deserved? 'You are quite correct, Sir James, although *unsophisticated* is not the word I would use for Miss Woodward. She may be completely ignorant of polite society but she has a range of other talents that are going to take the *ton* by surprise, I suspect.'

'If her grandfather lets her loose before he's had

them shaken out of her, perhaps you're right. But I know his Grace's methods. He'll have chaperons and tutors and lord knows what else lined up to turn her into a pattern-book young lady within a Season, mark my words.'

The sun moved behind a cloud, the dolphins gave a few last heart-stopping leaps and vanished and Quin felt a sudden wave of depression. Cleo was unique and to turn her into just another well-bred female on display in the Marriage Mart seemed as great an act of vandalism as taking a Greek statue and recarving it into some sentimentally pretty garden ornament.

And I will have contributed to that. I will have made it possible. He struggled for the hundredth time with the sense that he was betraying her by keeping quiet about her grandfather. But she had no understanding of how things should be, he told himself, again for the hundredth time. She would probably try to bolt or do something foolish, but once she was safely with her grandfather she would soon discover the advantages of the situation.

But it wasn't enough, he knew it. Cleo dreamt of freedom, of the power to make her own decisions, to be her own woman. The fact that this simply was not a possibility for a well-bred lady was no answer to that dream, to that passion.

And yet he had given his word he would bring her back to England. His word, his honour and, plainly, his duty, argued for seeing he achieved it without risk of Cleo taking off and putting herself in danger or creating a scandal before he could retrieve her.

It was the first time his inclinations, his personal feelings, had been opposed to his duty, he realised. He had worked hard to secure his place on the ladder of his new career, to be accepted as himself, a man forging his own name and his own destiny, not in the shadow of the Malvern escutcheon.

Brace up, he told himself. *You gave your word and you will do your duty to your country or you aren't fit to hold the aspirations that you do. And it is the right thing for Cleo, whether she likes it or not.* To tell her that he was taking her to her grandfather might ease his conscience for a while, but then he would have to deal with the consequences when she rebelled, as she surely would.

'Brooding, Lord Quintus? Or seasick?' Cleo's voice right behind him brought him swinging round before he could get his expression under control. 'Oh! I am sorry, you really are upset about something, aren't you?' Her tone shifted instantly from the lightly sarcastic edge she always seemed to use to him now to something genuine and kind. Its softness hit him like a punch in the gut.

She held her broad-brimmed hat on her head with one hand, the other catching at the flying ends of the scarf that should have secured it. The breeze and the sea air had brought the colour up in her cheeks and the relief from the daily grind of her previous life was already beginning to show in the graceful, relaxed way she moved now.

'Upset? No, just thinking about…work. Various obligations.' He shrugged and managed a smile. *The obligation to continue to deceive you. The obligation not to touch you. The obligation not to kiss you. The obligation not to get to know you very, very well indeed, Augusta Cleopatra Agrippina Woodward Valsac, you infuriatingly unique woman.*

'How troublesome, I do hope it is not keeping you awake at night.'

The edge was back and with it something else, an undertone that had him wondering if she was kept awake by something herself. Fear of the unknown, no doubt.

Quin wrestled again with the temptation to tell her the truth in the hope it would quell that fear if she knew what her fate was to be. He could tell her that she need not concern herself about making a new life in a strange homeland, that she would be pitch-forked into a gilded cage of privilege and wealth. But that was what temptation did, gave you justification for doing the wrong thing, and he had to resist.

'Yes, it keeps me awake,' Quin admitted, adopting the neutral smile that was virtually the first thing that a budding diplomat learned. *I lie awake thinking of you, of that generous mouth against mine, making sweetness not sarcasm. I remember the soft curves of your body and the length of those lovely gazelle's legs and imagine them naked, twining with mine. I imagine that austere oval of your face transformed by your passion as you come beneath me, over and over again, crying out my name as I bury myself in you and the flame burns through my blood...*

'It is really very trying,' he added as he held her gaze and willed her not to look down to where his thoughts would not permit the slightest diplomatic cover-up. 'After the tranquillity of the desert a ship under full sail does not make a quiet or easy bed.' *Not when I am lying on the thistles of desire and the stones of an uneasy conscience.* His muddle of mixed metaphors made him smile a little and he saw her relax.

'I like the motion,' Cleo said. She seemed full of a natural perversity since they had boarded ship and was ready to disagree with any opinion Quin expressed. 'It is wild and different. We are going somewhere at last and I feel almost free. Soon I will be, completely.' She untied her hat and let the wind take her hair, whipping it into a banner of brown silk.

'Almost?' Quin queried as he turned back to his position at the rail. *Think about the here and now...*

Chapter Fourteen

'Madame da Sota does her best to shackle me. These clothes.' She made a sweeping gesture at the skirts of her high-waisted gown. 'The shoes. Wretched stockings and garters! Everything pinches or needs holding down in the wind. And I am not allowed to complain because that is unladylike and of course I must wear them. I do not expect I should have mentioned stockings and garters to you. It was much easier when I could wear what I wanted and put a *tob sebleh* on top.'

Quin tried to imagine Cleo at Almack's in Egyptian dress and found it was all too easy. He disciplined the smile that was tugging at his lips and made room for her when she spun round and joined him at the rail. Her elbow poked against his, a sharp pressure he could not ignore. *Just like her.*

'But you get on all right with *madam*?' he queried. 'She is not of the *ton*, of course, being a merchant's wife, but she is undoubtedly a respectable chaperon.'

'She is kind,' Cleo agreed. 'But she never stops talking and I am not used to that. You are much more restful.' The point of her elbow was removed as she threaded her arm through his and leaned against his shoulder. *She trusts me.* 'Where should I buy a house to live?'

'In London? It is usual to rent, but even so, a whole house in a good area would be very expensive. There are houses where one can rent an entire floor as an apartment though.' He was careful not to say *you*. Even so, it was hellish, spinning this web of make-believe for her when the first thing he must do when they reached London was to put her in a carriage and take her to her grandfather. Where did honour lie in all of this? Was there something flawed in him because of his birth that he could not see the honourable path clearly, as his superiors so obviously did?

'London is so very expensive, then?' Cleo snuggled against his side without the slightest self-consciousness, using him as a windbreak, he supposed.

How the blazes she managed to forget those moments of shared physical intimacy back in the camp outside Cairo he had no idea. He certainly could not, yet Cleo appeared airily unconcerned about past kisses and caresses.

'Very expensive,' Quin said, dragging his mind back to her question. 'Lodgings, servants, provisions.'

'Oh. Do you have a London house?'

'I have an apartment in Albany, which is apartments mainly used by gentlemen needing a *pied-à-terre*. It is just off Piccadilly in the St James's area.'

'But you will have one when you marry?' He nodded. 'A whole one? Then you are rich.' Quin shook his head and she laughed. 'Ah, you will marry a rich wife!'

'Perhaps.' Lady Caroline was certain to be very well dowered and a London house might come as part of the settlement. Her father, the Earl of Camden, owned one that was diagonally across the square from his own father's house. Quin grinned wryly at the thought of his father's reaction if he set up home there. The cuckoo in the nest ending up with a promising career, a lovely wife, noble in-laws—that would chafe.

'Thinking about her makes you smile.' Cleo leaned forward to look at his face properly. The wind had whipped up the colour in her cheeks, her eyes were bright and her hair whirled around her like the wild locks of a creature of myth.

'I was thinking that you look like a maenad with your hair like that.'

'A crazed follower of Dionysus?' she said and laughed. Of course, she would know all the classical myths and legends. 'Is that flattering, I wonder? Would I enjoy being driven into a frenzy by strange rites? Iron would not wound me, nor fire burn me. I would subdue wild bulls and tear men to death with my bare hands, draw wine and honey and milk from the rocks.'

Spray flew up as the ship plunged into the trough of a wave, showering them in droplets. Quin drew Cleo against himself in an instinctive gesture of protection and found he was lost in her beauty and her fierce spirit. Against the backdrop of deep blue sea, her hair streamed out like a living thing. Her eyes were wide and wild and she was laughing with the sheer joy of the elements. Free, unique.

Maenads lured men into the woods with their wild dances, then they turned on them, rending them until their blood drenched the earth. Caught in the exhilaration of the wind-swept, sea-soaked moment, Quin could understand why a man might take that risk.

He pulled her tightly to him and bent his head, caught the scent of milk and honey on her lips, smelled the crushed herbs and grasses beneath her bare feet, heard the roar of the sacrificial bulls in his ears.

Make love to her, every instinct screamed. *No one will know. You want each other...* The ground lurched beneath his feet and became the wooden deck of a ship. The scents of a night-time forest became tarred rope and sea salt, the roaring was replaced by the flap of a sail and the scream of a gull.

'We'll be over the side in this sea,' Quin said and was surprised to hear how steady his voice was. 'We've changed tack, which is why she is rolling so much more. Come and sit on this hatch cover—much safer.'

Cleo looked at him out of wide sea-grey eyes, her face pale under the golden tan, her lips parted. She had felt it too, that wildness, that reckless attraction. *Thank God we're on a ship,* Quin thought. *Nowhere to go, no privacy. No risk of this getting out of hand.*

'My clothes are wet,' Cleo said. 'I will go and change. I expect we will meet at dinner.'

Quin watched her go and forced his mind into some semblance of calm common sense. He could not seduce the granddaughter of a duke—not that much seduction would be needed, it seemed. He especially could not seduce the granddaughter of this particular duke.

The ship gave another lurch and settled into a new tack. Quin began to pace up and down the deck, glad of the exercise as a distraction from physical and mental discomfort. Leaving aside the moral issues, he was on a mission and he could no more compromise it out of desire than he could take money from a foreign power or gossip about state secrets.

To be utterly practical, he lectured himself, *you cannot afford to make a mull of this.* He had worked too hard to reach his present position and to risk it now for a few snatched kisses, perhaps a tumble in some empty cabin, was insanity. He was a mongrel pretending to be a pedigree animal. One day, with the right wife by his side, and with hard work and good fortune, he would rise to the top of his profession, serve his country well, gain his own title, sire sons to carry it on and shake off the stigma that he felt like a brand, however politely the whispers about his birth were ignored by society.

And he had to believe this was for the best for Cleo, however much she might try to kick over the traces when she discovered she was being handed over to her grandfather and not released into the life of independence she fantasised about. She was a well-bred young lady, however unconventional her upbringing, and she had a place in the *haut ton*. It was her destiny, Quin assured himself, and he owed it to her to make sure she achieved that position. She had saved his life and she had trusted him enough not to betray him to Laurent.

He just wished the nagging feeling would go away that he was clipping the wings of a falcon and pushing her into a cage. If only he did not have to deceive her.

'How long will we have ashore in Syracuse?' Cleo asked as the ship glided to anchor in the bay. She tilted the parasol *madam* had lent her to shield her eyes and studied the town that rose from the bay, a hill studded with buildings in golden stone.

'The ship sails tomorrow as soon as they have filled the water casks and unloaded some cargo. I will need a few hours to make calls. I can see no reason for you to go ashore, Miss Woodward.' Quin glanced at her, then back to the letter that had been rowed out to him from the shore.

'Shopping, exercise, sightseeing,' she said, modulating her terse words with her best smile. It was wasted as Quin folded the paper and tucked it into the breast of his coat.

'You need nothing, there is the entire deck to walk on in the fresh air and the sights of Syracuse are infested with sailors, beggars, pickpockets and the riff-raff of a dozen nations.' He glanced at her with scarcely concealed impatience. 'I do not have the time to escort you and I do not know the crew well enough to trust any of them either.'

'It cannot be worse than Cairo.'

'True. No one is shelling it, there does not appear to be hand-to-hand fighting in the streets and I believe it is free of the plague, but then one can say that of many cities around the Mediterranean and I would not want you wandering about in any of them.'

Quin looked quite disgustingly fit, healthy and well groomed. The wind-blown man who had strolled around on deck, and occasionally even climbed the rigging, was suavely formal now. Not that she was going to show him that she thought so.

'Why are you dressed like that?' The wave of her hand took in pristine white linen, knee breeches, black stockings, buckled shoes and a strange flat hat under his arm. The embroidered baldric supporting a dress sword was visible between the edges of his coat as it crossed his chest, a flamboyant dash of colour beneath the midnight blue of his tail coat.

'I am off to see the representative of the King of Naples and this is the correct outfit for a formal call.' He interpreted the lift of her eyebrows correctly. 'It is always good diplomacy to make oneself known where possible and not attempt to slink in and out of port. That only raises suspicions.'

Cleo glanced down at her limp skirts, made by be-mused Cairo seamstresses in approximation of the newly fashionable high-waisted gowns of France and England, as described by *madam*. This city with its Bourbon king and flourishing trade would be certain to have fashions that were up to the minute. There was no time to have anything made up, but she might be able to buy fabrics and make sketches and sew some-thing herself.

Quin must have heard her sigh. 'I am going to be busy all day. I do not have time to escort you, Cleo, so you will just have to make up your mind to amuse yourself on board.'

She would not put it past him to tell the captain not to allow her on shore, Cleo thought, watching Quin talking to the man as he waited for a rowing boat to be brought alongside.

Infuriating, but not impossible, she decided, as she made her way down to her cabin. 'Maggie!'

'Yes, miss?' Maggie emerged from the cabin she shared with *madam*'s maid. '*Madam*'s lying down, she's got a headache.'

'Maggie, are you still friendly with that sailor you were flirting with?'

'What, the first mate? Yes, you could say we were friendly-like.'

'Friendly enough for him to have us rowed ashore

without, shall we say, advertising the fact to the captain?'

'His lordship not co-operating? I'll see what I can do.'

Half an hour later the rowing boat bumped against the quayside and Cleo scrambled ashore, her hand held out to steady Maggie. 'Straight up there,' she pointed. 'That's where Lord Quintus went. If the king's representative lives in that area then that is where the fashionable quarter will be, I have no doubt.' She unfurled her parasol. 'And there should be pastry shops where we can have coffee before we start.'

The street curved uphill, filled with a crowd of local people. Cleo dug into her memory for her rusty Italian and tried to understand the accent. There were intriguing little shops and stalls, people seemed cheerful and busy and there was nothing alarming as Quin had suggested. *He was just trying to keep me on board,* Cleo thought as they came into a long, rectangular open space with towering stone buildings on their right.

'There,' Cleo said, nodding towards a small group of elegant ladies entering a shop. 'Can you smell the coffee? We will start there. I might even buy some cakes for his lordship to show him I bear him no ill will for making such a fuss about nothing.'

Quin strolled out of the palazzo into the cathedral square and started to write a dispatch in his head while he eased his stiff shoulders. Stifling Bourbon court etiquette, the need to think about what he was hearing through layers of subtlety and misdirection, and the heat of an Italian afternoon, all served to put a dull ache behind his eyes and a stiffness in his neck. The square, surrounded by its golden stone buildings, and paved with the same material, threw back light and heat in a burning dazzle.

He felt restless and dissatisfied, even though the meeting had gone well. *Trapped*, that was the word. Ridiculous, because he enjoyed the diplomatic cut and thrust, the subtleties and the deception and knew he was good at it. He even enjoyed the formality and ritual when it was done well.

It was probably lack of hard exercise, Quin told himself as he took a side turning into a shadowed alleyway. A swim would be good, but the water in the harbour was not enticing. Perhaps there time to take a rowing boat, go along the coast a little, find a cove with clear water over sand…

The cry was faint. It might have been the call of a child or a seagull and yet there was something about it that jerked him out of his reverie of cool water. It came again, louder this time. *'Aiuto!'*

Help! It was a woman. He would have responded anyway, but there was a familiarity about the voice, even raised, even in Italian, that brought the hairs up on the back of his neck. *Cleo.* Quin began to run, cursing his stiff formal shoes as they slid on the cobbles and in the rubbish of the gutters. He cannoned off corners, ignoring the pain of bruised shoulder and skinned palm. The voice came again, closer, unmistakably Cleo, informing someone in vehement, confident Italian that their ancestry involved a donkey and a camel and they would regret ever crossing her path as their doubtless pathetically small balls would not survive the experience.

Quin was grinning as he rounded the final corner and found himself in a square so small it was almost a large courtyard. It was deserted except for four men who looked like fishermen and, facing them, Cleo, a knife in her hand. At her feet Maggie was crouched, her teeth bared at the men. Above his head a shutter banged closed. There was going to be no help from the locals.

The group shifted and spread apart when they saw him, moving with the ease of men accustomed to brawling and quite happy with the prospect of a fight.

'Quin!' Cleo flicked him a glance, then fixed her eyes on the men again. 'They are after our purses and everything else you may imagine. Maggie's hurt her ankle. The shorter one with the blue neckerchief is the leader. They don't seem to speak English.'

She reported with the economy of a soldier back from reconnaissance, all useful information and no hysterics. Quin drew the dress sword from its scabbard, a slim, fragile-seeming needle of steel.

'Lo chiami una spada?' Blue Neckerchief pulled a blade from his belt, a heavy knife that looked capable of gutting a big tuna with a stroke.

'Yes, I call it a sword,' Quin said mildly in Italian as the other three drew their own weapons, equally large, equally unsubtle. 'Can you make a distraction?' he added in English.

Without a word Cleo stooped, picked up a handful of dusty grit and threw it at the nearest man, a fat, deceptively jolly-looking type. He batted it away, laughing at her, and then staggered back as she followed it up with a cobblestone. The second man made a dive at her and she slashed with her knife, catching him across the back of his hand. He fell back cursing.

'I said make a distraction, not start a war,' Quin said on a huff of laughter as he lunged at the fourth man who had swung round to look at what Cleo was doing, presenting an undefended left side.

His sword was a rapier. It was light, thin, vulnerable to a blow from something heavy, but as a stabbing weapon it was unsurpassed. The point sank into the bulk of the man's bicep so smoothly that he did not start yelling until Quin pulled it back in a flowing fencer's move and then slashed at his face when the man spun round to face him. The cut was just where he had intended, across the forehead so blood flowed down into the man's eyes, blinding him.

One down, no, two. Cleo was fending off one man while the one she had hit with the cobble was on his knees, arms over his head, as Maggie pelted him with everything she could reach, from stones to what looked like a dead rat.

Cleo had been right, Blue Neckerchief was the leader. He stepped back, eyes flickering from side to side and let the one Quin thought of as Bloody Hand pick up the fight.

'Run while you can, my friends,' Quin advised and shifted position so he could keep both men in view at once, rapier raised in a textbook pose. He wanted them to think he was an academic fencer. Bloody Hand spat on the cobbles, then shifted his knife and came in fast. Quin lifted his weapon out of the way, spun round and kicked, hard and accurately, and the man collapsed on the cobbles, clutching his groin and retching. His knife clattered away, skidding on the stones, and Cleo lunged for it, grabbed it and tossed it back to Quin, who caught it left-handed.

No point in pretending now that he didn't know how to fight dirty. Blue Neckerchief pulled a short cosh from his pocket and edged forward, grinning a gap-toothed smile of pure malice. He was clearly not happy about losing his prey, still less having three of his men injured, but he was plainly looking forward to gutting Quin.

'Come on,' Quin encouraged him. 'Or are you only capable of attacking girls? And you need your friends to help you with—' He broke off as the man barrelled forward, stabbing with the knife while he beat at the slender blade of the rapier with the cosh.

The second it touched the sword Quin tossed the weapon away, throwing the man fractionally off balance, then spun out of the way of his thrusting blade. Quin brought his clenched left fist, holding the knife hilt, down on the angle between neck and shoulder and felt the collarbone break. The man fell to his knees and Quin followed through with a right hook to the jaw as he went down.

Chapter Fifteen

Quin looked round at a frozen tableau. Four men on the ground, Maggie, a cobblestone clutched in her fist, and Cleo, his rapier in her hand, poised like an avenging Fury.

'Thank you,' he said as he got his breath back and held out his hand for the sword.

She passed it to him, her face white under the golden tan. 'No, thank *you*.' Then she ran to Maggie's side and helped her to her feet.

'Bloody hell,' Maggie said, hopping on one foot. 'Cracked my ankle bone, the—' The string of curses she produced were hopefully unintelligible to Cleo. Some of them were new to Quin.

'I'll carry you.' He sheathed the rapier, scooped her up in his arms and looked round for Cleo, who was gathering up scattered belongings. 'Come on, before the neighbours decide to come out and join in.'

She was uncharacteristically silent as they navigated the twisting alleyways to emerge on to the quayside. Quin realised he was grinning again. Damn it, he was enjoying himself. A thoroughly satisfactory fight, the only injury on his team a sore ankle, his arms full of an appreciative young woman who was batting her eyelashes at him and Cleo safe and sound, the hellcat. It occurred to him that not only had he repaid her a little for saving his life, but that now he had the opportunity to tease her just a trifle as she thoroughly deserved. He tightened his lips, banished the grin for a scowl and strode towards the waiting skiff.

'That did not go well,' Cleo said as she wrapped a soaking cloth around Maggie's ankle. *Madam*'s maid scuttled into the cabin with a tisane in one hand, picked up a fan in the other and informed them snappishly that she couldn't help, *madam* was having a dreadful migraine and would they have the kindness to be quiet?

'I thought it went very well,' Maggie retorted and stuck out her tongue at the maid's retreating back. 'We won. Ouch!'

'I think it is only bruised,' Cleo said. 'Quin is livid and I can't say I blame him. I've got some salve somewhere.'

'Horse liniment. Use it for everything in the army. There, in my brown bag.' Maggie levered herself up on her elbows and wriggled her toes experimentally. 'What do you think he will do?' she asked as Cleo soaked a rag in the evil-smelling liquid and put it on the bruise under the wet cloth.

'Lock us in the cabin at the next port, I imagine,' Cleo said. 'At least our shopping was not damaged— even the apricot pastries survived.' *Which is more than my relationship with Quin will after this. Whatever that relationship was...* 'I'll take the rest to Quin.'

'Peace offering?' Maggie's smile was knowing.

'Apology, I suppose.' Cleo put down the sticky box of pastries and sat on the end of Maggie's bunk. 'I thought it would be safer than Cairo and that he was making a fuss about nothing.'

'He fights well, doesn't he? Very elegant. And dirty.' Maggie dug into the box and came out with a pastry. Golden preserve trickled down her fingers. 'Yum.'

'You haven't tasted it yet.'

'Him, I mean. Good looking, moves like a dream, has a really useful kick...'

'Controlling, deceitful, untrustworthy...'

'Intelligent, good in bed.'

'How would you know!'

'Isn't he?' Maggie asked with unconvincingly round-eyed innocence.

'He is good to hold and to be held by. Very calm, very strong. He kisses...' *and my bones melt* '...well. He is also exceedingly strong-minded. I am going to be delivered to England like a packet of sweetmeats and he is only going to allow himself to nibble the corner of one of them.'

'Lick the sugar off,' Maggie said with a snort of laughter. 'He could nibble my corners at any time.' She cocked her head to one side and regarded Cleo in the gloomy cabin like a Cairo sparrow watching for a crumb of flatbread. 'Is he married?'

'No.' Cleo twitched the box of pastries away from Maggie's searching fingers. 'But he is going to be. There's some lady he has his eye on and she has all the right qualities and a rich influential papa.'

'And you—'

'I have a father who has been unwittingly aiding and abetting the enemy, I have been brought up in the poor quarter of just about every Near Eastern city you can name, I have no social graces at all, no influential relatives who acknowledge me… Anyway, I don't trust Quin as far as I can throw him if my interests and his collide, as he has already proved. And *I* don't want to marry him.'

'Don't you?' Maggie shrugged. 'You could have fooled me.'

I am blushing. Of course I don't want to marry him. He tricked me. I don't like him. Cleo bit her lip. *Yes, I do, fool that I am. And I desire him.* She took a pastry out of the box and bit into the flaky, yielding sweetness. 'Pastries are more reliable than men. They make you happier, anyway. And why would I want to get married again? The first time was quite enough, thank you.'

She lifted the lid of the box. Two left. And Quin was not going to become any less annoyed with the passage of time.

'I'm going to try to sleep.' Maggie lay down and closed her eyes. Then one opened, just a crack. 'Good luck.'

'Don't use all the liniment,' Cleo muttered as she went out, clutching the battered box of pastries. 'I am probably going to need it.'

The captain had given Quin a cabin right in the bows of the ship. Cleo negotiated companionways and wriggled round cargo until she found herself at the door. Goodness knew what she was going to say to him. Probably she would get her ears blistered and then she would lose her temper and throw the pastries at him. She knocked.

'Come in!'

The cabin was roomier than hers, triangular in shape and lit by two good-sized portholes. Cleo blinked in the light and realised they must be right up in the bows. Quin was sitting writing at a table that let down on straps from the bulkhead. He had taken off coat and waistcoat and rolled up his sleeves to the elbow and beside him the dress sword hung by its intricately embroidered baldric from a peg, swaying to the motion of the ship as though it had a secret life of its own.

When he saw who it was he stood, the chair bumping back against the bunk. 'Cleo? You should not be in here.' The frown was still there, two marked lines between the straight slashes of his eyebrows, his mouth unsmiling.

'I brought you some apricot pastries.' She offered the box and when he did not take them she put them on the bunk.

'And that is what made the risk of robbery and rape worthwhile, is it?'

'No.' She took a tight hold of her temper and reminded herself that Quin had rescued her from a situation of her own making. 'I bought fabric and fashion plates and thread and ribbon.' *And fine lawn underclothes, not that I am going to mention those.*

'That's all right then. If I had known it was something *that* important—'

'There is no need to be so sarcastic. It might not matter to you—you've got trunks full of fancy clothes, apparently. You aren't going to feel like something the cat dragged in when you meet strangers.' To her horror her voice almost wobbled. She must be more afraid of what was to come than she had realised if she needed the support of fashionable clothes and pretty ribbons to support her.

'Those clothes aren't so bad.' He frowned harder as he contemplated the odd cut and lumpy waistline

'If I had to wear Egyptian dress, that would not be such a problem, I would merely look foreign and strange. These,' she said with a sweeping gesture at her skirts, 'look like laughable imitations of the real thing.'

'I see. Do you have enough supplies to make something better or shall I escort you ashore again?'

What had come over him? 'Thank you, but we were on our way back when we missed the main street to the harbour.'

'When we get to Gibraltar there will be ladies there who can help you fit yourself out more suitably for England. Quite a few have accompanied their husbands to the garrison.' Quin sounded almost as if he was concerned for her frivolous feminine needs.

Cleo sat down on the edge of the bunk. 'Why are you being kind to me? I was wrong to go ashore, I admit it. Maggie has a badly bruised ankle as a result and things could have been much worse,' she added scrupulously.

'I owe you my life, perhaps twice over,' Quin said. He spun the chair around and sat down, his arms crossed along the back of it.

Cleo stared at the defined muscle and sinew under the tanned skin, the dusting of dark hair. She had tried so hard not to look at him when she was nursing him. Now it was as though she held a magnifying glass up to his skin. She shrugged, the movement repressing her instinct to lean forward and touch his arm. 'That was different.'

'True,' Quin agreed. 'Certainly I was not enjoying myself on those occasions.'

'Enjoying?' She looked at his face and saw he was smiling. 'I don't understand.' This was not good. She had thought she was beginning to be able to read Quin, to understand him. Now... 'I am confused.'

'I was walking down the hill away from my meeting feeling as if I'd been stuffed into my clothes. My shoulders were stiff, my head was full of facts and hints and I just wanted to do something irresponsible and free and physical. Starting a brawl in a foreign city minutes after leaving a diplomatic meeting counts as all of those, I suspect.' The smile had become a grin.

'We might all have been killed!'

'I very much doubt that, not with your skill with a knife and Maggie's lethal tricks with a dead rat.'

There was a light in his eyes that she remembered from the moment when he had sent the felucca weaving its dangerous course through the barges full of soldiers, from the tense minutes after he had hoisted the makeshift flag and brought them safely into the British camp. She had glimpsed it in that fight as well.

'You enjoy the danger. Why are you not a soldier if you like to fight?' And he had made her think he was angry with her, displeased over her trip ashore when all the time he had been enjoying himself, the wretch. *More deception.*

'I prefer not to kill people.' He unfolded his arms and leant back in the chair. 'I enjoy the challenge of problems. I like the moment when the solution comes clear. When that sometimes resolves itself into physical action I relish it, too.'

'You understand yourself very well, it seems.' She

wished she had the same clear self-knowledge. Freedom, yes, she knew she wanted that. But what then?

Quin's smile became wry. 'Too well sometimes.'

'You know what you want.'

'Oh, yes. I know that.' The smile faded altogether.

Cleo thought back to the night on the felucca when he had woken her, talked in his sleep. He had sounded bitter and driven. He might know what he wanted, but it did not seem to give him peace. 'Quin…' She put out one hand as if to reach him.

Quin's smile came back, bright and teasing. And false. 'I want those apricot pastries.'

'I don't think you deserve them,' Cleo retorted. If he was going to pretend everything was all right, then she was going to let her resentment of his teasing out. 'I only brought them because I was sorry for dragging you into a fight and now I discover you enjoyed yourself and tried to make me feel guilty.'

Quin leaned to the side and stretched out his arm, snagging the box off the bed before she could snatch it away. 'Hmm. Two. I'm prepared to share.'

He offered her the box and then took the remaining piece. For a few minutes they ate in silence. Quin seemed focused on the pastry, catching crumbs, using his tongue to find the escaping fruit in the corner of his lips, his eyes half-closed like a cat enjoying its dinner. *Sensual.*

I've never seen that side of him. Perhaps there were not so much many *sides* to him as *layers,* like this flaky pastry. And somewhere there was the real Quin, the one that perhaps she had never glimpsed yet. He was a master at hiding his feelings. *He was honest when he told me about his father,* she argued with herself.

Or was he? another part of her wondered. She had felt sympathy, liking, but those could be manipulated as easily as hate or love. Or desire. Somewhere was the real man and she had to find him because he was the one she needed to trust.

The silence when they finished eating felt heavy, loaded with unsaid words. Cleo shifted on the bunk, restless.

'You've a crumb.' Quin reached towards her face. 'Just here.' His fingertips brushed at her cheek and then stopped. He leaned closer as his palm cupped her cheek.

Cleo made herself meet his gaze and saw that the light was back in his eyes. It was as if embers had leapt into flame. His whole focus was on her and she swayed, leaning into the warmth of his hand. 'What is it?' It was a whisper, all she had breath for.

'I fear I am not going to be able to give you what you want when we reach England.' The brief blue fire had flickered and gone now. His gaze met hers, heavy and dark. 'I fear you will be disappointed.'

'In what I find there, or in you?' His hand was still touching her face, the fingers caressing her cheek.

'Both. I think you will be confused because I do not think you know what you truly want. This world I am taking you to is so very different to what you are used to.'

'I know what I want.' It was hard to form the words with the mesmeric movement of his fingertips sending her nerve endings into tingling confusion. 'Why will I be disappointed in you? Should I not trust you?'

'You never have, have you?' His fingers stilled.

'No.' She shook her head and his hand dropped to

rest on her shoulder. 'And I was right, was I not? You hid the reason you came to Egypt, you were selective with the truth about who you were. There is still something that you are not telling me, I can sense it. And you even deny this.' She reached for his hand and brought it to her lips, savouring the texture of his skin.

'Cleo—'

'You want me and I want you and yet you will not admit it.'

'I admit it.' Quin made no move to free his hand. She could feel the pulse, strong, steady. Perhaps a little fast for a fit man.

'Then why do you not do anything about it? I am not some sheltered virgin. I am a widow, I am of age and I am travelling to London to start my own life on my own terms. Why cannot that include a lover?'

'I would be taking advantage of you,' Quin said. Behind the words she sensed his mind working furiously. *Seeking for excuses.*

'You are not trying to seduce me, you do not coerce me, so how would you be taking advantage?'

'I am virtually the only man you have been on familiar terms with since your husband died, other than your father and Laurent. It is only natural that there is a certain…awareness between us.'

'Such sweet reason. Shall I then wait until I arrive in London and find a variety of men to choose from? You will secure me invitations to all the best parties so I may view the cream of the available gentlemen, perhaps.'

'Only if you wish to set up as a high-class courtesan!' Quin tugged his hand free and stood, stooping under the low deck. He shifted the chair further away and sat down again. 'How do you expect to make a suitable marriage with that attitude?'

'You think I want a marriage? You sound like Madame da Sota. You and she might think that is what all this is about—keeping me respectable so I can catch a second husband—but I do not.'

'Of course that is what should happen.' The colour was high on Quin's cheeks, as though she had somehow embarrassed him or caught him out in some way. 'You are of good family, you are still a young woman. A beautiful young woman. Of course you will marry, and marry well, once you have settled into London society.'

'I will not marry again.' This time it was she who stood, waving Quin impatiently back to his seat when, with automatic courtesy, he began to stand too. 'I will *never* marry again. Never.'

'You loved your husband so much?'

'I hated him.'

Chapter Sixteen

Cleo stood at the porthole, her back to Quin, and stared out at the busy harbour. 'Oh, I thought I loved him at first, but then, I knew nothing about men. The only model of marriage I had was my parents, but I knew no one could be as eccentric and selfish as my father. I believed I would have a companion, a lover, a friend. Of course, life in an army camp would be hard, but I was used to that, I was prepared to work. But nothing was what I expected.'

'He did not love you?'

'Of course not. Now I realise Thierry had been ordered to marry me, and why. It was simply to make sure that there was nothing to stop my father co-operating fully with the French authorities. Thierry didn't want a lovestruck virgin who hung on his arm asking for affection and attention. He wanted the experienced camp whores, or the women of the town who knew how to please a man and demanded nothing more than a coin.'

'Are you saying that you are still a virgin?' Quin asked.

'Oh, no. Why spend good money on sex when you

can have it for free at home? He taught me how to make love, he showed me, for a few wonderful nights, what pleasure a man and a woman could have together.' Someone was sailing a small skiff right past the ship, his wife or girlfriend cuddled up close to him as he sat at the tiller. The woman turned up her face and Cleo heard her laughter, clear across the blue water. Happy lovers.

'Then he stopped bothering about my pleasure and after a few days, stopped caring whether I was tired or sore or unwilling. I was there to cook his food and wash his clothes and…everything else.'

'You mean he forced you?' Quin's voice had that dangerous calm she had heard before, on the river, in the courtyard.

'Yes.' The skiff had tacked into the wind and the couple were kissing now. Young, hopeful love.

'He hit you.'

'Eventually he did, after a few days when I recovered from the shock and he discovered that curses and pushes and shoves met with resistance.'

'Dear God.' His voice was a whisper. 'How long did this go on for?'

'One night. The next day I started carrying a kitchen knife with me everywhere. He thought I would not use it, but he was wrong. I slashed his arm for him and after that he decided I was too much trouble and went back to his whores.' She shrugged. 'He was no more work than my father was from then on.'

'Cleo.' Quin's voice was right behind her. She had not heard him move. 'Cleo, not all men are like that.'

'Of course not,' she agreed. 'My father never lifted a finger to my mother. I am certain you would never hit a woman. But all men are as selfish, of that I am certain. Marriage is on their terms, for what money or land it brings, for their comfort and convenience and for the production of their heirs.'

Is that your skiff? she wondered, as the girl in the boat moved with confidence to lower the sail. *Was that your dowry?*

'And women are protected and provided for. The children are theirs to love.'

'Yes.' Cleo turned and leaned back against the bulkhead. 'For as long as the wife does exactly what her husband expects of her. She exists to support the life he wishes to live.'

Quin was so close she could see the faint shift of muscles beneath his skin as he kept his face calm, his tone reasonable. 'You tar us all with the same brush?'

'You told me you intend to marry a woman because she is *suitable*, her father has influence and she will bring you wealth. Do you love her?' He shook his head. 'Do you even *know* her?'

'We are acquainted.'

'Poor woman.' His eyebrows lifted, but she swept on. 'Sir James back in the camp outside Cairo—where was his wife? Waiting at home with the children, I suppose. I wonder if she would have liked to travel?'

'Cleo, you are being unreasonable. This is what marriage is, a sharing that might not be exactly equal, but which does have benefits for both parties,' he said.

'Then I want no part of it.'

'You want to be the selfish one.'

'No!' She slapped her open hand against his chest to try to shake some sense into him. 'I want to share, to be equal, to have my own interests and my own life as well as being with a man whose own life I am involved in. I want what Mama thought she was going to have when she eloped with Papa. I wish for the moon, I know that perfectly well.'

'And you discount the benefits of marriage to a woman then?' Quin frowned. 'Respectability, protection, financial security…'

'Children, sex?'

'Cleo! A lady does not speak of sex.'

'Exactly my point. Or one of them. I would like to make love with you, but I must not mention it. You, on the other hand, may.'

'Not to an unmarried lady—'

'A widow. Have you never had an *affaire* with a widow?' Quin's lips set in a hard line. 'Yes, I can see that you have.'

'But not one under my protection, that would not be honourable.'

'So, in fact, this is all about *your* honour, not about the woman's thoughts, needs, wants,' Cleo stated. 'I think you were accusing me of being selfish just now.'

'Checkmate,' Quin said. 'But if I were to be perfectly ungentlemanly and said I did not wish for a liaison, that I did not desire you, then you would be angry with me.'

Cleo realised that she was enjoying herself. This was like verbal chess and, maddening as Quin was, he was at least prepared to play. 'It would be hypocritical of me to be angry,' she told him. 'Unless I thought you were lying, of course. And you are, aren't you, my lord?'

For a moment she wondered if she had pushed him too far. Then the corner of his mouth twitched, producing that almost dimple that she was beginning to find dangerously endearing.

'You are a witch, Augusta Cleopatra Agrippina Woodward. Yes, I desire you. No, I am not going to have an *affaire* with you because I am simply an old-fashioned gentleman, hypocritical attitudes and all.'

She found she was smiling back at him, charmed by what, for once, she guessed was the pure, unvarnished truth, not some clever twisting of the words. 'Oh, Quin.' They were close enough for her to be able to put her palms flat against his chest as she stood on tiptoes to reach his mouth and that dimple.

He accepted the brush of her lips, which she expected, but his arms came around her and he pulled her close, found her mouth with his own and kissed her, his tongue sliding between her lips, open on a gasp of surprise. The kiss was thorough, confident, and his arms held her very firmly. When Quin freed her mouth she said, 'You said you were not going to have an *affaire* with me!'

'I know. I said nothing about not making love to you, though.' He stooped, swept her up in his arms, ducked his head under the low deck beams and went to the door where he slid the bolt across. 'Now then, Cleo. You said something about you desiring me and me desiring you, if I recall.'

'Yes, but—' The words escaped her as he placed her on the bunk.

'You have changed your mind? A lady's privilege.'

'No! But you play with words—'

'It is my profession. I have to be good with them.' His fingers were busy with the strings of her shoes and then his hands slid up her calves to her garters. 'Lie back, Cleo, I am quite good at this as well.'

'Braggart,' she muttered and collapsed back on to the pillow. 'Oh, what are you doing?'

'Making love.' He lifted her and caressed her and somehow—magic, perhaps?—her gown had gone, and her chemise, and he was saying something appreciative about a lack of stays and then his mouth was on her breast and Cleo lost the will to think, only to feel.

She twisted, whimpering under the onslaught of lips and tongue and teeth, clutching at Quin's shoulders as she arched up to him. Then in a fleeting moment of sanity as he moved from one nipple to another, she realised that her hands were gripping the cotton of his shirt, not the bare skin of his arms.

'Quin, let me…' She pulled at his shirt, tried to find the fastening of his breeches.

'Oh, no.'

'Oh, yes! You are wearing altogether too many clothes and I am wearing none at all. *Ah*.' He silenced her by the simple expedient of kissing her and stopped her roving hands by catching both wrists together in one strong-fingered hand that trapped her arms above her head. Cleo arched against the restraint, aroused by his strength.

His free hand slid down, over the curve of her stomach, over the aching mound, and her legs parted wantonly, even as she tried to free her hands so she could caress him. She was wet and wanting and desperate. *In a minute,* she told herself. *In a minute he will let me make love to him...* And then he slid two fingers into the desperate heat and his thumb moved with devastating accuracy and Cleo screamed, the sound caught by his kiss.

She surfaced—for surely she had been drowned in a hurricane—and found her hands free and Quin's warmth gone from her side. And then she felt his hands on her thighs and the heat of his mouth where his fingers had been and she reached, desperate, to touch his hair. Anything else was beyond her. 'I can't...' she whispered, but the coiling, tightening pleasure–pain was possessing her, fast, deadly, overwhelming.

'Quin,' she cried as he took her over the edge and back into the whirlpool. 'Quin!'

'I am here,' Quin said and moved to gather Cleo's quivering body into his arms. 'I'm here.'

She had been so beautiful in the throes of passion, so intense, so abandoned and primal. And so responsive. He ached, but pushed the need away. It was a nagging reminder that he should not have done this, that it had given him satisfaction when it should all have been for her.

Cleo's eyes opened and she smiled at him, a sweet, trusting caress of a look that had him smiling back, frustration and conscience forgotten. '*Mmm*, that was so good.' She stretched like a cat in his arms and he thought of the goddess Bastet, feline, feminine and powerful. Then her fingers found the waistband of his breeches and she began to tug at his shirt. 'How can I make love to you if you won't take your clothes off?'

'You can't. I do not want you to.' Quin set her on the bed and stood up. 'This was not about me.'

'Not about...' She sat curled up on the rumpled bunk completely naked, still flushed with passion, and stared at him. 'Why?' she murmured, as though to herself. Then her furrowed brow cleared and her eyes that had been inward-looking with thought became sharp and angry as she focused on his face. 'Of course. Make love to me and I'll stop making demands. Befuddle my brain with sex and I'll curl up like a well-stroked cat and not ask that you engage with my anxieties and my desires. Commit physical intimacies and you will not risk me trying to create mental ones.'

'Cleo, it is not like that.' *Hell, is that what I was doing? Surely not.* His conscience stirred, uneasy. *I gave her pleasure, I showed her I return her feelings of attraction. No, that is not enough to justify it.*

'Is it not?' She was flinging on clothing as if a fire alarm had been raised. Quin winced at the sound of tearing cotton as her nails caught in a stocking, but she dragged it on regardless and knotted her garters with a jerk. 'Whenever I tell myself I was wrong about you, that I was foolishly suspicious, you have the perfect knack for destroying my trust in you.' Cleo cast around, one shoe in her hand. 'Oh, where is my other shoe?'

'Here.' Quin handed it to her and bit back the words that were forming. It would be hopeless to explain what he did not understand himself, pointless to apologise when he could not decide whether she was being utterly unreasonable or not. He had never met another woman like her.

Cleo cast a distracted look at the mirror hanging on the bulkhead, pushed her fingers through her hair and whirled round to confront him. 'Will you kindly let me out?'

For a long moment Quin stood there, his hand on

the bolt, and thought about letting common sense go to the devil. Something far more powerful than lust was urging him to take her in his arms, kiss her, undress them both and to hell with the consequences.

The moment of recklessness lasted only seconds. Quin unbolted the door and stood back as Cleo swept out without looking at him, then closed it behind her with meticulous care. He was closer to completely losing his temper than he could ever recall and he was not too sure who he was most angry with: himself for being a bloody fool or Cleo for asking far more than he was prepared to give her, or any woman. Or perhaps it was the nagging instinct that he had just lost something important.

Quin scrubbed his hand across his aching head, then flung open his trunk and rummaged until he found the thin cotton trousers and *galabeeyah* he had worn in the desert. He changed and went barefoot up on to deck.

'How long before we sail?' he asked the captain, ignoring the man's raised eyebrows.

'Four hours at least, my lord. Several of the water casks need replacing.'

'Can you lend me the small skiff and someone to sail it? I want to go along the coast to swim.'

'Certainly, my lord.' The idiosyncrasies of aristocratic passengers were obviously to be tolerated, given the price the man had extracted for their passage.

It took only minutes to find a sailor and for the skiff to be sailing out from the harbour and along the coast to a shallow bay. The man, who obviously thought he was mildly deranged, threw the anchor over and dropped the sail while Quin stripped off his clothes. He took a shallow dive into water that was clear, calm and cool to the skin, warmed only by the spring sunshine, not the heat of summer.

Quin surfaced and began to swim, hard and fast, parallel to the beach. He was grateful for the salty freshness, even as it stung the grazes from his collision with a wall that morning.

He pushed himself hard, working on speed and the accuracy of his strokes, focused on nothing but the physical sensation, the burn and stretch of the newly healed scar on his arm, the slide of the water, silky over his naked skin.

When he finally stopped and hung there, treading water, blinking against the salt in his eyes, the skiff was a child's toy in the distance. Quin turned on to his back and began to swim towards it, eyes open and staring up into the perfect blue of the sky, marred only by the occasional white dot of a wheeling gull.

He let his thoughts free again to run over what had happened, as he might have probed an aching tooth with his tongue, braced for the stab of pain. He was the wrong man for that mission into the desert. Or, perhaps, simply the wrong man for Cleo. She would have been better with some swashbuckling romantic who would have carried her off without a thought for her father's fate, fallen head over heels for her and brought her to her grandfather with some impassioned declaration of love.

What she had got was a man determined to catch a spy, if he existed—cross off item number one in notebook—and to deliver Miss Woodward as a neatly wrapped parcel to the duke—item number two on the list—before proceeding with the next well-planned phase of his life: marriage—item three.

The neatly wrapped parcel had come badly un-
wrapped. The memory of undressing Cleo disturbed
the even rhythm of his stroke to the extent that he swallowed sea and stopped to tread water and recover. She
was too intelligent, too unconventional and too...*Cleo.*
He liked her when she wasn't driving him to thoughts
of drink or murder. He was certainly in lust with her.

Quin floated on his back and contemplated where
that left him. *At arm's length from Cleo, that's where,
contemplating the nightmare she's going to be for her
grandfather and thanking my lucky stars she will cease
to be my problem the moment I hand her over.*

He turned over and struck out hard for the skiff.
Time to get back to the boat and back to normal. When
he hauled himself back on board he scrubbed himself dry with the cotton trousers, pulled on the *galabeeyah* and settled back to enjoy the journey back to
the harbour.

The sun shone, the sea was calm, he had a plan.
Why, then, was he feeling so damnably blue-devilled?
*Because I have justified deceiving her, of course. Be-
cause I have chosen duty and ambition over desire and
friendship and romantic wrong-headedness.*

Chapter Seventeen

'What is wrong?' Maggie asked from her perch on the bottom of her bed where she was rolling pairs of stockings together.

'Quin.' The mixture of anger and passion on top of too many apricot pastries and the tension of the fight in the town had left Cleo's stomach churning.

'He seduced you? What was it like? I should imagine he is magnificent in bed.'

'No, he did not seduce me. I told him I wanted to make love.'

Maggie peered at her. 'Surely it wasn't a disappointment?'

'He made love to me and it was wonderful. But he would not allow me to make love to him.'

'Why ever not?'

'He didn't really want me, I suppose. Or his wretched sense of honour is more important. Or perhaps simply his common sense. But if course, being a gentleman, he *obliges a lady,*' Cleo said with an exaggerated drawl. 'And it stops him having to listen to me talking about what I want to do when we get to

England, having to hear about all the unsuitable, unladylike things that are important to me.' She shifted
so she could curl her arms around her legs and rest her
chin on her knees. 'When I realised, we had a row. Or
I tried to have a row, he just looked down that aristocratic nose of his and maintained a dignified silence
while I ranted at him.'

'Where is he now?'

Cleo shrugged. 'I have no idea.'

'Do you think he knows how you feel about him?'
Maggie stuffed the stockings in a bag and hung it on
a nail on the bulkhead.

'I made no secret of it. He would have to be very
dense indeed to miss it. And whatever else he is, his
lordship is not stupid.'

'No, I don't mean that you are angry with him,'
Maggie said in a tone of exaggerated patience. 'Does
he know you are in love with him?'

Cleo found her mouth was open and she closed it
with a snap, then tried to laugh. 'Of all the ridiculous…' She stopped and thought. 'Oh, no. I am, I love
him. I hadn't realised, How awful.' *And that is why I
ache inside. I love him.*

'Why? He's handsome, a gentleman, intelligent…
He would make a fine husband.'

'Husband! As if I wanted one of those.' *Brave
words, Cleo,* she mocked herself. *If he asked you, you
would say* Yes *without a moment's thought even though
it is completely impossible.* 'And besides, he has his
eye on some titled lady who will be the perfect wife
for a diplomat and she has a papa with money and influence. Why would he want me?' *Why, indeed? He*

*has just made it very clear he doesn't even want to
make love with me.*

'What are you going to do about it then?'

'Avoid him,' Cleo said grimly. How appalling if
Quin guessed. She would sink with mortification. She
had her pride and sometimes that had been all that had
kept her going.

'But you're a lady,' Maggie protested. 'I know
you've been living a bit…rough, but you aren't—
what's the word?—ineligible.'

'He needs a hostess, someone who knows all about
society. I have no idea who is who and I didn't even
know which piece of cutlery was for what when I had
dinner back in the camp. My parents eloped and made
a scandal and my English relatives do not want to know
me. And I do not have any money and certainly no
influence and Quin needs both in his career. He's a
younger son.'

Somehow it was important to convince Maggie that
it was absolutely impossible, because if she could convince her, then perhaps she could also extinguish the
small glimmer of hope that persisted despite all the
cold water she poured on it.

'If he loved you, none of that would matter. Grab
what happiness you can, I always say, life's short
enough.'

'It would matter to me,' Cleo discovered. 'I couldn't
allow him to throw away his career because of me.'

'That's all very fine and noble.' Maggie did not
look convinced.

'No, it isn't. We'd be miserable, I would feel guilty,
everything would go wrong. I am just being selfish.'

'Well, what I think is—'

Maggie's thoughts were cut short by *madam*'s maid bustling in. '*Madam*'s up and feeling a lot better and asking for you. Ma'am.' She always added the title as if it was an afterthought.

She can see I am not a proper lady, Cleo thought as she stood up and began to unpin her tousled hair. *I would never fool anyone in London society for a moment.* 'Please tell her I will join her just as soon as Maggie has done my hair. Such a breeze on deck.'

It took them three days to reach Gibraltar on smooth seas and with a favourable, light wind. Cleo stayed with the other women and avoided being alone with Quin. He made no move to speak with her apart and his manner at meals was polite yet distant. She fixed a smile on her lips and made a careful point of neither ignoring him nor of seeking him out. Her heart might be aching, but she had her pride.

'Such elegance of manner, Lord Quintus,' Madame da Sota pronounced as they sat under an awning on deck one afternoon. 'Such a gentleman. Typical of the English aristocracy. I have had the most interesting discussion with him about the politics of Greece this morning.'

'Indeed,' Cleo agreed in a colourless tone as she finished a seam in the gown she was sewing.

'Did you see Gibraltar when you sailed to Egypt, Miss Woodward?' *madam* enquired with one of her rapid changes of subject.

'No, *madam*. I think we must have gone overland to Italy, which I can recall as a child, and then we moved to Greece and into the Balkans later.'

'So you do not remember England?'

'I have never been to England, ma'am.'

'My goodness! And who will be chaperoning you when you arrive, Miss Woodward?'

'Er...' She had given it no thought. Presumably there were agencies where one could hire a respectable duenna.

'Me,' said Maggie firmly.

'But there is your son and your parents,' Cleo protested. She had assumed it would be impossible for Maggie to stay with her.

'Freddie's better off where he is. I'll visit, of course I will, but he's spent more time with them than with me. I won't drag him away from where he's settled, just so I can have him to myself.'

Cleo was beginning to know Maggie now. The bright smile and the determined tilt of her chin were hiding an aching need to see her son and an equally strong-willed determination to do what was best for him.

'He could come and have a holiday in London,' she said. 'He would like that, I imagine. Most big cities have lots of things children enjoy and you could be together.'

'Forgive me, Miss Woodward. Maggie is an excellent maid, I am sure, but you will need a lady companion.'

'Yes, of course.' A lady companion, as far as she could see, would be a complete nuisance, and an expensive one at that. If she had Maggie, then surely all the proprieties would be observed.

'Shall we try the gown on and then I can pin the bodice to the skirt, Miss Woodward?' Maggie said, the perfect lady's maid.

'Yes, we had better check it. If you will excuse us, *madam*?' She hustled Maggie and her armful of fabric into her cabin. 'Would you really consider coming to live with me? I don't know what the wages are like in London, but I am sure I can pay you the right amount as well as what I owe you for this voyage.'

'Don't worry about that. His lordship gave me five sovereigns and my passage all found, so I'm right and tight until you can sort things out with your bankers.' Maggie shook out the separate pieces of the walking dress. 'Will you put it on? This'll show his lordship that he's dealing with a lady.'

'A pigeon in borrowed plumes is still a pigeon and not a peacock,' Cleo said, holding out her hands. 'Look at them. *Madam* keeps tutting over them. They are brown and I have calluses and my nails haven't all grown to the same length yet. And my hair is in no style at all and my face is tanned and...'

'Do you care so much what he thinks?' Maggie was busy unfastening Cleo's gown.

'He? You mean Quin? No, of course not. I am above such things.' *Liar, you want him expiring with desire, you want him struck dumb with your beauty and elegance. You want...him.*

'We can study the hair styles of the ladies at Gibraltar and I can try to copy them. You might even be able to find someone to cut your hair. And there are sure to be merchants with all the cosmetics and creams that English ladies use.'

'The problem is going to be getting ashore to do all this studying and shopping.' Cleo stood still while Maggie tossed the skirts of the new gown over her head and then helped her into the bodice, taking care with the pins and the basting stitches.

'I'll fix him,' Maggie said as she stepped back to study the set of the bodice. 'If he says we cannot go, I will take him aside and tell him it is essential for *female reasons*. He won't ask what, he'll be too embarrassed.' Maggie grinned.

'You are obviously far more skilled at managing men than I am,' Cleo said as she put her own gown back on.

'They are all quite simple really,' Maggie said as she began to pin the sections of the garment together. 'It is just discovering how their brain works and then making that a target. His lordship is a gentleman and so he does not want to embarrass a lady. Simple.'

Simple? Quin? I do not think so. Cleo began to measure out braid and ribbon and wondered if she dared risk crossing him again. *But what can he do to me? He has promised to take me to London and things can hardly be worse between us than they are at the moment, surely?*

May 15th 1801—the Thames, London

'Home,' Maggie said. She leaned on the ship's rail and inhaled deeply.

Cleo huddled into the thick shawl she had bought at Gibraltar and shivered. Inhaling lungfuls of smoky, damp, river-smelling air was a treat she could well do without.

'Good to be back in a city without heat and dust, isn't it, Maggie?' Quin joined them at the rail, looking, to Cleo's surreptitious glance, exceedingly smart. She had thought that all English gentlemen were incapable of getting themselves dressed without the attentions of a valet, let alone turning themselves out in prime style, but Quin managed it. He had even had his hair cut at Gibraltar.

'Is this winter?' Cleo asked, convinced that her nose must be blue. They had avoided each other since the ship had passed through the Straits into the Atlantic, unless mealtimes and accidental meetings made exchanges—carried out with painstaking courtesy—essential.

Quin had agreed without argument to Maggie's stammered request for an essential shopping expedition and had even arranged for them to go with the Governor's married niece and one of her footmen as guide and escort.

Cleo had enjoyed Mrs Denver's company even though she was disconcerted to discover that Quin knew her.

It had been even more disconcerting to have to carry on a conversation with a woman who assumed that Cleo knew just as much about Quin as she did. No, she had never danced with Lord Quintus, but she was certain he was most accomplished. No, she was not familiar with his family, but she was sure his brothers were all that were charming. No, she had no idea what Lord Quintus's plans were after he arrived in London. *Except courting a bride,* she could have said, but instead, bit her tongue.

'Did you not buy a cloak with all that shopping you did?' Quin asked now. She must have shivered, or perhaps it was simply her question.

'No. It never occurred to me it would be this cold.'

'This is summer, but I have to admit it is not as hot as it might be for mid-May. I'll find you something warmer.' Quin strode off and came back five minutes later with a black cloak of fine wool with a deep-blue lining the colour of his eyes. He swirled it around her shoulders but left it to her to fasten the clasp under her chin. 'It is a good twenty inches too long for you, be careful not to trip.'

Cleo told herself she was glad of his impersonal touch. 'Thank you. I will take care not to trail it in the mud.'

'You will not need it in the carriage,' Quin said, his attention apparently on the wharf that was rapidly approaching. 'Good, they are there.'

'Who are?' Cleo scanned the crowded dock that seemed quite as chaotic in its way as the Cairo waterside.

'I wrote as soon as we arrived in Gibraltar and told my secretary to make certain we were met, even if it meant coming down and waiting every day for a week. We do not want to be hanging around in this area. It is not what your gr— What is suitable for a lady. Excuse me, I will go and make certain all the luggage is on deck and ready to be swung ashore.'

'What was he going to say just then, I wonder?' Cleo puzzled.

'I don't know, but if that little collection of carriages is his lordship's, then he's plump in the pocket and no mistake,' Maggie said and pointed to three large coaches that, even at a distance, Cleo could recognise as expensively shiny.

'At least we'll be arriving in style at this lodging house he knows,' she said with some satisfaction. 'That will assure us of respectful treatment.'

* * *

It seemed that not only was Quin plump in the pocket but he commanded excellent service. They were off the ship and on to the dock less than an hour after the first mooring lines were thrown ashore. The luggage was stacked into a small, orderly mountain guarded by a stocky individual who Quin addressed as Sam, and Mr Baldwin, introduced as Quin's secretary, ushered them towards the largest coach.

'Everything is organised as you instructed, my lord. Godley is awaiting you at the Albany apartment and I have not accepted any invitations on your behalf for the next week. Miss Woodward's luggage will go in the first coach and yours, accompanied by myself, will proceed direct to Albany in the second.'

'Thank you, George. Admirable as always.'

That seemed to be a joke between the two men. Mr Baldwin grinned, transforming himself from dry and serious secretary into a cheerful young man. 'I endeavour to give satisfaction, my lord,' he said, adjusting his expression back into solemnity.

Quin helped Cleo and Maggie into the carriage, flustering Maggie by insisting she sat beside Cleo in the forward-facing seat. The vehicle was as sleek inside as it was outside, with well-sprung seats in crimson plush, a carpeted floor, brocade hanging straps and numerous cunningly arranged pockets in the doors. Cleo did her best not to stare and contented herself with running her gloved hand over the soft pile of the seat. What luxury to be able to afford something like this, and the horses to pull it, and the grooms and drivers to manage it.

She told herself that she was lucky to have been

liberated from a dusty tent in the desert and that a respectable apartment, money to spare and her independence were luxury enough.

'Look,' Maggie pointed to the right. 'St Paul's Cathedral. This is the City of London where all the merchants and trade is conducted. The banks are here and the lawyers.'

'Is this where the house you are taking me to is located?' Cleo asked, trying not to gawp out of the windows like a complete rustic. Time enough to sightsee when she was on her own.

'The City is not considered suitable for a lady's residence,' Quin said. 'Living there would indicate that you are not of the *ton*. You do not wish to appear shabby genteel.'

But I am not of the ton, Cleo thought, but did not say it. If he thought there was somewhere she could afford in an even better district she was not going to protest.

The carriage went downhill, its wheels rumbling on cobbles, then climbed again, surprising her by how hilly London seemed to be. 'Where are we now?' she asked, looking out on crowded pavements, shops, swinging signs—inns, perhaps?

'Just passing Temple Bar,' said Quin, puzzling her. Temples in London? 'Now we are in the City of Westminster.'

'Strand,' Maggie said. A few minutes later, 'Pall Mall, look, there's Carlton House…St James's Street. Now I'm lost, I've never been up here.' She fell silent, wide-eyed.

'We are going to an area called Mayfair,' Quin explained.

The rough-and-ready bustle of the city had vanished. The streets were crowded, certainly, but with carriages as smart as the one they were in, gentlemen on horseback, elegant ladies with footmen at their heels.

'My lord…' Maggie began. She sounded uneasy. Quin raised one eyebrow in silent question. 'Er, nothing.'

'Here we are.' The carriage rolled into a vast square surrounded by what looked like rows of palaces all joined together. There were high iron railings around a garden, or a small park, in the centre and ornate ironwork at the front of every house. 'Grosvenor Square,' Quin said as they came to a halt.

The groom came to open the door and let down the steps and Quin helped her down, leaving the man to assist Maggie.

'This is very…opulent,' Cleo managed. Surely this place could not be a lodging house, however respectable? Something was wrong and every instinct was screaming at her to run.

'One of the foremost addresses in London,' Quin agreed, ushering her up the steps. Her feet seemed to drag and she felt her body leaning backwards as though resisting a strong wind, even though all that was holding her was Quin's hand, firm under her elbow. The door opened before Quin could knock and Cleo found herself bowed into a hall that appeared to be entirely carved out of marble—floor, stairs, columns in chilly black-and-white perfection.

Where has he brought me?

Chapter Eighteen

'You are expected, my lord.' A man in formal clothing bowed. 'Miss Woodward. Welcome. I am Cranton, the butler.' He turned to Quin and took his hat and cloak. 'If you will follow me.'

Where to? As though in a dream Cleo trod across the polished floor. The butler threw open a pair of double doors almost twice her height and intoned, 'Miss Woodward, Lord Quintus Deverall, Your Grace.' And then they were in a room that seemed to be some kind of library, gloomy with heavy wood, the brown and gilt of hundreds of book spines and the swags of curtain draperies like crimson thunderclouds looming above.

A tall, slender man in his mid-sixties stood in front of the desk. Cleo took in close-cropped iron-grey hair, a high-arched nose, clear grey-green eyes that seemed somehow familiar and a thin, unsmiling mouth.

'Your Grace.' Quin stepped forward, his hand on her arm urging her to keep pace. 'May I present your granddaughter, Augusta Cleopatra Agrippina Woodward? Miss Woodward, your grandfather, the Duke of St Osyth.'

'No!' She wrenched her arm free of Quin's hand. 'No, you told me you were taking me to respectable lodgings. You told me—'

'It is difficult to imagine a more respectable lodging than this,' the duke remarked. 'The Queen's House, perhaps?' His lips curved a little, but the smile, if that was what it was, did not reach his eyes. 'This is your new home, Augusta. Welcome.'

'No. I was promised independence, I was promised…' She whirled to face Quin. 'I am leaving now. I will find my own lodgings.'

'Paying with what, exactly?' The duke strolled towards a conversation group of chairs and a sofa by the unlit fire. 'Do, please sit down, Augusta, then Lord Quintus and I may sit also. Tea, I think.' He tugged at a bell pull. 'Your nerves are obviously deranged from the journey. Was it very tiring?'

This is probably a bad dream, Cleo told herself. She wanted to run and yet, under that cool grey gaze, so like her own, so like Mama's, she found herself on the sofa. 'I have money. It was arranged with Papa when I left Egypt. A respectable sum, I only have to call on the bankers.'

'I control all your assets, Augusta. You will have a very generous allowance, naturally. There is no need for you to concern yourself with money while you are under my roof.'

'My name is Cleo and that is what I am trying to explain: I do not wish to be under your roof, Your Grace.' *If this is a nightmare, it is an extraordinarily real one,* she thought with the beginnings of panic taking over from the confusion.

'Cleopatra is an outlandish name. Augusta is eminently suitable.' The duke sat, crossed his legs and steepled his fingers. He regarded her over them. 'You are an unmarried woman, Augusta, and therefore in my care. I will manage your money, your activities and your education, which appears to be sadly lacking. When you leave my safekeeping it will be on the arm of your husband. Do I make myself clear?'

'Yes, Your Grace, you make yourself perfectly clear.' Hot panic was knotting her insides, but she kept her voice as cool and detached as his. 'And I repeat, I do not agree to live here, to be controlled and ordered by you. I am twenty-three, a widow and—'

'And penniless,' her grandfather said. 'There is one way of making a living for a woman with no money, my dear, and that profession you are most assuredly not going to follow.' He glanced towards the door. 'Deverall, please, come and join us for tea. You have obviously had a most onerous duty delivering my ungrateful granddaughter safely.'

'On the contrary, Your Grace. Miss Woodward undoubtedly saved my life when I was wounded and was a great help in avoiding interference from the French troops.'

Cleo swivelled to face Quin as he sat down, the anger seething in her stomach to the point of pain. 'You—'

She was interrupted by the door opening. The butler entered with a footman at his heels. 'The refreshments, Your Grace.' There was silence while the tea service was placed on a small table between her and Quin, and tiny savouries and cakes laid out.

'You are a liar and a spy and a deceitful, conniving toady,' Cleo threw at Quin the moment the door closed behind the servants. Quin's lips firmed into a hard line, but he said nothing.

'Augusta, Lord Quintus was simply doing his duty. His mission was clear: to establish whether or not your father was a traitor and to return you to me. And never let me hear you call a gentleman's honour into question in such a manner again.'

Or what? she felt like retorting. But that would be childish and there was nothing of the nursery about this situation. She kept her shoulder turned to the duke and spoke directly to Quin. 'I never trusted you and yet I made allowances, I gave you the benefit of the doubt over and over again. I could have left you to die. I could have turned you over to Laurent. And all the time, fool that I am, I was—' She caught herself just in time before her hurt and her anger and her fear let those five damning words escape. *Falling in love with you.* 'I was obediently doing just what you asked.

'Yes, I understand you had to stop the correspondence passing through my father's hands. And, yes, I see that deception was necessary until you had established his innocence.' A thought struck her. 'What exactly were you supposed to do if he was guilty?' Quin's eyes narrowed, but he remained silent. 'Oh, I see. An assassin as well as a spy. But what have I got to do with this? My mother's family cast her off and showed not the remotest interest in me for twenty-three years.'

'When the position you were in was brought to my attention as a result of the intelligence about your father's correspondence I deemed it time for you to be removed from his ambit,' her grandfather interposed. 'I had understood that his way of life was eccentric, I had not realised that it had descended into squalor.'

'Squalor!' Cleo threw up her hands, palm outwards. 'Look at these. Are those the hands of a woman who has allowed her surroundings to descend into squalor? I worked, Your Grace. I cooked and I cleaned and I washed. I did it for my father when my mother died, I did it for my husband when I was tricked into marrying him and then I did it again for my father when I was widowed. And my mother did the same, for years. Where were you while we were doing that?'

'Your mother made her choice when she ran off with that wastrel,' the duke said, his voice frigid. 'You were, all of you, remote from England.'

'Oh, I understand now.' Cleo felt the anger drain from her, leaving her calm and strangely cold. 'Out of sight, out of mind. But then Father threatened to create a scandal and all of a sudden the Ashfordham family name is at risk, so I have to be removed from Egypt and turned into a milk-and-water miss who is of no trouble to anyone.'

Her grandfather's stony expression told her that she had hit the target squarely. He opened his mouth, presumably to deliver another frigid set-down, when Quin got to his feet.

'If you will excuse me, I believe this is a family conversation and I am *de trop*. Good day, Your Grace. Goodbye, Miss Woodward. I am certain you will soon feel at home here.' He turned towards the door.

'Deverall, I am most obliged to you,' the duke said, getting to his feet. 'You, and the department, will not find me ungrateful.'

'Thank you, Your Grace, but I can assure you the satisfaction of delivering Miss Woodward safely back to her family is more than reward enough.' There was a snap in his voice and she could tell, for all his politeness, that he was angry. 'This is where she belongs, not in Egypt, and it was my pleasure to see her here safely.'

Despite his words just now, Quin bringing her to her grandfather would result in the advancement of his career, she could see that. A duke must have great power and influence and when the price for securing that influence was simply the liberty of one insignificant female, why, not a single diplomat amongst them would question it for a moment.

She made herself stand and walk to where Quin stood. He watched her come, unmoving, even though he must have been expecting a slapped face. When she reached him she stood on tiptoe and kissed his warm cheek, inhaled the familiar scent of him. Under her lips she felt the muscle contract. 'I forgive you,' she murmured with acid-drop sweetness. He shook his head, his eyes dark with some emotion she could no read. 'After all, betraying a woman who means nothing to you, in return for such patronage as the duke can give, makes perfect sense.'

'No, Cleo, that is not how it was. How it is,' he said, his voice low, for her ears only. His eyes were dark with what she had come to recognise as pain. Doubtless her words had stung. 'Cleo—'

'Goodbye, Quin. I hope I never see you again.'

'You appear to have won, Your Grace.' Cleo returned to her seat as the door closed behind Quin. She poured herself a cup of tea and tried to deal with her churning emotions. She wanted to believe Quin so badly and yet her grandfather had made it clear there would be payment for her return. 'Would you care for tea?'

'Thank you.' The duke sat and watched her as she prepared the cup, added a slice of lemon—surely he did not indulge in anything like sugar or milk—prepared a plate of savouries and little cakes and came and placed them on the table at his elbow.

She sat again with careful attention to her skirts and smiled her sweetest, falsest smile as she selected two morsels for herself and picked up a tiny silver fork. 'You see—I do not drink from the saucer nor stuff food in my mouth with my hands. Perhaps I am not quite the savage you think me.' He made an ironic inclination of the head. 'Nor am I an idiot, Your Grace.'

'I never thought you were, Augusta. Your father, for all his faults, is an intelligent man, within his restricted focus. Your mother was a bright young woman, until she lost her mind and eloped with him. But neither am I gullible. You will not lull me into a false sense of security by behaving meekly now, not after that little exhibition.'

'I was deceived and I find myself, against my will, somewhere I have no wish to be. My money has been withheld. Do you expect me to murmur, *Yes, Grandfather, whatever you say, Grandfather*? I am angry and I am upset and I am not going to hide the fact.'

'You wish me to admit that I was at fault? Very well. As soon as I received news of your mother's death I should have sent agents to remove you and bring you to me. Do you wish me to apologise? I do so. I had no idea you were living the life of a drudge or had been married off to some Frenchman—again, both the result of my failure to bring you back to England and secure you a suitable husband.'

'I would not have come. My objection, Your Grace,

is not to your prior lack of attention, but to my imprisonment now. I do not wish to be here, it is as simple as that.'

'You have no choice. Your only course of action is to make your life in England, become an English lady, behave like the granddaughter of a duke. How else can you survive? There is nowhere that you belong any more, Augusta, except here.'

I belonged with Quin, she thought, wondering at the pain that tore through her. *I love him, even though he has deceived me. What can I do?* The realisation that her grandfather was right, that unless he released her money to her she had no options save this one, was painfully obvious once she moved past the emotions that racked her and applied only reason to her plight.

'Very well, but upon conditions.' She was an adult and she would negotiate, not meekly take orders like a child. 'My name is Cleo and I will not answer to any other. Maggie Tomkins is my maid and I will continue to employ her and she will receive the wage suitable to my closest servant. And if I have not remarried by my twenty-fifth birthday in eighteen months' time you will give me access to my money and release me from your control.'

'You think to negotiate with me, do you? Very well. Your maid, I agree to. Your Aunt Madeleine, who is a widow, is here and will see whether she needs any assistance to bring you up to scratch. Your name, I suppose, we must tolerate. It is at least fashionable if the new craze for all things Egyptian lasts. Your other condition is, of course, nonsense. You will make a suitable marriage to a gentleman of my choosing.

'You may call me Grandfather and you will apply

yourself to becoming a lady. You will give proper attention to every offer of marriage I approve. If you have found no one you are prepared to marry by the time you reach your twenty-fifth birthday then you will move to the country and become the companion of your Great-Aunt Millicent.'

'But—'

'There is no other respectable occupation for the spinster granddaughter of a duke. That is my final word.'

It was a prison sentence. But if she kept turning down suitors she had time to learn about this strange country and its ways, time to plan and accumulate money, somehow, so that when she was banished she could escape. In time, perhaps, she could forget Quin Deverall.

'And if you show yourself unfit to learn and fail to comport yourself as a lady, then you will go to the country immediately.'

Her stomach knotted with a pang of something very like fear. How naïve to believe she could lay down terms to this man. Her grandfather meant what he said and he had the power to carry out his threats—no one was going to naysay a duke.

Cleo swallowed back the protests. She had to buy time and he had to believe she was obeying him. Her grandfather tugged the bell pull again and waited until the butler appeared. 'Ask Lady Madeleine to join us if it is convenient to her, Cranton. Now, Cleo, we begin.'

Two weeks and I could swear there is not the smallest space in my brain for one more fact about the peerage, one more rule about table settings, one more

*dance step. There is certainly not an inch of my body
unpricked by dressmaker's pins.*

Cleo climbed another step and then stopped, her
nose almost between the shoulder blades of the matron in front of her.

'This will be a complete crush if the queue for the
receiving line is anything to go by,' her Aunt Madeleine said in a self-congratulatory tone. 'I knew I could
trust Almeira Hazelcroft to host something suitable for
your first appearance.'

She glanced sharply at Cleo, who sent up a silent
prayer that her face showed nothing but polite enjoy-
ment, that her deportment was perfect, that she was
holding her fan correctly. It had been made quite plain
to her that her continued residence in London depended
entirely on the effort she made to learn everything that
was required of her and that she never let her upbringing show for an instant.

'I will not be fooled by passive resistance, Cleo,'
her grandfather had warned. 'You have shown a re-
bellious, outrageous temperament that must be utterly
eradicated. Do you understand me?'

Yes, she understood him. And she found she feared
him as she had feared nothing else in her life because
she sensed he had the power to completely crush her
true self out of existence. There were even long, sleepless hours when she feared he could force her into a
marriage she did not want through sheer strength of
will.

It had taken a fortnight of intensive lessons and fit-
tings before she was deemed ready for this trial. If she
failed to demonstrate that she could behave in every
way as befitted a duke's granddaughter then this was

over before it had begun, for it would soon be June and the *ton* would be planning its summer escape from the heat and dust of London. If she could not cope with a ball, Lady Madeleine had pronounced, she certainly would not stand up to the constant scrutiny of a house party.

The crowd moved up several steps and shuffled to create a little more space, turning to look about them and wave to friends. Cleo, flanked by her grandfather on her right and her aunt on her left, achieved two more steps and found she had a clear view of the top of the stairs.

Quin.

Chapter Nineteen

Quin was talking to a man in scarlet dress uniform, his own corbeau-blue tailcoat and crisp white linen in startling contrast to the military magnificence. How foolish to be taken by surprise. Of course she should expect him to attend a function of this sort: he was intending to court a bride and where better to encounter her?

Anger, longing, misery mixed uncomfortably with her existing nerves. Cleo put up her chin, dropped her shoulders and drew herself up to her full height. She was not going to be sick, she was certainly not going to burst into tears. When Quin turned his head and looked directly at her, bowing his head in unsmiling greeting, she inclined hers a trifle and then looked away.

At least she could be certain he would not approach her here, not after the way they had parted. Her long jade ear-bobs swayed and she focused on the unaccustomed sensations she was experiencing. The pull of the earrings on her lobes, the weight of her hair, skilfully coiled and pinned with tiny jade-headed clips, were slight discomforts that helped her recall her posture. The warm air on her shoulders and the exposed swell of her bosom reminded her to handle the silken folds of her sea-green gown with grace.

Her aunt had decided that she was so tall that there was no point in attempting to disguise the fact and, as she was a widow and not an unmarried girl, pastels need not be adhered to. *Neither fish nor fowl,* she thought now. *Neither a virgin nor a matron.* Quin's teasing from one day in Egypt came back to her. *Queen of the Nile.* If she could concentrate on being Cleopatra, then her fear of disgracing herself would not show.

They arrived at the landing, turned left and reached the receiving line. Cleo shook hands with her hosts and was swept into the crush of the ballroom.

Sheer will-power carried her along in the wake of the duke until he stopped in an alcove with a number of gilt chairs framed by ferns. 'Will this do, Madeleine?'

'Admirably, thank you, Papa.' He strolled off and her aunt sat down. 'Stand slightly behind me with your hand on the back of the chair, allow yourself to be seen,' she commanded. Ladies approached, were introduced. Some sat and beckoned to daughters or nieces to join them. Cleo dipped curtsies, bowed, tried to remember names. And smiled.

She was being stared at, she knew. From the other side of the ferns she heard a conversation, the whispers not quite low enough.

'They say she and her father were stranded in the desert and rescued from savage tribesman by a French officer! Can you imagine! And so she had to marry him to secure his protection for herself and her father. And then there was a battle and he was killed and her father—the scholar Sir Philip Woodward, you know—he bravely took a small boat down the Nile—'

'My dear! The crocodiles!'

'I know, I was aghast! But fortunately they encountered our valiant army besieging Cairo and were saved. And Miss Woodward—she is not using her French name, and who can blame her, poor child?—was escorted home by some wealthy merchant's wife. Not good *ton* of course, but utterly respectable.'

'Good heavens. So now she is with her grandfather, St Osyth. Quite a catch, I imagine, despite the French husband. Handsome girl. Have you seen her gown? One of Madame Rochester's, if I do not mistake. And that jade set—unconventional, but I suppose as she is actually a widow...'

'Cleo, my dear!'

'Yes, Aunt Madeleine?'

'Lady Jersey is coming this way.'

One of the patronesses of Almack's, one of the leaders of the *ton*. Cleo felt herself shivering with nerves. If she got this wrong, she was doomed from the outset.

The next half hour passed in a daze. Cleo maintained her poise, her smile and, apparently, her wits, although she had no clear idea of what she said to anyone. Lady Jersey was pleased to be interested and amused by her exotic story, gentlemen joined the group. *Perhaps I can do this after all.*

'Lord Dryton, good evening.' Lady Madeleine fluttered her fan and beamed on the gentleman who had just joined the group.

That was very warm. Suspicious, Cleo tried to study him without staring. Dark, olive-skinned, lean with firm lips and deep lines from his nose to the corners of his mouth. He bowed to her aunt and smiled. Cleo took an involuntary step back. *I do not like you, my lord.*

'Lady Madeleine, such a pleasure to see you again. Do, please, introduce me to the young lady I believe is your niece. I have been hearing such exciting tales of perilous escapes.' His voice was deep and pleasant, but his smile did not reach his eyes. They seemed to slide over her body before returning to her face.

'Of course. Cleo, my dear, here is a good neighbour of ours in Somerset, Lord Dryton. My lord, Miss Woodward.'

She curtsied as she had been taught and found a smile to curve her lips. 'My lord.'

'You have had an exciting time of it, it seems, Miss Woodward.'

'The stories of crocodiles were exaggerated, my lord,' Cleo said. *But I think I have one standing in front of me.*

Lord Dryton shot her a look from under his dark brows as though he suspected her of levity. 'Excellent. You will do me the honour of a dance, I hope?'

'My lord.' She proffered her empty dance card and he wrote his name against the dance immediately after supper, bowed and left.

'Deverall, my dear fellow. You are back in town.'

Cleo dropped her reticule and someone picked it up. She murmured her thanks. *I must not show any particular interest in Quin.*

The rest of the group glanced in his direction, several people nodded and smiled and the buzz of conversation grew. Quin was obviously known and liked. Cleo's hands moved of their own accord—to reach out and touch him or to slap that clean-shaven, handsome face with its easy diplomatic smile? She clenched them on her fan.

'Miss Woodward.' He inclined head and shoulders in a slight bow.

'Lord Quintus,' she returned, amazed to find she could speak with perfect control. 'We meet again. Lord Quintus was on the same ship that I travelled on from Alexandria, Aunt Madeleine.'

Lady Madeleine knew the true story, of course, but her self-control was perfect. 'Indeed, my dear?' There was a smile on her lips and a clear warning in her eyes.

'It was a fleeting acquaintance, ma'am, to my regret,' Quin said. 'I am a martyr to seasickness and spent most of that wretched journey confined to my cabin.' That little lie was going to get him unmercifully teased by some of his acquaintance, Cleo could tell from the grins on the faces of the men. 'I must do my best to make up for my lack of utility now. Might I beg the honour of a dance, Miss Woodward?'

The correct behaviour for dealing with requests to dance had been drilled into Cleo. Provided her chaperon had approved the gentleman, then she must accept if there were any dances left on her card. She'd had not the slightest excuse for refusing Lord Dryton, nor would Quin believe her card was full. Even pleading fatigue when the time came would not save her from either man—she must still accept, but ask to sit out and talk. Aunt Madeleine appeared to approve of Quin as a partner so there was no help there.

She was supposed to look at her card, pretend it was almost full, even if it was not, but she could not play those games with Quin. Cleo looked him straight in the eye and said, 'They are all free but one, my lord.'

Her aunt gave a little moan as Cleo offered him the card and waited for his choice. He was wearing cologne, subtle and provocative.

'This set then, if I may?' He wrote his initials against the dances immediately before supper. 'And this.' He added the last country dance set, handed the card back, bowed and stepped back out of the group as the other men pressed forward, all eager to claim a dance now her chaperon had signalled her availability.

The dancing master they had found for her had been excellent and demanding. Cleo had drilled every day for a fortnight and gave silent thanks for the fact that she was fit and supple and had good natural co-ordination. It was different dancing to a full string orchestra and in a crowded ballroom, but she was fortunate in her partners and there were no mishaps to earn her a reproof when she was returned to her aunt after the quadrille.

Quin, she had seen, had been dancing with a lively, freckled brunette and the pair of them appeared to be able to negotiate the tricky dance with ease and chat while they did so. She found her gaze was following him and kept her eyes forward with an effort. He looked as home on the dance floor as he had when moving around the felucca.

He returned the freckled girl to her mama and came to collect Cleo for the country dances before she had come to any decision about how to treat him.

'What is wrong?' he asked, low-voiced, as they waited for the set to form.

'Wrong?' She glanced down at her skirts, lifted one hand to her nape as though to check her hair was still pinned securely. 'What do you mean?' He shot her a quizzical look and she realised he was not deceived for a moment. 'Perhaps you think I should be pleased to see you. I can assure you, Lord Quintus, that only the constraints of good manners stop me slapping your face.'

'You look perfect,' Quin told her. Either he did not believe she would do anything so rash or he was a magnificent actor. 'You are beautiful.'

'Why, thank you, my lord.' She knew she was colouring up, just as though that was a genuine accolade. 'Praise from you is to be treasured.' Anyone overhearing would have taken that at its face value, unless, of course, they had heard the tremble of anger in her voice.

Quin moved closer and the familiar scent of him swept through her senses. 'I know you are angry with me and I understand why. But it is more than that, isn't it? You are afraid. Tell me, what is wrong?'

'You put me in a position where I had to accept a dance with you when all I want is never to see you again, that is all,' she murmured back.

'That might well make you irritated,' Quin agreed. 'It would not make you fearful—and you were that already on the stairs. Don't deny it, Cleo. I know you too well.'

'Do you? No, I do not think so.' She knew her expression was under control, but to her own ears her voice held a betraying thread of yearning. *Don't let him realise. Please don't let him see I love him.*

'Cleo—'

'We cannot talk here.' The music struck up, partners bowed and curtsied.

'No.' Quin took her hand and moved into the first circle. 'But I have reserved the supper dance.' He tightened his grip on her hand as though he thought she would make a bolt for it.

'You may relax your grip, my lord. Or do you think the prospect of crossing swords with you over a plate of cakes would send me into retreat?'

'Nothing makes you flee, Cleo.' Then he fell silent as if he realised that she needed every ounce of concentration to weave through the measures of the dance.

I can do this. Their circle formed, advanced, split up and reformed with half of the dancers from the adjoining group. A pretty blonde stepped forward to take her place in the centre.

'Lord Quintus,' she said with an enchanting smile. 'You are back in England!'

'As you see, Lady Caroline.' Quin advanced and took her hand and the circle closed around them. Cleo's hands were taken by the men on either side and somehow she kept on dancing.

Lady Caroline Brooke, the woman Quin intended courting, the prospective bride who would be perfect for his career. *How lovely she is.* Her blonde curls bobbed around her pretty, heart-shaped face with the movement of the dance steps and her skin was flushed pink with the exertion of the dance. As the central pair turned Quin's eyes met Cleo's. He had remembered he had told her about Lady Caroline, she realised. And he could see she had guessed who the other woman was. *But what does it matter? He does not know I care.*

'How nice to see you back in England again, Lord Quintus,' Caroline said brightly as he turned her under their clasped hands. 'You must call.'

'You may be sure of it.'

To Cleo's ears that sounded remarkably like a declaration.

'What are those?' Almost two hours later Cleo sat
and studied the intricate little pastries on the heaped
plate Quin placed before her. She knew she was pink-
cheeked and she knew she was breathless, but she
could only hope he thought that was the result of the
energetic set they had just danced. 'I…I mean, thank
you, Lord Quintus, that looks delightful.'

'Those are an assortment of savouries, including
a fair number of lobster patties, which I thought you
might like. They are delicious but, naturally you must
only nibble at them, pretending you have no appetite,
despite the fact that they are the product of Gunter's
fabled kitchens.'

'I know. Yet another ridiculous convention. Ladies
have no appetites. Of any sort,' she added darkly, and
Quin swallowed a laugh choked on pastry crumbs.

She told herself she could do this, pretend to be indifferent, as though she was prepared to forgive him
in a ladylike manner, but wanted no closer acquaintance with him than an exchange of small talk over
supper. Fortunately she had danced every set between
the country dances and the moment when he came to
claim her again for the supper set. Her shock at coming face to face with his prospective bride must surely
be hidden by now.

Quin looked around as if confirming that their little
table squashed into a corner was out of earshot of any
of the nearby tables, each with their chattering group.
She had wondered at him choosing it when so many

better-placed tables had been available, now she realised he was preparing for a tête-à-tête.

'Cleo, tell me what is wrong. And don't pretend it is simply that you want to run me through with a dagger or you are exasperated by lessons in ladylike behaviour.'

She pushed a patty around her plate with her fork. 'Why should I confide in you? You will probably go straight to my grandfather and report whatever I say to him.'

'No, I will not. Cleo, you know I did the right thing in bringing you to him. The only possible thing. My fault was in not explaining to you beforehand, but I thought you would run away from me.' He hesitated, and she had the inexplicable feeling that what he said next was somehow of deep significance. 'Cleo, I give you my word of honour that I am not hiding anything from you and that what you tell me will go no further.

'Are you so very unhappy?' Quin asked. 'Truly I believe this is the best for you, the safest thing. You probably still feel very alone, but that will pass. This will all become familiar, you will make friends, make a new life.' He laid his hand over hers on the table and Cleo stiffened, then left hers where it was. A dangerous indulgence if he could read her erratic pulse aright.

'Yes, I am unhappy,' she agreed, making no attempt to lighten the words with a brave smile.

'Does it seem intolerably superficial and frivolous?' She shrugged.

'What is wrong, Cleo?'

'I feel better now the evening is half over. But you see I have to do this perfectly or my grandfather will exile me in the country with my great-aunt. I thought

I would have at least until my twenty-fifth birthday, eighteen months away, to find a husband he approves of. He told me that if I do not behave as he thinks fit, or fail to consider honestly proposals made to me, then I will be banished earlier. This is my first major social event. At first I feared that I would get it all wrong, that I would fail at the first hurdle and it would all be over before I can find a way to get some money together and somehow live my own life.'

'It must seem daunting, a mountain of things to learn, a quicksand of social pitfalls.' There was no sympathy in his voice, only bracing encouragement. 'You are good at languages, this is just another language to learn,' he said as she sat silent. 'You are doing wonderfully already. You dance well, you look both elegant and beautiful. Soon you will feel at home and realise that this is where you belong. You see your grandfather in the light of an ogre, but he is not that really, is he?'

She had been a fool to think Quin would help her, or even understand. This was his world, of course he assumed she would learn to think of it as the natural, right, place to be.

'You are quite correct, I am sure.' Cleo smiled polite thanks for the advice and made herself eat a patty. It was exquisite, of course. So was the luxury she was surrounded by.

Quin lifted his hand from hers and gestured to a waiter for more champagne. 'Give it time and you might even find a husband you can tolerate.'

Chapter Twenty

He intended it to be light-hearted, she could tell, and that was good because it meant he did not have the slightest suspicion that she could accept no other man, feeling as she did about him. With the realisation that she had been unjust to resent his secrecy had come the even more painful understanding that she could love him without reserve. *I wish I could hate you, I really do.* It would be so much easier if she did not ache for him, yearn for him.

'Perhaps I will. Whether there is one who can tolerate me is another matter.' Cleo smiled to show it was a joke and her cheeks felt stiff and unyielding. 'Was that your Lady Caroline in the first dance of the set?' She managed not to wince as she said it.

'She isn't mine. Not yet. Perhaps not ever.'

'But she would be perfect, I am sure. And she seems to like you.' This was like driving pins under her own fingernails. What was she doing? But perhaps it was best to be sure, to kill stone-dead any lingering, weakening hope. Hope that was entirely without foundation. After all, Quin did not even desire her enough to make love to her when she had begged him. 'She is very lovely and assured. And you said the connection to her family could only be advantageous.'

'Yes,' Quin agreed, frowning at his champagne as if it had gone flat. 'She has been her father's hostess for the last year, now her mother's health does not permit her to entertain much, and her languages are very competent. I heard her talking to a number of diplomats at a reception last year.'

'You had better fix your interest with her before someone else snaps her up. I am amazed she is still unspoken for.'

'Her mother's illness took her out of society for a while or I suspect she would have been. As you say, I must begin my campaign. I have a set of dances reserved with her later this evening, which means I should call with flowers in any case. That will save me encountering her father accidentally on purpose and starting things off that way.'

'Excellent,' Cleo said and managed what she thought was an entirely creditable smile.

'Miss Woodward?'

She looked up into the face of the man who had taken the next set, the man she had been trying not to think about all evening.

'Dryton,' Quin said with a smile that she recognised as one of his diplomatic expressions. Did he not like the earl either?

'Lord Dryton,' Cleo said, injecting as much warmth into her voice as possible.

'I am sorry to disturb your conversation, Miss Woodward, but the orchestra is reassembling and I believe I have the pleasure of the next set.'

'Of course.' She gathered up her fan and reticule. 'Thank you so much for a delightful supper, Lord Quintus.'

Quin rose as good manners dictated, but she had the odd feeling that he was squaring up to the other man. 'It was entirely my pleasure, Miss Woodward. I will surrender you to Lord Dryton's…safe hands.'

Was that a hint, a warning that Dryton was not safe, or simply some male sparring? Cleo put her hand on her partner's proffered arm and left the supper room without looking back.

The evening wore on, the room became hotter, more crowded, the dancers less inhibited, even the chaperons became more relaxed. Cleo's feet ached, her head was spinning, but she kept smiling somehow. 'Here is Lord Quintus for his second set,' her aunt remarked complacently. 'You are doing very well so far, Cleo. Your grandfather is pleased, I believe.'

'Thank you, Aunt.' She looked up to see Quin was almost at her side. 'Lord Quintus.'

'Miss Woodward.' He bowed to her aunt, took Cleo's hand and led her on to the floor, through the crowd of couples forming up into sets, and across to the far side by the windows. 'You seem a trifle flushed, Cleo. Would you prefer to sit this dance out? I can fetch you a glass of lemonade to that alcove by the open casement there.'

'Thank you. Yes, I…I am finding this a trifle overwhelming. But is that not an indiscreet thing to do?'

'A separate room or the terrace certainly would be.' He guided her through a screen of ferns and palms to a bench seat. The breeze whispered through, cool and smelling of grass. 'But here we are in full view, if only in glimpses through the greenery. It is quite unexceptional. One moment and I will fetch the drinks.'

He returned with two glasses of lemonade and they sat for a while, turning the condensation-dewed glasses in their hands, letting the fresh air blow away the mingled odours of too many hot, scented bodies.

'I have not forgiven you, you understand,' she said abruptly. It was as though the words were the continuation of a conversation. 'You took me to him because you were ordered to and because you wanted his patronage. You sold me.'

Quin ran his hand over his mouth and chin as though to control the first words that came to him. 'My orders were to establish the truth about the suspicions regarding your father's correspondence. But my department needs the duke's patronage. He is a very influential man and not one to cross. They had let him know the situation and he insisted that I bring you safely back to England.'

There was a bleakness in his eyes that belied the calmness of his tone. 'I saw both as my duty and I hold by that still. To do anything else would have been to connive at your ruin, Cleo. I could not leave you there and I could not simply abandon you to your own devices here in England—you have seen enough of society now to know that would be impossible.'

'You lied to me by omission.' He was hurting too and that only fuelled the bitterness she felt. Cleo clenched her hand and felt a seam in her tight satin glove split.

'If I had told you the full truth, you would have tried

to escape the ship. I might have lost you in some port and never found you again,' Quin said.

'You could have helped me. Listened to me. Was that story you told me about your birth, your father, all lies too?'

'No, it was the truth.' He was maintaining his expressionless, diplomat's face and yet it seemed to her that she could see the nerves beneath the skin, the flow of the blood in every tiny capillary as if she was flaying him alive.

So much pain... Hurt him more. 'Then you should understand what it means to be an outsider.'

'I do not want to be an outsider,' Quin said. 'I want to make my own life within this society. I will be my own man and to hell with who my father is or is not.' He took up his glass and drank. 'My true father behaved dishonourably,' he said as he set the glass down again. 'I have undertaken to serve the government and the king as a diplomat and *I* will not behave dishonourably in that duty. To have helped you to your ruin would be wrong in every way—for you, for your grandfather, for the diplomatic service and its reputation.'

'So my happiness, my trust...' *My heart. My love.* 'Those weigh like a feather in the scales against your honour. Of course they do.' *Of course. He does not love me, he does not know I love him, why should he ruin himself for me?*

'My honour is all I have. It is what I am.' He said it softly, but the words were like chiselled stone.

'And women do not understand male honour, do we? I made the mistake of confusing...friendship with whatever it actually was between us. I am not sure of the word, but I was your objective and you…you were both our hunter and our judge.'

'I hope I was your friend,' Quin said slowly. He seemed to be picking his way through the words as if something in there was sharp and dangerous. 'I hope I still am. Can you tell me why you are afraid?'

He could see her fear? She had tried so hard to hide it.

'Fear?' Cleo stood up and set down her glass so sharply the fragile stem cracked. 'I am not afraid of anything, my lord. Or perhaps I am. Yes, I am afraid of relying on others, of becoming weak. I can see that my fate is in my hands and mine alone and to repine about shattered trust or friendship that never was is foolish and weakening. The second dance is about to start. Shall we join it?'

'As you wish.' Quin stood. For a long moment she thought he would say more, but he merely offered her his arm and brushed aside the ferns so she could regain the dance floor.

'I must say, this is promising. You have done better than I expected, Cleo.' Her aunt surveyed the massed flowers decorating the drawing room. 'Seven bouquets from gentlemen with whom you danced last night.' She went from vase to vase inspecting cards.

'Hmm. Willoughby, Axholme—the younger son unfortunately. Charles Bignor—hopeless, a complete fribble. Philpott, Drewe, Deverall.'

Quin sent me flowers?

'Ah, this is excellent—Dryton. Now that is an alliance your grandfather would be most approving of.'

'He has only danced once with me, Aunt. I am sure

the flowers are the merest courtesy. I…did not like him very much.'

'Hothouse orchids are never the *merest courtesy*, foolish girl!' Her aunt seemed more amused at her ignorance than annoyed. 'And what is there not to like, might I ask? He is a political ally of the duke, he has extensive lands, over thirty thousand a year, and I understand most silly girls find him good looking.'

He has hot eyes that seem to undress me and hands that wander just beyond the bounds of comfort and he is too smooth. And Quin does not like him.

'Lord Dryton is a widower, with children.'

He had not told her that. In fact, he had said very little, only looked. And touched. She had felt like a slab of meat on the butcher's block being assessed for freshness and flavour. She had learned about him by listening to the ballroom chatter.

'And you are a widow. He has two daughters, he needs an heir.' Lady Madeleine tapped the card against her teeth, lost in thought. 'I must tell Papa, he will wish to be prepared if Dryton makes an offer. You will write to thank him for the flowers, of course.'

'I will write to all the gentlemen,' Cleo said. She went from bouquet to bouquet again, pretending to study the cards. Quin's offering was a subtle and lovely blend of yellows and greens, a compliment to the colours she had worn the night before.

The card bore one line of strong black letters. *In friendship. Quintus Deverall.* 'If you will excuse me, Aunt, I will go up to my room and do it now.'

The ball had changed something in her grandfather's attitude to her, Cleo realised the following day.

He had obviously been impressed by her behaviour, or perhaps by her attaching the interest of Lord Dryton. At breakfast he was positively unbending, offering a teasing remark about milliners' bills.

Cleo decided she would see if the good humour extended to a relaxation of the bounds around her. 'It is a lovely day, Grandfather. Might I walk in Hyde Park? I believe that is an unexceptional place, is it not?' She looked earnestly at her aunt for guidance. 'I would take Maggie and a footman, naturally. But perhaps you need me to assist with something…'

'You are looking a trifle wan,' her aunt said, putting down the letter she had just opened and regarding her, so Cleo thought, like a village woman sizing up the freshness of a piece of fish. 'Yes, you may go. It will be quiet enough at this hour, but remember not to acknowledge any gentleman to whom you have not been introduced.'

'Yes, Aunt.' She had no illusions about being supervised, the footman would be instructed to take careful note of who she spoke to and what she did. But it was freedom of a sort and a way of testing the restrictions around her. A space to think and plan, but not to dream. Dreams were a deceiving weakness.

At last. Quin folded his newspaper and stood up from the seat amongst the shrubs of the Grosvenor Square garden where he had been pretending to read for the past hour.

Cleo's unhappiness was costing him sleep and instinct told him more was troubling her than homesickness for the familiar, if uncomfortable, world of the desert encampment.

It was none of his business any more, he had told himself for the hundredth time last night. She was her grandfather's responsibility now and if he interfered it would be deeply resented. And misunderstood.

He locked the gates behind him with the key he had borrowed from his friend Alderswick who owned the house on the corner, and followed Cleo and her small escort along Upper Grosvenor Street towards the park. It had been a gamble coming here, for she could have been spending the day inside or have driven off to some engagement, but the sunshine had made him optimistic and the decision had paid off.

It would not be wise to speak to her, naturally. Nor would it be kind for she was unsettled enough as it was, without presenting her with the source of her anger and resentment. But he needed to see how she looked.

Quin crossed Park Lane and took the track to the Riding House while Cleo, with Maggie and the footman behind her, strolled down to the small circular reservoir. It was frustratingly difficult to see her face at this distance. She had a charming bonnet with a brim that shaded her face, she was twirling a parasol, riders and trees kept getting between them... With a muttered oath Quin cut through behind her and took the direct path across the open park towards the end of the Serpentine, gambling that was where she was heading by way of the more shaded paths.

His luck was in again that day. Cleo passed him as he sat, newspaper raised, by the edge of the track along the Serpentine. She did not spare him a glance, he noticed through a slit in the fold of the newssheet. Her face was intent, as though she was thinking deeply and not noticing her surroundings and he recognised the way she held herself from the times in Egypt when she had been weary beyond words, but kept going by sheer will-power.

'My lord! Oh, excuse me, my lord, for speaking.' It was Maggie, of course, and he had been inexcusably careless, letting the paper fall as he stared after Cleo.

Cleo spun round. 'Qui— Lord Quintus! What are you doing here?'

Nothing for it but to brazen it out. 'Why, enjoying the sunshine as you are, Miss Woodward. Good morning.' Maggie was beaming and the footman, who must know he was the man who had rescued the duke's granddaughter from Egypt, obviously saw no cause for concern in Quin speaking to his mistress.

'May I join you? I confess to finding the Parliamentary reports have little attraction in comparison to a walk in your company.'

'Of course, my lord.'

He thought she had gone pale, and her smile was forced, but Cleo's chin was up and she kept her tone pleasant. She had courage, his Cleo. *My Cleo?* Quin pushed the thought away, unwilling to examine that feeling of proprietary pride.

He offered her his arm and she rested her gloved fingers on it with perfect grace. 'Something amuses you, Lord Quintus?' He must have smiled.

'I was thinking that those fingers, so prettily sheathed in pale primrose kid, are the same ones that cleaned my wound, milked the goat and hefted water jars,' Quin said, jolted into honesty.

'Yes. My aunt insists I retain my gloves at all times until the calluses have vanished.' Her voice was cool.

Damnation. 'I did not mean to refer to that. I admire the way you worked, the strength in those fingers. Their care.' *Their touch.*

'Really? But what I was doing was so unsuitable for a lady, was it not? I had to be removed from it, after all.'

'That does not mean I do not value the way you lived your life under those circumstances. Your character.'

He expected a tart retort, that she would pull her arm free. Instead her fingers tightened convulsively and she made a small sound, horribly like a smothered sob.

'Cleo? Damn this bonnet!' Quin ducked his head to see her face. 'Cleo, don't cry, please.' *I never meant to make you cry. Never.* He glanced behind, but Maggie and the footman were chatting and laughing on the edge of the Serpentine, pointing at the antics of the ducks. No one else was near and there was a small shrubbery just ahead.

Quin guided her in and found it enclosed a small circle of grass, surrounded by benches. A child's hoop lay forgotten. This must be a place where the nursemaids gathered with their little charges, but it was deserted now.

He guided her to a bench and she sat down without protest, even when he removed her parasol, snapped it shut and began to untie her bonnet ribbons. 'That's better, now I can see your face.'

'I can't think why you want to,' she muttered. 'And I am not crying. I never—'

'Cry. I know. Here, have my handkerchief and remove the gnat from your eye or whatever it is that is irritating it.'

'It would take rather more than a square of linen to remove you, Quin,' she snapped with so much of her old spirit that he grinned despite himself. 'Have you no work to be doing instead of lounging around in the park?' Her eyes narrowed as she stared at him. 'Oh, of course, you *are* working, aren't you? You have been following me. No wonder Grandfather was so complaisant about allowing me out, he knew his spy was in place.'

'You think I would— Yes, you do, don't you? No, Cleo, I am not spying for the duke, my word of honour on it. I was following you, I admit. I waited in the square, hoping you would come out, but that was for my own…satisfaction.'

'Very well, I know your word of honour is absolutely sacrosanct.' She blew her nose and stuffed his handkerchief into her reticule. He could not tell if she was being sarcastic, but he guessed she was. 'But how does spying on me give you satisfaction, pray?'

'I was worried about you. I am worried still. You are not happy.'

'Of course I am not happy! Do you not listen to a word I say to you? I told you how it would be and I was right. My grandfather wants me to marry Dryton, I am certain of it.'

'That rake?'

'Are there any other by that name? Yes, *that* rake. He is, apparently, eminently suitable. But if it is not him, it will be another, chosen, just as you have decided to choose a bride, for bloodlines, fortune and influence.'

'Cleo, damn it—' She levelled a look at him. 'And don't prim up at me like that, you are enough to make a saint swear. Cleo, darling… Oh, hell.' He kissed her.

Chapter Twenty-One

Kissing Cleo was like coming home…and it was like exploring some exotic new land. He had kissed her before, knew her taste, knew the softness of her lips and the sharp nip of her teeth and the languorous, adventurous sweep of her tongue, but something had changed. There was a heat and a wildness in her and a rightness in what they were doing. Her fingers speared through his hair, sending his hat flying, his found the fastenings of her pelisse and then the bodice beneath, found soft, warm flesh rising to meet his caress.

'Cleo.' He dragged his mouth free and stared down at her, into the stormy green depths of her eyes before she pulled his head back down and he was lost again.

A frantic flapping of wings, so close they brushed his cheek, made him straighten. 'Only panicking pigeons,' he said after a moment. 'Must have seen a sparrowhawk.'

Cleo curled in tight against his chest, for once, it seemed, at a loss for words, then she sat up and began to put her clothing to rights.

'Cleo, I am sorry.'

'Why do you always apologise when we make love?' she demanded, jamming her bonnet back on and pushing wisps of hair back with angry stabs of her fingers. 'I want you, you want me, yet you are such a hypocrite about it.'

Quin opened his mouth to reply and she snapped, 'And don't you dare say *honour* or I will never speak to you again.'

'Which would be an excellent thing!' She turned away, but not before he saw her teeth close hard on her lower lip. 'Cleo, I'm sorry, darling.'

'Don't call me that.' He could see her fight for composure, then she turned back. 'Can't you tell Grandfather what a rake Dryton is?'

'It won't make any difference. The duke is of a generation where gentlemen were expected to behave like that and ladies were expected to ignore it. He'd only find someone else anyway.' That was not the solution, but what was? He could not allow her to be forced to marry into complete unhappiness and yet he had no right to help her.

'Very true,' Cleo said. 'I can see that I will have to take things into my own hands. Can I trust you not to tell Grandfather we have had this conversation?'

'Of course.' He could see from her face that there was no *of course* about it. 'I swear. Cleo, what are you plotting?' Something dangerous, something that would ruin her, he was horribly certain and if he hadn't been so damned worried about his precious honour and duty in the first place then she wouldn't need to.

'Don't worry, Lord Quintus.' Tidy again, she reached for her parasol and stood up. 'I am not considering a career on the streets.'

He let her go ahead of him, watched as she went to join Maggie and the footman and turned back towards Grosvenor Square. He did not follow her.

Quin arrived on the Duke of St Osyth's doorstep two days after the encounter in Hyde Park within an hour of receiving a curt summons from his Grace. He knew himself to be immaculately turned out and his expression calm as the butler opened the door and pronounced, 'You are expected, my lord', but his internal state was anything but tranquil.

He had been trying to think of a way to influence St Osyth, a way of helping him understand his granddaughter, but he could come up with nothing. Now he decided to just tell the man straight that he was driving Cleo to despair.

The butler swept him straight into the duke's study. Quin bowed slightly. 'Good morning, Your Grace.' *Might as well be hanged for a sheep as a lamb*, he thought as he smiled and waited for the older man to speak. *Go down with all guns blazing and tell him what you think of him for putting political and dynastic consideration before his granddaughter's happiness and well-being.*

The duke got up and waved him to a chair. 'Sit. Damn bad business, this.' He seemed more worried than hostile.

'Your note was not explicit, Your Grace.' His stomach clenched. *God, I'm too late.*

'She's bolted. Cleo, I mean. Left during the night last night, through the kitchens, it seems. That half-trained woman of hers went with her.'

Thank heavens for that small mercy. Maggie was

streetwise and tough, although that hadn't stopped the pair of them getting into trouble in Syracuse, he thought with a stab of real anxiety.

'That is extremely worrying, Your Grace.' *I sound like some smooth diplomat. War has broken out? How inconvenient. A young woman is alone and unprotected in London? How worrying.* Quin gritted his teeth on the angry words. 'Have you any inkling why?'

'Taken against the man I intend her to marry, I suspect, foolish chit. Anyone would think she was some lovelorn girl barely out, not a widow of three and twenty.'

'Perhaps she has run to a man?'

'She doesn't know any except you.'

Was that an accusation? Quin took a deep breath through his nose, held it until the urge to call the man out subsided, and said, 'I can assure you, Miss Woodward was not on my doorstep this morning. I have not seen her for days.' *And she won't come to me, she doesn't trust me.* 'Has she money?'

'A few sovereigns. She left her aunt's jewels and she took only walking and morning gowns, nightwear, that sort of thing. Enough for a couple of portmanteaux.'

'Might I suggest Bow Street, Your Grace? Or a private enquiry agent.'

'Damn it, I am St Osyth! I won't have some grubby lout prying into my business. You find her, Deverall.' He glared at him. 'Money no object, just send me a round total of your expenses at the end of it. No scandal, that's all.'

Quin found he was so angry that he dared not speak.

'You aren't tied up with some mission or another,

are you? Not leaving on the noon tide for Russia?' the duke snapped when Quin remained silent.

All he had planned was the courtship of Lady Caroline and that could wait. Everything could wait. 'No, Your Grace. I was merely…' *Controlling myself.* 'Thinking. Have you any idea where her woman lives?' Cleo might have gone there, but he doubted it. She would not want to bring the duke's wrath down on the head of Maggie's family. The duke shook his head. 'Did she leave a note? Has she made female friends?'

'No note. And she's been too busy for such fripperies as friends. Time enough for tea parties when she's married.'

Quin took a firm hold on his temper at the thought of Cleo, lonely and adrift on this emotional desert island where he had stranded her. 'I must take my secretary into my confidence, Your Grace. He is perfectly discreet and with his help I can work faster.'

'Very well. Keep me informed twice a day.'

Quin stood, 'I will let you know when I have something to report. Anything else is simply a waste of time better spent searching. Good day.'

Damned old autocrat, Quin fumed as he ran down the steps and hailed a cab. 'Albany and fast.'

George Baldwin was sitting at his desk when Quin strode in. 'The invitations—'

'Leave them. Miss Woodward is missing.'

'Miss Woodward? As in the Duke of—'

'Exactly. She has left home and nothing, not a whisper of this, must get out.'

'Not a man, I assume?'

Quin shook his head. 'I've got to think.' He slumped into a wing-back armchair, flung one leg over the arm and closed his eyes. *Cleo. Would she try to leave London? No, she knows nowhere else and besides, she'll understand the way a great city can hide people. She will try to earn her living honestly, but how? She has no qualifications for anything except...*

'Languages!'

'My lord?'

'Miss Woodward speaks French, Italian, modern Greek and Arabic.'

Baldwin, always fast on the uptake, reached for three books from beside the desk. 'Let's see what the directories have for translators and educational services.' He glanced up from where he was beginning a list. 'We'll find her, my lord. Don't worry.'

Quin reached for another book and began to search, unsettled by that reassuring smile. It was as if George thought Quin had lost someone of his own. He flattened the pages open at the right spot and pushed it across to George. *Who do I think I am fooling? Myself, probably. This is Cleo. My Cleo, and she is all that matters.*

Quin studied the list in his hand and checked the address in Wimpole Street. Eight down, six more to go. He wondered how George was getting on with his list since they had met for a snatched mutton chop and pint of ale at the Red Lion just off Piccadilly. The brass plate on the door was well polished and respectable, as was the location. *Throcking and Trimm. Confidential translation services. Linguistic tuition.*

He thought he would probably still be repeating his

story in his sleep. 'Good afternoon. I am travelling to the eastern Mediterranean on family business and require some basic Arabic tuition. It is urgent and I do not care what age, sex or nationality the tutor is.'

'Good afternoon, sir. I am Mr Trimm.' The gentleman behind the desk in the office appeared to have been polished to a high gleam from the top of his bald head to the toecaps of his boots. 'Kindly take a seat and I will check our files. Arabic is not a common language, you understand… Ah.' He riffled through and removed a slip of paper. 'We have one tutor at the moment for Arabic, but I am afraid they have only just joined us. I have not yet had the opportunity to assess their work. However, by next week I am sure I will have fully tested their abilities.'

Mr Trimm put down the slip and Quin strained to read it unobtrusively upside down. Impossible.

'I am in rather a hurry and none of the other agencies I have approached have been able to help me. A young man, is it? Perhaps I can interview him myself if you let me have his direction.'

'A lady, actually. I am afraid we cannot give out addresses. However, I can write to her and ask her to attend the office tomorrow, if that would suit?'

'Excellent,' Quin said. He lifted his hat as if to replace it on his head. 'About two?' The hat dropped along with his gloves and cane as he made a show of catching it. The little bud vase on the desk overturned, spilling water across the surface. Quin's elbow knocked the filing drawer, sending it to the floor and Mr Trimm, with a small shriek, dived for it.

Quin leaned across the desk, righted the bud vase,

dropped a copy of *The Times* on the puddle of water and spun the index slip around.

> *Mrs Anthony*
> *Walker's Lodging House*
> *3 Trivett Street*

He pushed it back and fell to his knees, murmuring apologies.

'Not at all, sir, not at all. I will just pick this up and then I will take your details. Oh dear...'

Quin slipped quietly out of the door and hailed a cab. *Mrs Anthony—and Cleopatra...it has to be her.*

'I imagine school is like this,' Cleo said with a sigh and blotted the fair copy of the translation before looking to see what else she still had to do. Arabic into English. Greek into Italian, English into French. Mr Trimm was very thorough, but then, it had seemed a most respectable agency and the rates he had quoted seemed reasonable.

'Wouldn't know—dame school wasn't like that.' Maggie shook her duster out of the window. 'This place isn't bad, but they could do with a bit more spit and polish.'

Two rooms—one shared bedroom and what was optimistically described as a parlour—and the right to cook their own food in the kitchen and have a shovelful of coals every day, would take all of Cleo's money in three weeks. Earning was essential, although Maggie declared that she'd soon find a job in one of the inns and chop houses in the area.

'There's someone at the front door—sounds like a

row,' Maggie said unnecessarily as raised voices penetrated from the landing. The thin panels rattled as someone knocked and their landlady's voice could be heard raised in protest.

''Ere, I don't hold with callers in rooms. There's a parlour downstairs for that. This is a respectable house, I'll have you know. I'll not have some rake upstairs!'

'But I am a very respectable rake, madam,' a familiar voice said.

Cleo dropped the pen, heedless of ink splatters. *'Quin.'*

'Well, that's that,' Maggie said with a grimace. 'We're too high up to climb out of the window. I'd best open the door and we'll see if we can make a break for it when we get outside.'

Cleo shouldn't have been glad to see him, elegant and faintly smiling while Mrs Walker brandished a large wooden spoon and threatened to call the Watch, but she was. So very, very glad, just for a second. Then the unhappiness flooded back.

'Good afternoon, my lord.'

'Good afternoon, Mrs Anthony, Miss Maggie.' Quin stepped inside and closed the door firmly on the furious landlady. 'I suggest you pack immediately for I do believe she means to call the nearest Charlie with his stick to have me thrown down the stairs.'

'You have come to take me back to Grosvenor Square.' It felt better to be standing. Cleo put her shoulders back and her chin up.

'No… Pack and come back with me to Albany and we can talk. Cleo, don't look at me like that.' Quin reached out and touched her cheek with the back of his hand.

Her eyes stung, her lids felt heavy. Cleo closed them for a moment until she had the tears under control. Quin would take her back, of course, but at least it was a respite. 'How did you find me?' she asked when she had her voice under control.

'I thought about how you might earn your living and then Baldwin and I worked our way through all the likely agencies until I found Mr Trimm.' Quin was talking in a calm, conversational tone as he ushered them out and down the stairs, pausing on the landing to juggle the portmanteaux into one hand while he offered several banknotes to Mrs Walker. The landlady changed from fury to fawning in the time it took her to look at what she had in her hand.

'George is holding the fort,' Quin continued as he opened the door of the waiting hackney carriage and helped them in. 'The duke has been sending messengers demanding news of my progress at hourly intervals, which is a trifle wearying.'

'My grandfather came to you for help?'

'He summoned me,' Quin said and leaned across to drop the blinds. 'He told me to cancel whatever foreign trip I was about to embark upon and find you.'

'He is the limit! The arrogance of the man is incredible—as if you would just drop everything and do as he asks.' Cleo thought for a moment. 'But you did, didn't you?'

'I was worried about you, Cleo. You and Maggie together are bright and you are brave, but you are not used to the perils of London and he told me you had little money. After that morning in the park I knew you were desperate.'

Nice sentiments. Quin had warned her about Dryton, he was kind to her—but he still answered to her grandfather. She was sore with disappointment and fearful of what would happen now, but most of all she was saddened that it had been Quin who had tracked her down.

There was no point in quarrelling about that now. 'Grandfather told me I must consider proposals,' she said bitterly. 'I disliked Dryton on sight, but I suppose all the rest will be as bad. It is so hypocritical, these double standards for men and women.' She fell silent, wishing the blinds were up so she could at least look out of the window and pretend this was not happening. *Coward.* 'Quin—'

'No, I do not, if you are about to ask me if I keep a mistress,' Quin said. 'I am not a monk, I have liaisons. I believe that marriage vows are made to be kept,' he added.

That is nice for Lady Caroline, Cleo thought. *Has he asked her yet?* Perhaps the duke's imperious summons had interrupted his courtship. He must be so weary of her. 'You had best take me back to Grosvenor Square. I cannot see there is anything to talk about.'

'I think there is,' Quin said. The carriage turned sharply and then stopped. 'Here we are. Pull down your veil, Cleo.'

She stepped down into a rectangular courtyard of red brick with what looked like an impressive house at one end. Quin paid the driver and brought them through the wide door under its elaborate fanlight. In front of them stretched a long paved corridor, open at the sides.

Quin nodded to a porter and led them along it. 'My

chambers are along here. Hurry, I do not want you seen.' He opened a door, calling, 'George!'

'My lord.' The secretary Cleo remembered from her arrival in London appeared from a room in his shirt-sleeves. 'I beg your pardon, Miss Woodward. Excuse my undress.'

'George. Pack a bag, take money for a few days and escort Miss Maggie here to her family, send to let me know where you are and stay in the area until you hear from me. I want Miss Maggie looked after and I do not want you involved in this any more than you are already.'

'Miss Cleo needs me,' Maggie protested as the sec-retary nodded and disappeared back into the room

'She has me. The duke is not a man to take kindly to being thwarted. If he should decide to cast blame on you for this, I want you somewhere safe. I wouldn't put it past him to have you arrested for kidnapping or procuring if the mood takes him.'

'Ready, my lord. I've taken fifty pounds from the strong box. Off we go, Miss Maggie.'

'But—'

'Go,' Cleo urged. 'Lord Quintus is right, I do not want you blamed in any way. I will write,' she called as George took Maggie's arm, checked which was her bag and hurried her out, still faintly protesting.

She was alone now, with only Quin between her and her gilded prison.

Chapter Twenty-Two

'In here.' Quin opened the door to a sitting room. 'Off with your bonnet and pelisse and make yourself comfortable. We have planning to do.' He tugged the bell pull as she obeyed, still too tired and shocked to protest. Everything was happening too fast and none of it was good, not even being with Quin. That just hurt.

'My lord?' A dapper little man, a valet, Cleo supposed, came in. 'Ma'am.'

'Miss Woodward, this is Godley. Godley, you have become exceedingly unobservant, I trust? Excellent. Please make up the bedchamber Mr Baldwin uses when he stays over. Hot water, of course, but first tea, I think.'

'You want me to stay? To hide here?' Cleo looked around at the very masculine room with its leather chairs, desk, bookshelves and tray of decanters. There was a small table with packs of cards in the window and a gun rack on the wall. A riding whip and several canes were stuck in a stand. It suited Quin. Its smell of leather and wood smoke and a faint hint of citrus made her think of his skin...

'I suspect that keeping you here in bachelor apartments will be noticed soon enough. But one night will let you rest, I think. Ah, tea and crumpets. And cake, wonderful. Thank you, Godley.' He sat back and studied Cleo.

She stared back. *I must look a sight. I'm tired, and wearing my plainest clothes and I haven't been able to wash in more than a basin of warm water for two days and I'm at my wits' end.*

'Eat.' Quin poured her tea when it became obvious that she was not going to do the ladylike thing and take control of the tea tray. He slathered butter on to two crumpets and passed her the plate. 'Don't let them get cold. You need food and a hot bath and a good night's sleep, Cleo.'

The crumpets were delicious, hot and light and buttery. She drained her cup and Quin refilled it. Finally she found her voice. 'Eating and bathing I am capable of. I doubt I could sleep.'

'You expect me to send a note to the duke the moment your eyes are closed?' Quin studied the cake plate as though it was of absorbing interest. When he lifted his gaze to her she was shocked at the sharp intent in his eyes. 'I suppose I cannot blame you.' He put down his cup and saucer. 'Shall we discuss what is to be done now, then?'

'You have a plan?' Cleo asked. How ridiculous that she still clung to the hope that he could save her, set her free, show that she mattered more than his career, his good name. *How selfish you are, Cleo Woodward,* she chided herself. *And how foolish.*

'Yes, I have a plan. You tell me what you want to do and I will help you do it.'

* * *

'But I was doing what I wanted…' Cleo looked as though she was holding on to her temper by her fingernails, but Quin suspected she was simply holding herself together by sheer will-power. *She must be exhausted and frightened*, he thought. And being Cleo she would not want fussing over.

'You were doing the only respectable thing you could think of under the circumstances. Tell me what you would do if you had control of that money your father gave you.'

'If! Oh, very well, if we must play foolish games. I would find a small house in some respectable town. One with a theatre, perhaps, good shops, a library, pleasant company. I would be a widow again. My husband would have died in Egypt. Perhaps I would give language lessons to young ladies… What is the point of this?'

She wants so little and I could provide it so easily. Quin spoke rapidly, working it out as he went. 'I will give you the money to do that. I will put it all in George's hands so I can tell your grandfather with a clear conscience that I do not know where you are. George will find you a house, manage the funds for you.'

'But what funds?'

'I will provide you with sufficient.'

'I cannot take money from you! What does that make me?' He expected anger, he had not foreseen the tears that sparked in her eyes or the look of hurt.

'It makes you the lady to whom I am in debt for my life twice over. The lady whose life I have interfered in and to whom I now wish to make some small recompense.'

'I should say *no.*' Cleo stared into her teacup as though seeking to read wisdom in the dregs. She got to her feet and walked away from him to stare, apparently entranced, at a set of atlases on the bookshelf. He could almost hear her thinking. Quin willed himself into stillness and watched the tall, slender figure. She was tired, he could tell by the infinitesimal droop of her shoulders, the less-than-perfect balance of her spine. He wanted to hold her, kiss her, undress her and wash her in the warm bath water, then towel her dry and tuck her up in bed to sleep while he paced through a sleepless night of frustration.

The wave of tenderness, the acceptance of restraint. It began to puzzle him that he cared so much. Perhaps the way he felt was the weight on his conscience lifting, the realisation that he could help Cleo.

'Do you give me your word that this isn't simply a ruse?' She turned as she spoke and he saw the mistrust and, beneath it, something utterly naked and vulnerable.

She expects to be hurt, used, betrayed, he realised. *Her father, her husband, the French officials, her grandfather—and me. We have all deceived her for our own purposes. No wonder she cannot trust.* 'I give you my word,' Quin said and saw the flicker in her eyes as she noticed his hesitation. He saw, too, the moment when she decide to risk it as she had before. Surely it meant something, that she was prepared to try again when he had betrayed her before?

'I think I would like one of your hugs,' Cleo said, and ran into his arms.

Quin held her tightly to him, buried his face in her hair and breathed in warm woman, plain soap, the faintly spicy scent of her skin, the indefinable something that was Cleo. He wanted to kiss her, but that was not what she needed now, so he contented himself with stroking her back and murmuring nonsense until she relaxed with a sigh and pulled back a little.

'Does this mean I am forgiven?' Quin asked.

'Forgiven? Yes,' she agreed.

'But you haven't forgotten and you still are not certain of me, are you?' He was a fool to keep pressing when he knew he was not going to like the answer.

'No,' she said slowly, her eyes still locked with his. 'I have learned that you are very clever with words and with the finer points of truth and honour.'

Well, you asked for that, don't dig any deeper. 'Come, the water will have heated. I will call for your bath. The room is this way.'

She followed him into the second bedchamber. Godley had made up the bed and turned down the covers. There was the tub before the fire and a pile of towels, soap and his big sponge. 'Go behind the screen and start undressing and I'll help with the water,' Quin said.

Cleo looked around the small, very masculine room, smiled at him and slipped behind the Cordoba leather screen.

Quin and Godley carried in the buckets until the tub was three-quarters full, placed two jugs of rinsing water by the side and then the valet took himself off.

'Cleo, the bath is ready.' It was very quiet behind the screen.

'I need help.'

He should have thought. Without her maid Cleo was at the mercy of buttons and pins she could not reach, stay laces she could not untie. Quin stamped on the rush of arousal that the thought of undressing Cleo provoked. 'Right. I'll shut my eyes.'

'There is no need.' She came out from behind the screen, barefoot, her hair down and braided into one long plait. She was a trifle pink in the cheeks, but remarkably composed.

But of course, she had been married and they had been intimate... 'Turn around then.' He began on the buttons at the back of her gown. Tiny, infuriating things.

'I almost saw you bathing once before, when we first met.' Was he talking to help her nerves or to keep his need to take her in his arms under control? 'I lay on top of that dune, burning up with fever, trying to think rationally about whether I should watch any longer or make my move. I was so far from my right mind that it took me several minutes to realise what you were about and that I was within an inch of making a Peeping Tom of myself.'

Cleo laughed, the first happy sound he had heard her make since he had found her that day. She stood there in her shift and petticoat, twisting her long plait into a coronet on top of her head and skewering it with a pin. Quin thought he had never seen anything more feminine, more sensual or more tempting.

'Stay now.' She wriggled out of the gown and laid it over a stool, then came back so he could tackle her laces.

It was his fantasy become real. 'No!'

'But you will,' she stated, looking back over her shoulder as the corset came loose. 'Quin, we want each other, we both know it. I am not some innocent little virgin. I have been married, I understand what physical desire is—and I feel it now. So do you.'

'How can you mistrust me so much and yet want this?'

'I trust you to make love to me, to make me feel better tonight, to show me that you care for me. It… hurt when you would not lie with me.'

What was right? Quin shut his eyes on the sight of her and found her scent made his head spin. Yes, he wanted her, had wanted her since he set eyes on her. She was a grown woman who knew her own mind and she wanted this, now and with him.

'It hurt me, too,' Quin said and opened his eyes. 'I would be honoured to lie with you.'

Cleo smiled, shy and suddenly vulnerable as she shed her few remaining garments and stepped naked into the water. It was painful, the beauty, the desire, the need for her.

'Quin?' She looked back over her shoulder again, unconsciously seductive, an uncertain water nymph.

Quin pulled himself together, determined never to make her feel unsure ever again. 'Why do I see you in terms of classical mythology?' he said as he took off his coat and cufflinks and began to roll up his sleeves. 'First a maenad, now a water nymph.'

'Because you are overeducated?' Cleo suggested, laughing up at him, and he fell to his knees and laughed with her.

'No,' Quin retorted, working up a lather. 'Because you are beautiful and timeless and…ancient.' He began to soap her back, loving the slide of his palm over the elegant curves, running his thumb down the bumps of her spine. She was still too thin.

'Ancient?' she protested.

'Eternal, like one of those wonderful Greek statues.

So alive, so old and yet so young, looking as though they knew the wisdom of the ages.'

'Quin, that is lovely.' She dropped her head back so she was looking up into his face. Quin abandoned the soap, rational thought and self-control, slid his arms around her and kissed the soft mouth offered to him so freely.

Oh, yes, I want you, Quin thought as Cleo's lips opened to him and he explored her with his tongue and lips and breath. There was desire, a white-hot wire through his veins, heating his blood, hardening his aching body into readiness, but there was also tenderness, caring, the overwhelming feeling that he had come home at last.

She arched against his hand and he realised he was cupping her left breast, small and prefect, the nipple hardening against his palm, the skin as soft and smooth as a fresh fig with the bloom still on it.

'Cleo.'

'Ah, yes,' she murmured as though her name had been a question, and curled her arms around his neck so it was easy to lift her from the water and hold her against him. 'I'm soaking you,' she protested, but she did not try to free herself.

Quin stood, snagged a towel from the pile and dropped it on to the bed before laying her down. He brought more towels and began to dry her, arms and legs and face first, then her breast and waist, catching her up against him so he could stroke the towel down her back. When he laid her back down she moved her legs apart a little, watching him from beneath the sweep of her lashes, sensual and relaxed.

'You are like the cat goddess Bastet, again,' he murmured, patting the dark curls dry, the breath thick in his throat.

'Again?'

'There have been moments when I have thought of you like that.'

Something passed across her face, an expression too fleeting for him to catch. 'You mean you have thought of me with…desire before now?' she asked. There was that look again—uncertainty and past hurt.

'You think I did not, from the beginning? What about Cairo and on board ship? That first kiss at Koum Ombo?'

'You stopped at Cairo and on the ship, you did not want me, you were only being kind.' Cleo sat up and curled against the pillow, pulling the towel around her.

'Kind!' Quin tossed the rest of the damp towels into a corner. 'I was being frustrated and attempting, Heaven help me, to do the honourable thing. Do you really think I didn't want you?'

'Not *me*,' she said, her gaze on her clasped hands. 'I realise you wanted sex, men always do, but I thought it was easy for you to stop because it was just me.'

'Hell, Cleo.' Quin was not sure whether to laugh or drop his head in his hands. 'There I was, nobly suffering agonising balls' ache and sleepless nights and you were insulted by my restraint?'

'You were frustrated?' She sat bolt upright, curled her arms around her knees and smiled at him, her eyes sparkling with very feminine pleasure.

'And aching. Cleo, I want you. I have always wanted you, even when you were torturing me with wet sheets and sharp implements and icy looks.'

'Then come to bed with me now.'

I could drown in those eyes, he thought. Quin stood up and began to strip off his clothes.

At last. His naked body was surprisingly unfamiliar, despite the fact that she had handled it while he was unconscious. A conscious, active man was something else entirely, Cleo mused as she allowed herself the indulgence of openly watching the play of his muscles as Quin lifted the wet shirt over his head, bent to his shoes, tugged off his breeches. *He was not lying about wanting me.* She felt her own body soften and grow moist.

'Hurry,' she whispered.

'Stop it,' Quin said as he lay down beside her. 'You are doing nothing at all for my self-control.'

'I don't want your self-control.' She shifted down the bed, opened her arms to him, and, wantonly, her legs.

Quin's weight over her was bliss. His heat and the texture of his skin, the pressure against her belly, the teasing friction of hair against her nipples turned longing into desperation. Her body was tightening painfully, as close to the edge as if they had been making love for an hour.

She arched up, inciting him, needing him inside her, needing to surround him with love and passion and urgency. Quin shifted and she felt him slide between the wet, swollen folds, pressing, caressing, but not penetrating. He gave a deep sigh and rested his forehead against hers.

'You are so beautiful, Cleo,' he murmured and took her mouth in a deep, demanding kiss even as he began to move against her, tightening the coiling desire in her to desperation point. She wanted him inside her and yet she wanted him to keep on doing exactly what he was doing; she wanted his mouth on hers, possessive, demanding, and she wanted to scream his name, bite the muscled arms that caged her.

And then Quin tilted his hips, changed the angle of the pressure until there was nothing in her consciousness except that one pulsating focus of need. Lights flashed behind her closed lids, the spiral knotted, broke, unravelled and she screamed his name against his lips and lost herself utterly.

Cleo came to herself to find that Quin had not moved except to raise his head. She looked up into his eyes, dark with desire, and freed one hand from the sheets she had twisted it into to touch his cheek, wondering if this was not a dream.

'Don't cry,' he said softly.

'I'm not.' It seemed she could speak.

'Must be rain then.' He kissed the corners of her eyes and then brushed his mouth to hers so she could taste the salt. Then, lips still brushing hers, he eased himself into her in one long, slow, perfect thrust.

It had been a long time since Thierry and Quin was not, she thought with fleeting apprehension, a small man, but he was perfect for her body. She focused on relaxing, accepting, and then she found those almost forgotten inner muscles and began to use them to caress Quin, even as her hands slid over his shoulders and her tongue thrust against his.

He groaned, deep in his chest, and began to move in long, hard, slow strokes. Cleo gasped, tried to hang on to some kind of control and failed, convulsing around him as he arched over her, thrust one more time and came with her, his shout muffled in her hair, his body wrapping hers within his powerful embrace.

I love you, she whispered silently as she cradled his head against her breast and let her trembling body grow still and calm in the shelter of his.

Chapter Twenty-Three

Cleo woke in the dawn light and lay watching Quin as he slept beside her. They had woken and made love twice in the night, once gently, once with an explosive passion that shook her to the core.

Now the morning stubble darkened his jaw, his lips were slightly parted and his hair was tousled in a way that would have been endearing if it was not so erotic. *Oh, my love, how am I going to manage without you?*

As if she had said the words aloud Quin's eyes opened. He lay without speaking, looking at her. The light waxed and suddenly spilled through the gap in the curtains, across her face. Cleo blinked and Quin came back into focus. He was looking at her as though he had never seen her before, as though she was something strange and wonderful and yet…frightening. But that was absurd, she had never seen Quin frightened.

'Quin?' She touched his face and he pulled her to him, rolled on top of her and sank, without hesitation, into her body. Then he lay there, caging her with his body, looking down into her eyes.

'Oh, Cleo,' he murmured. 'What a fool I have been.'

He kissed her before she could speak and kept kissing her as he made slow, achingly tender love to her.

Goodbye, she thought. *He is saying goodbye.* And then what he was doing with his body, with his hands and his mouth, made all thought impossible.

'More toast?' Quin was watching her with amusement and a tenderness that made Cleo's heart stutter. *He feels even more guilty now we have made love.*

'You have fed me until I am fit for nothing but a day in bed to sleep it off,' she protested, pretending lightheartedness as she gazed at the wreckage of Godley's idea of an intimate breakfast *à deux*.

'There are things to be done, so I'm afraid that is out of the question. We had best take the carriage out this morning,' he added and got up from the table, his expression suddenly back to what she thought of as the *diplomatic mask*.

'Yes, of course.' Lawyers and banks, she supposed. 'I will get ready and find a veil.'

In the gloom of the closed carriage Quin was silent. His profile seemed somehow distant and austere as though he was preparing for some unpleasant task. Cleo gave herself a little shake for Gothic imaginings.

The carriage came to a halt, the groom opened the door and let down the step and Quin got out, then turned to hold out his hand to her.

Cleo stepped down, glanced around, then froze. The house in front of her with its ornate railings and wide front door was very familiar. She looked wildly from side to side, there was no mistake. This was Grosvenor Square and her grandfather's house.

'No!' She tugged at Quin's hand and he released

his grip. '*No*. I trusted you. I believed you.' *Oh such a fool, such a fool for love.* She began to back away. He could run her down in a moment, she knew that, but she was not going to go without a struggle.

'Cleo, think. You trusted me yesterday, last night. Trust me now.' Quin made no move to seize her. 'Listen to your feelings, not your fears.'

Cleo edged a little further along the pavement. Mama used to say, *If something seems too good to be true, it probably is.* She should listen to her common sense—of course Quin would not sacrifice his brilliant career for her, discard a beautiful, sophisticated bride for her.

'My feelings? What do you know about feelings other than how to manipulate them? You gave me your word—how have you managed to twist that this time?'

'Last night I meant what I said, that I would find you a house and give you the means to start a new life.'

'And now?'

'I changed my mind. Come, we cannot discuss this here.' He took her arm and pulled her towards the garden, took a key from his pocket to open the gate and guided her inside.

'Changed your mind?' She could hardly speak for the bitterness of the pain. 'After last night? After this morning?'

'I realised this morning just why I have been so damnable confused and unhappy about all of this,' Quin said.

'*You* have been confused and unhappy? Well, that at least we share!'

'I can only ask you to forgive me for not telling you the truth in Egypt, on the voyage. I can only tell you that I never wanted anything but your welfare and hope that you believe me. I did what I thought was right and all those rights made one dreadful wrong, Cleo. But I know this: to let you go off alone to spend the rest of your life in hiding, living a lie—that would be the worst wrong of all.'

'And so you bring me back to my cage.'

'I bring you back and hope that you can trust me one last time. Hope that what I thought I saw in your eyes, and felt in your lovemaking, is not some illusion.' Quin took a step and caught her hands in his. 'Come with me now. Forgive me. I swear, if you do not want the solution that I will offer, then I will take you out of there, whatever it takes.'

'No.' She began to back towards the gate and he did nothing to stop her. She could not break eye contact with him as he stood there silent, watching her leave.

'Let George know how to contact you. He will make arrangements with whatever solicitor you choose. I will not be able to find you,' Quin said. His voice was steady, the look in his eyes was bleak.

That look stopped her in her tracks. *I love him and up to now I have given him nothing that was not easy to give, nothing that I did not want, in my heart, for him to have. I can give him this, my trust, and if I am wrong... To the devil with common sense,* she thought. *Love him and take the consequences.*

Cleo walked back and put her hand on Quin's arm. 'I will go with you.'

He smiled then, that elusive quirk of the lips that almost made a dent in his cheek, but not quite. 'Let us get this done.'

The butler admitted them. 'Welcome home, Miss

Woodward. His Grace is in the library, I will announce you.' He sounded relieved to see her, presumably her grandfather had been making life hell for all and sundry.

'Miss Woodward, Lord Quintus Deverall, Your Grace.'

It was too quick, she had not had the chance to collect herself, Cleo realised. She made herself unclench her fingers from Quin's arm. If he was about to hand her over like a stray dog, then she was not going to put up an undignified fight.

'You found her!' The duke came round the desk and shook Quin's hand. 'I knew I could rely on you, Deverall.' He frowned at Cleo. 'Where the blazes have you been, you wretched girl? You have completely compromised yourself: it is going to take a great deal of effort to salvage this mess.'

'Kindly do not speak to Miss Woodward in that tone, Your Grace,' Quin said. 'Miss Woodward has been in a respectable lodging house chaperoned by her maid. And then she has been with me.'

'Excellent.' The duke stalked back to his chair, then something in Quin's tone seemed to penetrate. 'With you?'

'Yes, Your Grace. With me. Cleo is indeed compromised and beyond your powers to cover up.'

All her grandfather's icy poise seemed to desert him. His face darkened and he thumped his fist on to the desk. 'You damned rake!'

'You will not swear in front of Miss Woodward, Your Grace,' Quin said calmly. He turned to her, went down on one knee and said simply, 'Marry me, Cleo.'

The world tilted and then righted itself. Cleo found

she could speak. 'Why? Because you have compromised me?'

'Because I love you. I must admit to being exceedingly obtuse. I only realised this morning, in bed.'

Over his head she saw the duke's face go red. 'You *what*?'

'Grandfather. I need to speak to Quin alone.' Could it be true? Could he really mean it?

'And I need to take a shotgun to him!'

Quin stood up. 'Excuse me, Your Grace. Cleo?'

'This way.' She led him out of the study and into the deserted dining room and locked the door behind them. 'Quin, if this is belated guilt for lying with me…'

'No, it is not belated guilt for anything, it is simply the first true thing I can be certain of in a very long time. I love you, Cleo. You have a great deal to forgive me for, I know that. The thing that I find hardest to forgive is that it took me so long to realise what I felt for you was not simply desire or liking.'

'It's impossible.' Cleo realised she was wringing her hands and forced herself to stop.

'What exactly is impossible about it?' Quin enquired. 'I have a courtesy title, a small estate, a healthy income and all my parts are in full working order, as you have seen for yourself. I do not keep mistresses, take snuff, gamble to excess, smoke and I am not going bald. And all my teeth are my own.'

He must have hoped to lighten the atmosphere, but instead his words moved Cleo from bewilderment to something near tears. 'It would ruin you, Quin. You heard Grandfather just now. He would descend on the Foreign Office and denounce you. You would have made an enemy of an incredibly powerful man, upset the government and you will never get preferment, much less end up an ambassador.

'And Lady Caroline,' she went on, desperate to lay it all out so he would stop this gallant nonsense and save himself. 'She is the perfect wife for you. What about her?'

'I have said nothing to her, nor to her father, that would lead them to expect a declaration. I am not in any way committed.' He smiled at her. 'Cleo, it is you I love, not her.'

'But I have so much to learn of society. I have no accomplishments, no experience.'

'You have languages and strong nerves,' Quin countered. 'You are not disconcerted by strange places and you have excellent health. You learn fast. Cleo, my love, the worst that can happen is the end of my diplomatic career. If that happens, then I have an estate and investments to fall back on. We won't starve, Cleo.'

'That is not what I am worried about,' she said vaguely. 'I know more recipes for rice and scrawny chicken than you can imagine, I can keep house on a pittance.' She realised what she was saying. 'How can I risk being the death of the one thing you really want in life and ruining your opportunity to make the break from your father that is so important?'

'I find those do not matter so desperately, not any more,' he said. 'I know who I am now, I know what I can achieve. I only need you to complete me.

'I thought my honour defined me, that somehow I had to be a better man than my father believed me and a more honourable one than my true father had been. Now I know that all that matters is listening to my heart and my conscience. I love you, Cleo. Can you forgive me?'

It was true, Cleo knew it in her bones, her blood, her heart. He loved her and perhaps he had for a long time. He had wanted, always, to do the right thing and now he was hurting and she could not bear that.

'How can I not?' she asked him and opened her arms. 'I love you and I have for so long, Quin.'

He walked into her embrace and closed his arms to hold her against his chest. 'I had hoped, last night. I feared I was deluding myself. Will you marry me, Cleo?'

'I will.' It was a promise and a vow and there was nothing else to say as Quin's kiss took her breath away.

'Enough of this sentimental twaddle,' the duke snapped half an hour later. 'I'll see you ruined, Deverall.'

'No, you will not, not unless you wish to make life more difficult for your granddaughter.' Quin dragged his gaze away from her face with an effort. 'You can ruin my career, but we'll not starve and society loves a romantic scandal—it is your dignity that will suffer if you try to hinder us.'

'You—the mongrel in the Deverall kennel daring to aspire to the granddaughter of St Osyth? *Pah*.' The duke flung himself down into his chair.

Quin smiled. 'I am a perfectly acceptable match for the daughter of an eccentric baronet and a lady who eloped and was cast off by her family.'

'Why, damn it?' the duke demanded.

'Because I love her,' Quin said simply.

'And I love him.' Cleo's fingers closed tight on his hand.

'Stop it!' St Osyth thundered. 'I can't bear it. The

pair of you are a sentimental disgrace, like some driv-elling pair of yokels. Cleo, you do not know about this man's parentage.'

'Yes, I do, he told me. Mine isn't much to brag about either. Besides, I would rather marry a man whose worth depends on his own intelligence, hard work and honour than some crony of yours.' She tucked her hand under Quin's elbow.

There was a long, simmering silence before the duke reached for the bell pull. 'I should send for my grooms and a horsewhip,' he said.

Quin made himself relax his fists. 'You are welcome to try, although I dislike the idea of hurting men who are only obeying orders.'

'Hah!'

Cranton entered. 'Your Grace?'

'A bottle of champagne. The best. And three glasses.' He waited until the door had closed behind the butler. 'I hope I know when to stop fighting for a lost cause. I wish you well of my granddaughter, Deverall. She'll lead you a merry dance.'

'You will not influence the Foreign Ministry against Quin?' Cleo asked.

'Stop it, Cleo,' Quin said. 'I will not beg for your grandfather's forbearance. I do not want his help.'

'Well, I want my money,' Cleo countered. 'The money Father let me have.'

'You'll have your mother's dowry,' snapped the duke. 'And don't you get on your high horse about that, Deverall.'

'I wouldn't dream of it, Your Grace. It is Cleo's by rights.'

'You'll get married in St George's in three months' time.'

'One month and Cleo will decide where.'

He saw Cleo bite her lip to hide the smile. 'St George's. It will be better for Quin's career if we have a big London wedding. And two weeks.'

'That will seem very rushed, tongues will wag.'

'Not if you put it about that I asked for Cleo's hand the day I brought her to you,' Quin said. 'You naturally wished her to acquire some town bronze before the engagement was announced. Just smile when you say it, Your Grace. Who would dare doubt you?'

'No one, if they know what is good for them. Well, Cleo. Your room is as you left it. I want to speak to Deverall about settlements.'

'I have to stay here?'

'Of course you do, Cleo.' Quin bent and kissed her. 'Trust him, my darling,' he whispered in her ear. 'You learned to trust me, he'll be easy in comparison.'

'There, Lady Quintus Deverall, is your new home.' Quin swung Cleo down from the chaise and pointed to a house nestling below the wooded shoulder of the hill. Golden stone glowed in the afternoon light and sweeping wings framed the central block.

'It manages to be grand and homely at the same time. I love it.' It was perfect. *Home, with Quin.*

'I haven't done much to it, I've been away too much, but you can do what you like to make it yours.' Quin leaned on the wheel and put his arm around her shoulders, pulling her close.

'Ours,' Cleo said and rested her head against his

shoulder. 'Will I be here very much alone? May I not travel with you?'

'Not when I am extracting beautiful women from foreign lands and kissing them senseless in the hope they'll admit to being spies,' Quin said. 'Otherwise, yes, of course.'

'You never kissed me senseless,' Cleo complained.

'Then I have not been trying hard enough.' Quin held the door for her to climb back into the chaise and told the postilions to drive on. 'Of course, we may decide to stay put when the children arrive.'

'We're back to the kissing then,' Cleo said. She had a niggling suspicion that decorating the nursery might be a priority, but it was too soon to be certain and they had only made love once. But still, she had hopes.

'I hope so,' Quin said and took her in his arms and proceeded to kiss her until the world was spinning. When the carriage came to a halt in front of the house she could only blink at it.

'I told the staff to make themselves scarce for two days,' Quin said as they reached the foot of the steps up to the front door. 'Food will appear, hot water will materialise, beds will be made, all apparently by ghosts.' He swept her up into his arms and climbed the steps. 'Even front doors will open by magic.' As he spoke the heavy panels swung open with a loud creak. Cleo thought she heard the quick scuff of footsteps and a muffled laugh, but there was no one in sight as they entered a wide hall with a staircase winding upwards like the coils of a nautilus shell.

'Are you hungry?' Quin asked.

'Only for you.'

'In that case, as you have been disappointed in my kissing—'

'I never said that!'

'—I intend to render you senseless, as requested.' Quin strode across the hall and up the stairs without, apparently, drawing breath. It was, Cleo decided, the most dashingly romantic sensation.

He shouldered open a door on the first landing. 'Your bedchamber, my lady. And rather more to the point, your bed.'

How he managed to undress her while kissing her, Cleo could never afterwards recall. And his own clothes seemed to melt away, although afterwards she found his shirt was ripped from neck to hem.

Her brain was most satisfactorily addled by the time he released her lips, only to start on her neck, then her shoulder and then her breasts. That was bliss, better than bliss. Quin could just stay there, kissing and nibbling and licking and gently biting and she would spin into one climax after another, she was certain.

But he abandoned her breast just when she was clutching the sheets and arching up into his mouth. He trailed kisses down her ribs, swirled his tongue into her naval, found an exquisitely sensitive spot on her hip bone, then proceeded down her left leg.

'What are you doing?' She managed to lever herself up on her elbows as he sucked her toes into his mouth and started to do improbably wonderful things to them.

'Kissing you,' Quin said as he moved to her right foot. 'It obviously needs more work as you aren't senseless yet.'

The back of her right knee was just as ticklish as her left, her hipbone just as sensitive on that side. And then he slid between her thighs, gently pushed her legs apart and began to kiss her intimately.

Cleo writhed and sobbed and begged, but Quin was relentless. He seemed to know to within a fraction of a second when the swirl of his tongue was about to tip her over into oblivion, to a hairsbreadth where the nip of his teeth was pleasure and not pain. The universe spun down to the place where Quin's mouth made love to her and then fractured into swirling stars and burning galaxies and he was in her arms again, and within her, and they were moving together in an aching harmony that ended, finally, blissfully, as they found a peak together and plunged off it, locked in love.

'Cleo?' Quin stretched with slow, luxurious delight, and looked down at his wife, twined about his body in sensual abandon.

'Mmm?'

'I love you.' It was very easy to say, when those three words were all he needed to make sense of the world.

'I hope so, after that,' she murmured against his collarbone. 'Have I told you recently that I love you, too?'

'I seem to recall it.'

'Are you happy?'

'Oh, yes. More than I can say.'

'Truly? She looked up, her eyes wide and soft, full of satisfied love.

'Truly. Trust me on that, Cleo.'

'Trust you, my love? Always and forever.'

* * * * *

Author Note

The military and political events in Egypt described here are as accurate as I can make them—and Napoleon really did promise his beleaguered Army of the East a shipload of entertainers to raise morale! Officers of the rank of general and above are real historical characters, everyone else is my invention.

I have used the place names that Europeans of the time would have used, taking an early nineteenth-century map as my guide. Their modern equivalents are given below in the order in which they are encountered in the story.

Koum Ombo—Kom Ombo
Shek Amer—Darau
Kene—Qena
Coseir—Kosir or Quseir
Benisouef—Beni Suef
Dashur—Dashur
Sakhara—Sakkara
Tora—now part of southern Cairo
Elkatta—El Khatatba

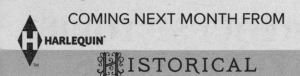

REQUEST YOUR FREE BOOKS!

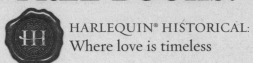

HARLEQUIN® HISTORICAL:
Where love is timeless

2 FREE NOVELS PLUS 2 FREE GIFTS!

YES! Please send me 2 FREE Harlequin® Historical novels and my 2 FREE gifts (gifts are worth about $10). After receiving them, if I don't wish to receive any more books, I can return the shipping statement marked "cancel." If I don't cancel, I will receive 6 brand-new novels every month and be billed just $5.44 per book in the U.S. or $5.74 per book in Canada. That's a savings of at least 16% off the cover price! It's quite a bargain! Shipping and handling is just 50¢ per book in the U.S. and 75¢ per book in Canada.* I understand that accepting the 2 free books and gifts places me under no obligation to buy anything. I can always return a shipment and cancel at any time. Even if I never buy another book, the two free books and gifts are mine to keep forever.

246/349 HDN F4ZY

Name	(PLEASE PRINT)	
Address		Apt. #
City	State/Prov.	Zip/Postal Code

Signature (if under 18, a parent or guardian must sign)

Mail to the **Harlequin® Reader Service:**
IN U.S.A.: P.O. Box 1867, Buffalo, NY 14240-1867
IN CANADA: P.O. Box 609, Fort Erie, Ontario L2A 5X3

Want to try two free books from another line?
Call 1-800-873-8635 or visit www.ReaderService.com.

* Terms and prices subject to change without notice. Prices do not include applicable taxes. Sales tax applicable in N.Y. Canadian residents will be charged applicable taxes. Offer not valid in Quebec. This offer is limited to one order per household. Not valid for current subscribers to Harlequin Historical books. All orders subject to credit approval. Credit or debit balances in a customer's account(s) may be offset by any other outstanding balance owed by or to the customer. Please allow 4 to 6 weeks for delivery. Offer available while quantities last.

Your Privacy—The Harlequin® Reader Service is committed to protecting your privacy. Our Privacy Policy is available online at www.ReaderService.com or upon request from the Harlequin Reader Service.

We make a portion of our mailing list available to reputable third parties that offer products we believe may interest you. If you prefer that we not exchange your name with third parties, or if you wish to clarify or modify your communication preferences, please visit us at www.ReaderService.com/consumerschoice or write to us at Harlequin Reader Service Preference Service, P.O. Box 9062, Buffalo, NY 14269. Include your complete name and address.

HHI13R

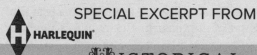
A Mouse, the heavier hand had scrawled next to the bit
about the ceremony, and underlined it.

Not of the upper ten thousand, her shocked eyes
discovered next.

Preferably an orphan.

Her stomach roiled as she recalled the look on
Lord Havelock's face when she'd told him, that fateful
night at the Crimmers, that she'd just lost her mother.
She'd thought he couldn't possibly have looked pleased
to hear she was all alone in the world, that surely she
must have been mistaken.

But she hadn't been.

She tottered back to the tea table and sank onto the chair
the waiter had so helpfully drawn up to it. And carried on
reading.

Not completely hen-witted, the sloppier of the two
writers had added. And she suddenly understood that
cryptic comment he'd made about finding a wife with
brains. Suggested by someone called…Ash, that was
it. How she could remember a name tossed out just the
once, in such an offhand way, she could not think.

Unless it was because she felt as though the beautiful little dainties set out on their fine china plates might as well have been so many piles of ash, for all the desire she had now to put one in her mouth.

Good with children, not selfish, the darker hand had scrawled. Then it was back to the neater hand again. It had written, *Modest, Honest* and *Not looking for affection within Matrimony.* And then the untidier, what she'd come to think of as the more sarcastic, compiler of wifely qualities had written the word *Mouse* again, and this time underlined it twice.

But what made a small whimper of distress finally escape her lips was the last item on the list.

Need not be pretty.

Need not be pretty. Well, that was her all right! Plain, dowdy mouse that she was. No wonder he'd looked at her like—what was it Aunt Pargetter had said—like his ship had come in?

Getting to her feet, she strode to his bedroom door and flung it open. Somehow she had to find a sample of his handwriting to see if he'd been the one to…to mock her this way, before he'd even met her. And then she would… She came to an abrupt halt by his desk, across the surface of which was scattered a veritable raft of papers. What would she do? She'd already married him.

Don't miss
LORD HAVELOCK'S LIST,
available from Harlequin® Historical
September 2014.

HARLEQUIN®

HISTORICAL

Where love is timeless

COMING IN SEPTEMBER 2014

The Gentleman Rogue

by

Margaret McPhee

INESCAPABLE, UNDENIABLE AND IMPOSSIBLE TO RESIST!

In a Mayfair ballroom, beautiful Emma Northcote stands in amazement. For gazing at her, with eyes she'd know anywhere, is Ned Stratham—a man whose roguish charm once held her captivated.

But that was another life in another part of London.

With their past mired in secrets and betrayal, and their true identities now at last revealed, Ned realizes they can never rekindle their affair. For only he knows that they share a deeper connection—one that could make Emma hate him if she ever discovered the truth....

Available wherever books and ebooks are sold.

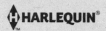

HISTORICAL

Where love is timeless

COMING IN SEPTEMBER 2014

Saved by the Viking Warrior

by

Michelle Styles

"THERE IS NO ONE. I TRAVEL ALONE. I LIVE ALONE. ALWAYS."

Battle-scarred Thrand the Destroyer has only one thing on his mind: settling old scores. But with the beautiful Lady of Lingfold as his prisoner, the unyielding warrior starts to dream of a loving wife and a home to call his own.

Cwen is also seeking justice, but she knows the fragile alliance she's built with Thrand will only last as long as they share a common enemy. Unless they can find a way to leave revenge to the gods to forge a new life together.

Available wherever books and ebooks are sold.